Dear Reader:

Hollywood High is more th[...] [...]ish parties, high-fashion, and [...] [...]ger than the sex, drama, and over-the-top antics. *Hollywood High* is about choices. It is about life lessons. It is about the need to be loved and the desire to fit in. Yes, the characters in this book are afforded the kind of lifestyle most teens (and adults) can only dream about. We make no apologies for that. They are young, rich, and famous because of who their parents are. Yet they lack parental supervision and/or healthy parental guidance. They are self-absorbed, spoiled brats who do whatever they want with little to no consequences. There is no denying this. They are products of their upbringing; period, point blank.

However, when you remove the shades, peel off the designer labels, mink lashes, and all of the bling that their parents' money can buy, London, Rich, Spencer, and Heather are simply teen girls who struggle with the same types of issues that many (not all) teen girls experience at some point in their lives. They struggle with self-esteem, identity, and weight issues. They struggle with peer pressure and acceptance. They have bouts of depression. They look for love in all the wrong places and faces. They do not know their own self-worth. They binge on alcohol and abuse drugs. They binge eat. They are promiscuous. And no matter how grown-up they want or pretend to be, they are merely young girls who want to be loved by their parents and accepted by their peers. Yes, they are wealthy. But they are far from perfect. London, Rich, Spencer, and Heather mask their hurts and pains and disappointments by attacking and putting each other down. And their whole worlds revolve around trying to outshine one another.

It is our sincere hope that readers see past the superficial trappings of each character's wealth and obnoxious, rude behaviors and see that within the pages of this fabulous series lie the lessons of life, love, and self-discovery.

Here's to Hollywood!

Yours truly,
Ni-Ni Simone & Amir Abrams

Hollywood High series

Hollywood High
Get Ready for War
Put Your Diamonds Up
Fame of Thrones

Also by Ni-Ni Simone
The Ni-Ni Girl Chronicles

Shortie Like Mine
If I Was Your Girl
A Girl Like Me
Teenage Love Affair
Upgrade U
No Boyz Allowed

Also by Amir Abrams

Crazy Love
The Girl of His Dreams

Published by Kensington Publishing Corp.

Put Your Diamonds Up

Hollywood HIGH

Ni-Ni Simone
Amir Abrams

Dafina KTeen Books
KENSINGTON PUBLISHING CORP.
www.kensingtonbooks.com

DAFINA KTEEN BOOKS are published by

Kensington Publishing Corp.
119 West 40th Street
New York, NY 10018

All Kensington titles, imprints, and distributed lines are available at special quantity discounts for bulk purchases for sales promotion, premiums, fund-raising, and educational or institutional use.

Special book excerpts or customized printings can also be created to fit specific needs. For details, write or phone the office of the Kensington Special Sales Manager: Kensington Publishing Corp., 119 West 40th Street, New York, NY 10018. Attn. Special Sales Department. Phone: 1-800-221-2647.

KTeen logo Reg. U.S. Pat. & TM Off.
Sunburst logo Reg. U.S. Pat. & TM Off.

ISBN-13: 978-0-7582-8852-3
ISBN-10: 0-7582-8852-2
First Kensington Trade Paperback Printing: August 2014

eISBN-13: 978-0-7582-8853-0
eISBN-10: 0-7582-8853-0
First Kensington Electronic Edition: August 2014

10 9 8 7 6 5 4 3 2 1

Printed in the United States of America

ACKNOWLEDGMENTS

We'd like to thank God for His grace and continued blessings. And to give a special thanks to all the readers and fans for the love!

1

London

Milan, Italy

"*Your body, beauty, and youth are your tickets to fame and fortune...*"

"Look into the camera, London," Luke Luppalozzi, a renowned photographer, cajoled as his camera clicked to life. I blinked my mother's voice out of my head. "Less stiff, more sass, London! Thrust your left hip...Give me seductress, darling!"

You nasty perv! Sounds to me like you want slutty!

I was at a photo shoot for a new fragrance—Pink Heat—for some new Italian designer, standing on a seamless swoop of heavy white paper that stretched along the floor for what seemed like miles, from a roll anchored to a beam. I was wearing a pair of six-inch pink spike heels and a slinky pink dress. My sculpted, milk-chocolate shoulders were exposed, shimmering from the glow of the lights. My long, shapely legs were bare. Around my slender, elongated neck hung a five-carat pink diamond necklace, a gift from my mother. Hair and makeup people had been at the ready from the moment I'd stepped through the doors four hours ago.

My shoulder-length hair was curled into cascading ringlets. Long, thick lashes wrapped around my large brown eyes. My sumptuous lips glowed and pulsed, coated in hot pink lipstick and glossed to perfection.

On the outside, I was *fiiiierce*.

On the inside, I felt everything but. I felt like someone had rolled me in a whole bottle of Pepto-Bismol. And I'd become the big pink Amazon. Ugh.

God, I wanted to love my life. Wanted to love the excitement. Wanted to love that I was in Milan... Italy, that is; among some of the world's elite fashion editors, being captured on film by renowned photographers for campaign and print ads—doing something most girls my age only dreamed of.

I wanted to love the fact that I was finally becoming the daughter that my well-coiffed, well-heeled, well-bred mother had always desired me to be. Flawless. Hair pinned, face painted, poised, and ready to take the fashion world by storm.

But right at the moment, I was too exhausted to care about any of that. My feet ached from wearing heels all day, standing in uncomfortable positions, being twisted and prodded to hold poses for the camera while gigantic industrial fans blew my hair this way and that.

Yes. I was a trendsetter.

Yes. I was a fashionista extraordinaire.

Yes. I was a lover of heels, handbags, and high fashion.

But on my terms. Not someone else's.

And, right now, at this very minute, this precise second, my mother defined everything about who I was. I wanted this for her. I wanted this for me, because *she* wanted this for me...for herself. This was her life, her world. And she insisted...no, demanded, expected, that I be a part of it. That I embrace my orchestrated destiny with grace and fervor and be forever swept into the glitz and glamour of it all.

But who I was was all back in California—six thousand forty-five-point-four miles; twelve hours and thirty-three minutes away. In La-La Land. At Hollywood High Academy, my elite private school, where I hadn't been for the last week or so in order to appease my mother's need to have me on the runway. God strike me for parting my lips and admitting this part, but...I'd rather be back at school *with* the Pampered Princesses—the "It Girls" of Hollywood High than be here with a bunch of snotty models.

Jeezus, the world must really be coming to an end for me to openly admit to missing the likes of Heather and Spencer! It must be the flashing lights! Yeah, that has to be it.

Yeah, we didn't always get along. And yeah, we fought. And yeah, most times I disliked Heather Cummings, the teen-star junkie; even looked down on her. She was the queen of trashy. Leopard prints and pounds of slut paint on her face. But, minus the fortune, she had fame. Everyone knew who Wu-Wu Tanner was. The fun-loving, animal-print wearing suburban teenager Heather had once played on the number one hit television show in America. But thanks to her druggie behavior and showing up strung out on the set, her show was canceled. And it's been downhill for Heather ever since. Still, like it or not, she had star power. What was left of it, that is. But I digress.

Anhoo yeah, I despised that dizzy-dumb, scatterbrain chick Spencer, the spoiled bratty daughter of the messy media mogul, Kitty Ellington. But she had heart. She had guts. And she was crazier than bat shit. And thanks to me, she'd gotten her face smacked off right in the middle of finance class when I convinced Rich that it was Spencer who'd stabbed her in the back and told her boo Knox that she'd had an abortion when she'd already lied and told him that she'd miscarried. It didn't take much coercion. Rich wasn't the sharpest knife in the cutlery drawer either. And she was as slutty as Spencer. No, no...she was sluttier. Still, she was my bestie. And sharing her with that floor-mop Spencer was *not* an option.

And what my mother failed to understand was, I *needed* to get back to my life at Hollywood High to ensure Rich and Spencer stayed enemies. Before Rich, who had the attention span of a bobblehead, went back to cavorting with my nemesis.

And speaking of Rich, why the hell hadn't I heard from her in two days? I called her four times. Sent her six text messages. And nothing! That was soooooo not good! It was an omen. I knew she'd wait until I got thousands of miles across the Atlantic Ocean to show her true two-faced ways. And her lack of regard for *me* and our friendship said one of three things: She was either somewhere chained to some boy's bed with her legs up in her famous V-split, or hiding out at some seedy ranch for sexaholics, or she was back in the manicured clutches of Spencer.

God, I couldn't stand that trampola. Everyone knew

her mouth was a used condom, thanks to the viral video of her sucking down watermelon shots in the girl's lounge at school with one of Rich's many boyfriends. But being here, away from my life in Hollywood, was more torturous than being friends with Spencer and Heather. So I'd take being around those two over the likes of the majority of the models I was surrounded by. And that really spoke volumes, considering my contempt for the two of them.

I was besieged by the likes of the living dead, pony-stepping the runways. A gaggle of models who recklessly eyeballed me and mumbled snide remarks under their collagen-plumped lips every chance they got about me receiving preferential treatment because I was the daughter of Jade Obi, one of the world's beloved international supermodels. Whatever!

They had no clue as to what life was like living with their role model, their adored idol. My mother.

Sure, being the daughter of a famous supermodel came with the advantages of a lavish lifestyle. I lived a privileged life. And being young, beautiful, and rich always made me a target. For the paparazzi. For the haters. And for my mother's ridicule.

She was imperious. She was controlling. She was rigid. She was—when I wasn't who she expected me to be—my worst nightmare. *"You're definitely not ugly. And you're far from old-looking, yet. Thank God you have my genes. But, fat... mmmph. You're well on your way...*

Diet is everything in this industry, London..."

And dieting I have done. For the last two-and-a-half years, she'd been monitoring my weight, measuring my inches, weighing my food portions, counting my caloric intake, keeping it all in a leather-bound journal, browbeating me to no end until I'd finally lost the fifteen extra pounds she required of me to be runway ready. Now weighing in at one-hundred-and-ten pounds, I had arrived. I'd made it back in front of the flashbulbs popping all around me. It didn't matter to her how I lost the weight as long as it was gone. Buried. To never return for as long as we both shall live. Amen. Amen. Amen.

"The sooner you can get this god-awful weight off and we can get you back on the runway and onto the covers of all the fashion magazines where you belong...You were born to be in front of the camera..."

Still, some of the models I'd seen since being here looked like crack whores in couture. Many of them stood over six feet tall. They were needle thin with sunken cheeks and protruding collarbones, speed racing off of caffeine and nicotine. Most of them, ice queens, shot daggers of icicles at me as I was led through the sea of miserable haters to my next photo shoot. From what I've overheard while waiting for casting calls among models vying for the same shoot, campaign, etc., many of them were snorting lines of coke and popping uppers to stay wafer-thin and to keep up with the grueling hours that went along with being a high-fashion print-ad model.

"Oh, my darling London. I am so proud of you!" My mother had bubbled over with joy in the backseat of the stretch Benz during the ride over here at six o'clock this morning. "You are going to be the next hottest thing. *Sei bella, mia cara Londra!*" She beamed as she stroked the side of my face, telling me how beautiful I was. "You are absolutely perfect."

I almost wanted to laugh at the absurdity of that word. *Perfect.* The *perfect* oxymoron, if I'd ever heard one. There was nothing *perfect* about me. Nothing perfect about this world I'd been thrust into.

No. There was definitely nothing perfect about this life. If it were, I'd be pencil thin instead of curvy like a dangerously winding hillside. I'd have ant-size breasts instead of the melon-sized jugs that fit perfectly in a 34 C-cup. I'd have the derrière of a wood plank instead of a bouncy booty that snapped necks and had a mind of its own, commanding attention without much effort.

"For the love of God, London, why did you have to ruin your body...You just had to go and screw up everything I've worked for...No one wants a fat, ugly, old-looking girl on their runway..."

While most models craved bee-stung lips, mine were already naturally plump, ripe, and kissable. Although they hadn't been kissed in two weeks. Still, my beauty was a blessing and a curse. A double-edged sword.

I'd been longing for the day my mother would look at me with the same pride beaming in her eyes as she did when I was a preteen on the runway. Before the sudden weight gain. Before the *setback*, as my mother called it. Before the swell of my breasts and the roundness of my hips morphed my body into that of an Amazon. A statuesque brick house.

I was thirteen when I first graced the cover of *Vogue Italia.* Seven months later, I was swelling like an angry river, bursting out of my size zero, quickly ballooning to a size four, then six, then eight.

"You're nothing now. You'll never be anything...At the

rate you're going, you'll never make it on the runway.
You'll only be good enough to shake and bounce for rap
videos..."

Those were more of her cutting words to me, on many
occasions. That is how she viewed me. That is how she felt
about me. And although I knew she loved me, I also knew
that love, her love, came with unrelenting conditions. And
most times with unbearable consequences.

No, there was no room for imperfection when you had
a mother like Jade Obi Phillips, who expected nothing less
than perfection. The perfect P's, according to my mother,
were: Poise. Posture. Position. Then tack on the perfect
image, the perfect body, the perfect skin, the perfect set of
teeth, the perfect partner, and the perfect station in life.
Follow this mantra, and you were guaranteed the perfect
life, according to the world of Jade.

Yes, my mother loved me. But she'd always love the
perfect me more...

"London, darling...smile..." My mother's voice drifted
over toward me as the photographer tried to have me
flash a toothy grin with my head slightly tilted to the right
while one foot was lifted off the floor in back of me. Her
tone was light and airy but laced with a tinge of attitude as
she stood behind the photographer, like a backseat driver,
trying to coax me, coach me, and get on my last damn nerve.

I forced a tight smile. I felt a headache pounding its way
into the center of my forehead. But I had to get through
this. Had to get this finished, the sooner the better. "Blow
a kiss into the camera...Hold the bottle up closer to your
cheek...Give me attitude...Now lick your lips and give
me Pink Heat, doll..."

I cringed. *Doll?* How cheesy!

The photographer, speaking in his thick Italian-accented English, was dangerously handsome for a man in his thirties. Tanned and built like an Adonis. But he was a horny toad who winked and licked his lips on the sly every chance he got! I simply rolled my eyes. Or pretended not to notice. *Look but don't touch!*

I tried to stay focused, tried to steel myself for the dazzling whiteness of the camera's flash. But I couldn't. My mind kept swinging back and forth between Justice—the one true love of my life, whom my parents despised...to Rich—my supposed bestie, who I hadn't heard from since I'd gotten here and who had not kept one Skype date with me for whatever reason...to Anderson—my parent-approved boyfriend who was refusing to take my calls because I couldn't and wouldn't choose between him and Justice. And to think I had kissed him. That I had lifted up on my tiptoes and pulled his face down to mine in the middle of a dance floor at his fraternity's campus party and was kissing him, my tongue slipping into his wet mouth. And he was kissing me back. And everything was heating. Everything was melting. And I was caught up in the flames. God, I hated him!

I hated him for everything he was. Smart. Articulate. Handsome. Thoughtful. I hated him for being a good kisser. Hated the way his strong arms felt around me. Hated him for taking my mind off of Justice, my off-again on-again boyfriend. The only boy I'd ever loved. The only boy I'd ever given myself to. The only boy who'd ever had my heart. And I hated Anderson for making me feel messy and sexy at the same time; for making my mind replay his hands wandering all over my body when I should only be thinking of Justice.

I had cheated on my man. So, yes, I hated my faux boyfriend, Anderson, for managing, with one kiss—okay, okay, *three* kisses—to ruin my life. I was a cheater.

And speaking of Justice, why haven't I heard from him? I have gotten not one call or text from him in almost four days. Four days! Four fricking *loooooong* excruciating days of not hearing his voice or seeing his handsomely rugged face on FaceTime or Skype was *killlllling* me!

And I had my mother to thank for my misery.

In less than two weeks, she had managed to turn my whole world upside down, inside out, and every which way in between. She'd literally stripped me of my life. And she had no damn care in the world.

"*Londra, fare l'amore per la fotocamera,*" Luke shouts in Italian, suggesting I make love to the camera. *Ohmygod! How vulgar!*

I sighed.

My mother shot me a scathing look that read *Do. Not. Try. Me. You had* better *pretend this is where you want to be.*

Before I could put on my mask and get with the program, my mother asked the photographer and his crew if she could have a moment alone with me. To motivate me, she claimed.

"What in the world is wrong with you, London?" she snapped when she thought everyone was out of earshot.

"I want to go home."

She blinked. "For the next two weeks, *this* is your home. Get used to it."

I pouted. "I miss my friends."

She scoffed. "Trust me. Those spoiled little girls back at Hollywood High aren't losing any sleep over *you*. Their worlds are going on without *you*. As a matter of fact, I bet you haven't heard from any of your so-called *friends* since you've been here. Have you?"

I folded my arms and turned away from her. I was done. However, my silence only encouraged her to continue her babbling.

"London," she hissed, grabbing me by the arm and turning me to her, "what would you rather do, huh? Hang with some loudmouth attention whore, is that it? Rich will have to buy her way out of school because she's been raised to be a mattress for the richest fool who'll have her. The only thing she'll ever be good for is performing Cirque du Soleil acrobatics in some boy's bed, having babies, and carrying razors under her slithering tongue—"

I snapped my neck in my mother's direction. "Mother, do I talk about any of your friends, huh? Oh, wait. You don't have any." I narrowed my eyes. "I don't care what Rich does with her life. That's not my concern. She's my friend."

My mother laughed in my face. "In this industry there is no room for friends, my darling daughter. Friends stab you in the back. This is a cutthroat business. You have enemies and allies. Nothing more. Do you think I made it as far as I have, being concerned about having friends? No. I made it to the top of my game by knowing the difference between friendships and alliances. Trust me. Rich doesn't know the first thing about being a friend. That girl is nobody's friend. And she's definitely not yours, darling. So the sooner you get that through that luscious head of yours, the better."

I sucked my teeth. "I don't care. I want to go home."

"And do *what*, huh? Become some double-chin piglet with ankles the size of ham hocks, wobbling off to some godforsaken factory job? You want to be some big biscuit-eating, dimpled-butt oaf with saggy air-bag breasts, like your father's side of the family? Would you rather scrub toilets for a living, is that it, London? I am trying to help you build a legacy. Not help you piss your life away on some two-dollar pipe dream of doing God knows what else other than what you were destined to do."

For a moment I had...Absolutely. No. Words. Was she effen *serious*?

She continued, "*This* is your life, London. So you had better get used to it. Now, if *you* don't want this life, then speak now so I can make arrangements to have you shipped off to England to boarding school. Because, make no mistake, my darling daughter. You will *not* be returning to Hollywood High. Now pick a door. And choose it very wisely. Because the choice you make today will be the one you will have to live with. Now, be the darling I know you can be. Make your mother proud. Give me what I want, London, or I make the next two years of your life a living hell."

I blinked. *Dear God, what have I done to deserve this? Have I sinned that bad?*

I wanted to scream. I wanted to stomp. Wanted to pound my fists. Wanted to kick. Have a full-fledged tantrum. Wanted to defy every last one of my mother's beauty rules and have a pig fest, eating up everything in sight. What I wouldn't have done to kick off my heels and flee and never look back. What I wouldn't do to be able to hide out in my suite and sit cross-legged on my king-size Baldacchino Supreme bed amid cake crumbs and smeared bowls of Chunky Monkey ice cream.

I'd do anything to be at the Saddle Ranch on Sunset

Boulevard, sinking my teeth into a big, juicy T-bone steak. Better yet, what I wouldn't do to be back at Muddy Moments, a run-down hole-in-the-wall in San Diego, with Rich and her future ex-boo, Knox, and Anderson, sucking down on a platter of their infamous honey-coated hot wings and a slab of ribs. And I didn't even eat anything off of a pig.

Yes, yes, yes! I'd kill to scarf down a family-size bag of Cool Ranch Doritos and a bag of Oreos...then I'd beg the evil fat gods to spare me from gaining an ounce. I'd boldly do all of those things then I'd post pictures of my lips slathered with chicken grease and rib sauce and dusted with doughnut powder all up on Instagram.

My mother wanted perfect. I'd show her a perfect mess! And for the grand finale, I'd give her my perfect escape.

"Well," my mother huffed impatiently. "I'm waiting. Now, what's it going to be, London, the runway or boarding school? The clock is ticking."

I swallowed, then begrudgingly replied, "The runway."

She fussed with the big curl at the end of my bang that swooped along my jawline. "I knew you'd see it my way. Now go take a moment to get your thoughts together. And when you come back out here, you had better be in the mindset to serve it to the camera. Do I make myself clear?"

I clenched my teeth. "Perfectly." I briskly walked off as she stood there saying something slick and crazy in Italian about me being a selfish, ungrateful brat. Whatever.

One of the many assistants swarming around the photo shoot rudely thrust a large white envelope at me as I made my way toward the makeshift lounge area. She said it was sent via courier. Curious, I stared for several seconds at the envelope with its typed address label, wondering who'd sent me mail. I turned it over, pulling the tab and opening it. Inside was a manila envelope with a set of large eyes elaborately drawn in black ink on the front of it. On the back in red ink the words FOR YOUR WEEPING EYES ONLY was written across the seal.

WTH? I reached over for a fingernail file someone left on the table and slit open the envelope, pulling out the items inside: photos.

I blinked. *OMG! What the fu...?*

I glanced at the anonymously photographed images of the nude chick in the on-all-fours pornographic poses. There was a tattoo of a colorful butterfly just above her booty crack. I blinked, blinked again. *Ohno ohno ohno...* I felt my stomach lurching as I stared at the guy's hand on the chick's naked booty cheek. Right on the webbed part between his thumb and forefinger was a tattoo of a small black dagger with red drops of blood dripping from its tip.

I screamed, crumpling the pictures tight in my fist.

It was Justice's hand!

2

Heather

*K*nock... *Knock*...
"Heather! Who is that?"

My eyes swept across the room and landed on my mother, Camille, who sat on the edge of the bed and nursed the bottom of last night's bottle of scotch.

"It's seven o'clock in the damn morning and somebody's knocking at my door?" She fumbled over the nightstand. "Where are my Aleve? Dear God, I have a headache. My throat is dry. And the last thing I need, Heather Suzanne, is for you to invite some junkie up in here!"

Knock... *Knock*...

I rolled my eyes to the water-stained ceiling.

"Who's that?" she spat.

"I don't know."

She shoved three pills in her mouth. "Did you pay the rent?"

Hell no. I needed that money! "Of course I paid the rent."

"Of course?" She snorted, washing the pills down with her last swallow of scotch. "The only *of course* I know about you is that of course you're selfish and of course you have no consideration for anydamnbody but you, yourself, and Wu-Wu!"

Her words gripped me by the throat and I swear while she was sleeping I should've gently placed a pillow over her slobbering face and smothered the life out of her.

Tonight for sure I'ma do her in.

"Yeah, I said it." Camille twisted her thin lips, her white face loaded with clouds of hot red blotches. "You, yourself, and that canceled Wu-Wu show."

Knock...Knock...

"I said who *is* that?" Her blue eyes bulged.

I leaned forward in my chair and it took everything in me not to jump up and drop a hard elbow in her chest. "I'm in here with you. How would I know?"

"Well, you better find out! And send them away. We're in no condition for visitors. No one needs to see us like this!" She crawled beneath the covers and pulled them over her face.

"Oh really?" I placed a fist up on my hip and rocked my neck from side to side. "And when did you think of this? Before or *after* you spent all of my money?"

Camille peeled the covers from over her face, stopping at her chin. "Your money?" She sat up. "*Your* money? You didn't have any money, Heather!"

"I had two checks that were due me! And I told you to put them in the bank, but you didn't! You did what you wanted to do. Just ran right through 'em! You didn't pay a single bill. Not one! And before you turned the judge against me and had me locked up—"

"You drugged me!"

"You deserved it!"

"I did the best that I could do!"

"Which is never good enough! Before I left we were living in a house. And yesterday, I'm released from rehab and my welcome home party is here. At Sleazy Eight!" *And you think I paid the rent to keep staying in this place? Never! Trust. As soon as I can, I'm getting out of here. You can believe that!*

"How dare you speak to me like this? You know what"—Camille sighed as she wiped invisible sweat from her brow— "I'm going to close my eyes and ignore the fact that you just spoke to me like gutter trash." She pulled the covers back over her head and settled into her pillow. A few seconds later the knocking returned.

Dang! They're still here?

I shook my head.

Obviously, they don't catch hints.

I walked over to the door and peered through the peephole.

My heart dropped.

Dear God...it's Satan in six-inch heels and a hazmat suit.

I turned away from the door and instead of opening it, I paced.

Knock...Knock...

I need a cigarette.

Scratch that.

A blunt would do me right!

I stopped in my tracks.

Not that I've ever had a problem with drugs.

It's Camille. She's the problem.

I started pacing again.

All of my life Camille's been on a mission to do me in. Plotting. Scheming. Having me put on probation for drugging her. Mmph, what else was I supposed to do? I didn't need her killin' my vibe. I needed to relieve my stress and have my skittles party in peace. So...I slipped her a nice mix of somebody's granny's heart medicine, Xanax, and Sudafed in her nightly shot of scotch and rocked her to sleep. Still. It wasn't my fault that she woke up handcuffed and stuffed in a paddy wagon.

Knock...Knock...

I wish Satan would just go away! I'm already dead and in my coffin. I don't need her driving the nails into it.

She has to know I'm flat broke. Flat. Broke. All my irreplaceables are gone. All my money has been tricked on Camille's daily bottles of scotch, Chinese chicken wings, lottery tickets, and cigarettes.

I spun around toward the door.

That's it!

She's here to rub it in my face.

Spiteful whore!

I can't believe it!

The last time I saw Lucifer, she lied and told me that Richard Montgomery was my father. Imagine that. Richard Montgomery. Former drug dealing street thug and ten-page rap sheet convict MC Wickedness, now known as CEO and owner of Grand Records and Montgomery Sports Enterprises. Mr. Number Three on *Forbes*. And this devil really expected me to believe that he was my father? As if Rich, Princess Ratchet herself, and I could ever share a bloodline.

Not.

Never.

Puhlease.

Rich and I could never be sisters. Because one thing's for certain and two things're for sure: Camille may be a washed-up and drunk Hollywood slut, but one thing she's not is a notch on Richard Montgomery Sr.'s belt.

Knock...Knock...

"Ahh!" I jumped as a black ceramic ashtray just missed me and slammed into the wall. Cigarette butts, ashes, and jagged ceramic pieces flew into the air and fluttered to the floor. "ARE YOU CRAZY!"

"That's exactly what I am!" Camille pointed at me, her voice now deep and sounding possessed. "And if you don't get rid of whoever that is, so help me baby Jesus, I'm going to tear your face off!"

I narrowed my eyes at Camille and sucked my teeth. I turned and looked back through the peephole, and still standing there was Satan, with an attitude.

This tramp had no shame.

God, I wish I had a black beauty!

I just need one.

Just one to take the edge off.

"Heather!" made its way from behind the door.

Just open the door. Tell her to go away. And then slam it in her face!

I twisted the knob, opened the door slightly, and in the shadow of the blinking neon sign that read Twenty-Four Hour Vacancies was my number one frenemy, Spencer Ellington, and it took everything in me not to thumb her eyes out.

How the hell did she find me?

She lifted the cloth medical mask slightly above her full

lips. "SweetskidrowWestHollywood! You can run, but you can't hide from Momma. Ain't no ghetto low enough to keep me from you, thanks to my private eye. I can smell the ratchet two miles away. Now, who shot the crack whore and forgot to kill her? Dear mother of Francis, what are you doing here?" She pushed the door open with the tip of a stiletto and pushed her way into the room. Immediately she covered her mouth and dry heaved. "Air! I need! Air!" She rushed over to the open window and stuck her head out. A few seconds later, she fanned her face and turned toward me.

"You really tore the seat out of your panties with this one, Heather. The Pampered Princesses have reached a new low. And I didn't think we could drop any lower than Rich and her sucking down hot wings, licking up blue cheese, and gargling beer!"

She curled her lips and her eyes worked their way over my bare feet, up my legs to my cut-off denim shorts and white tube top, stopping at the unruly curls in my sun-streaked hair. "Before you even say it"—I clenched my lips—"I know I'm at my lowest. I don't need you rubbing it in my face."

"Excuse you." She faintly placed a gloved hand over her heart, as if she'd been insulted. "Don't do that, Heather. Don't put words in my mouth. You can't read my mind because if you could, you'd know that I was going to ask you what is that animal humped up under the covers?"

Animal? "You mean Camille?"

"Camille? That's Camille? Is she"—Spencer cast her eyes down at her watch—"drunk? It's seven fifteen in the morning and your mother's drunk?"

Oh no she didn't! How dare she put down my mother! And God knows Camille isn't perfect but still... Can you say rude?

I placed both hands up on my hips and cranked my neck to the right. "Why are you here? And what. Do you. Want?"

"I'm here to save your life." Spencer reached in her designer clutch, slid out an envelope and placed it in my hand.

I looked at the envelope, unimpressed. "What is this?" I popped my lips.

"Open it," she insisted.

Reluctantly, I followed her instruction.

Oh... my... God...

I pulled out a three-million-dollar certified check and blinked in disbelief. I clicked my heels, twice, in case this was a dream. Spencer looked down at me and smiled, her full lashes fluttered and locked into my brown gaze.

Three million dollars?

My eyes filled with tears and I turned my back to her. There was no way I could face her.

Breathe...

Just breathe.

Deep breath in.

Deep breath out.

I can't believe it!

I really. Truly. Can't believe it!

Did this cheap, low budget, skimpy blond fish just hand me a certified check for *three million dollars*? Really? As if this was not Hollywood, California! Tinseltown! And by the time I finished paying my rent—My personal assistant.

My driver. My stylist. My makeup artist. My publicist. My palm reader, who keeps me aligned with the universe. My acting coach. My butler. My maid. My personal jeweler. My monthly entertainment. My Korean shoemaker and my exclusive Chinese handbag maker—I'll be broke. Was she serious? Or was I being catfished?

Spencer placed a hand on my shoulder. "Don't thank me now."

Trick, please. If I weren't so polite and gracious I'd toss this check back in your face and tell you to get the hell off of my property! Even if it is a motel room!

She continued, "You must be wondering what you did to deserve such kindness." She paced before me like a professor. "Well, the answer to that is nothing. You haven't done one thing. And truthfully, anyone who spends up all of their money and runs through it like pissy panty liners should be banished. Put away. And nobody should ever have to lay eyes on you again." She stopped pacing and turned toward me. "But I couldn't let you die in the streets, Heather. So, being that I'm nice like that, I decided to save your poor wretched soul with my generosity."

Whaaaaaat?!

Oh hell no!

Breathe.

Breathe.

Relax.

Release.

She's crazy.

Save me?

Before my legs kick this wench, let me turn away from her again.

I turned and she carried on, "It's not that I make a habit

out of playing Captain Save A Crackhead. But I figured I'd make an exception this time."

I'm not a crackhead and you haven't saved me, you cheap whore! This is an insult! You've torn up my life. Ruined my career. Called the police on my skittles party! And put a thirty-day disruption between me and my get-right. You were dead wrong for that, ole nasty dome licker. I should take a WWE clothesline to your head! Backhand your cheek to the floor.

Three million dollars?

Really?

And you think you saved me?

"Ah!" I jumped and spun around when her finger stabbed into my left butt cheek.

"That's really you?" Spencer looked at me in amazement. "Here I was thinking how outdated this wallpaper is, and it turns out that I'm looking at the back of you." She sighed and paused, looking up at the ceiling as if she were deep in thought. "You know what I'm going to do for you, Heather?"

"I couldn't imagine you doing anything more than you already have," I said, my tone dripping with more sarcasm than I intended.

She looked at me and smiled. "I'm going to get you a Brazilian booty lift."

A what?

"Don't thank me now. Thank me after your first twerk." She snapped her fingers.

Twerk? Excuse you, Miss Knees On The Floor, I don't twerk. I Tootsie Roll. "Are you serious? A booty lift?"

"Yes!"

Well, that's the least you can do.

"I also have something else for you," she said.

Hopefully it's the other half of this check. "What could that possibly be?"

"I've arranged for you to tape a pilot for your very own television show—"

Pilot? Did she just say my own television show? "What did you just say to me, Spencer?"

She gave me a sheepish grin and batted her lashes. "You heard me right, boo. You heard me."

Did she say my own television show?

"I said your own television show," she confirmed, as if reading my thoughts. "Now"—she tapped a heel—"who loves you, baby?"

My heart dropped as I squealed, "A pilot?" I looked over at the bed where Camille was coughing and stirring beneath the covers.

Spencer continued, "Yasssss, dahling!" She resumed her pacing. "You are to be in Brazil tomorrow. I'll have my assistant make all of the arrangements. Just be at the airport first thing in the morning." She handed me a business card with a Dr. Cortez and his information listed. "This is who you'll be seeing. And when you return you will be taken to the set of the—"

"New Wu-Wu show!" I jumped up and down. "The new Wu-Wu show!" I clapped my hands. "There's a God after all." I braided my fingers and shook my hands. "I knew God could never turn his back on Wu-Wu!"

Spencer rolled her eyes extremely slow and then sprang them open, glaring at me. "What. Did. You. Say?" She shoved her purse beneath her arm and roughly grabbed my face. "Are you brain-dead?"

"What?" I snatched away.

"Or are you testing me?"

"Testing you?"

"I'm not stupid."

Depends on who you ask. "I never said you were stupid."

"So then why are you testing my memory? You know and I know that Wu-Wu was burned down to the ground." She stamped her six-inch pencil heels into the carpet. "What? Did you think I forgot? Dear God, please don't make me have to Mace you for trying to insult my memory! I'm trying to be good to you, Heather. Don't make me get ugly." She paused. "And in case you forgot what ugly looks like"—she pointed to the hump on the bed—"it's Camille after a few drinks. Now, let's try this again."

"I want you to listen to Godmother. Hear me, and hear me well. Wu-Wu. Is. D-E-A-D. Dead. You understand me? Forget her. Kitty has given me permission to let you know that you are to become Luda Tutor. Medieval princess storms New York. You are lost in a time warp capsule and have been dropped in the middle of the twenty-first century. Luda Tutor does Brooklyn. Now don't let me hear you say anything else about Wu-Wu again."

I could hear Camille snickering from under the covers.

Spencer continued, "Now, I have one last surprise for you. Close your eyes and open your hand."

I hesitated but followed her request. I felt her place something in my hand. My eyes popped open and there was a set of car keys. She pointed out of the window to a black Lamborghini Gallardo. "That would be yours. And you may thank Godmother now."

I looked up at Spencer and she wore the cheesiest smile I'd ever seen. "Go on, Heather. Thank me."

Thank you? Thank you? First this effen trick gives me

three million dollars. A step above a welfare check. And now she has the audacity to give me a black car, when she knows I hate black cars! She knows that hot pink and leopard print are my favorite! Therefore, that heap of scrap metal should've been hot pink and leopard. But noooooo, it's black! And then she left the factory rims on it. No spinners. No gold wheels. Real basic. You know what, I should take this douche bag by the hand, walk her outside, and bash her face into the windshield! Thank her? Really? No, what I should do is flatten her face with the wheels!

I looked up at Spencer and just when I thought about knocking her front teeth out, I decided to be the bigger person. "Thank you!" I said and fell into her embrace.

"You know I'm here for you, girl." She held me tightly and patted my back. "Just don't cross me."

3

Rich

*Y*eah, boo.

It's been magical: the lovemaking. The kisses: breathtaking. Your touch: like fire. But this is where I get off.

I'm done.

We're done.

It's over.

And last night was it.

I know it'll be hard for you, but you'll have to get over me. Besides, you demand too much of my time. It's been every other day, sometimes twice a day, with you. That's overkill. Who does that?

I can't have you possessing my body all the time. Heck, even the times when we're not together I find myself craving your touch, your mouth, the pulling, pinching, and sucking of your luscious lips on my... See, here I go again... Peeking over this letter, looking at your hard, sleeping body in the hotel bed and won-

dering if I should take my clothes off for a third time since last night...

This is too much.

And then you asked me to break up with my boyfriend. Why are you hatin' on my relationship like that? In case you've forgotten, you know we had an agreement—which was: I call you. You don't stalk me. Demand things from me. But over and over again this is what you do. You are out of control. Seriously, every time I turn around there you are—all up in my space and my face, casting spells on me. And being ridiculous. Touching my... squeezing my... whispering in my ear that you want to ease your tongue in my... leaving purple passionate evidence of your sweet sucks all over my body, forcing me to hide out for days from my man.

And no matter how many times I tell you that MY hair—the hair that grows out of my scalp—ONLY reaches my shoulders, and the ends that travel to the small of my back are a five-thousand-dollar infusion weave of Brazilian virgin hair; no matter how many times I explain this to you, you don't get it. And when we're doing the naked twerk—you keep. Yanking. My hair. Back!

Why are you doing that?

You cannot be all up in my hair like that! That is sooooo whack. And I suggest you don't do that with the next chick you get with, 'cause she may not be as kind as me and the next thing you know you'll wake up with your face bashed in!

Black women don't play that!

Anyway, boo, be easy. I've left five hundred dollars

on the nightstand, just in case you spent all your
money on me tonight.
   Sweet kisses,
   Rich

I placed the letter in the fresh indent I'd left on the mattress, carried my heels in my hand, eased out of the door, and prayed that the sound from the automatic locks clicking in place didn't wake Justice.

I had exactly twenty-seven-and-a-half minutes to make it home, be seen by my mother when she made her morning visit to my room, shower, change, and be dressed for school. And I needed to get to school early. Especially since the new red carpet was being laid today and I was head of the Red Carpet Committee. Hollywood High was red-carpet fabulous. And as I was chairwoman of the RCC, I liked to keep things fresh and new; hence the new carpets. Last time, the headmistress…well, the headmaster…well, same thing, tried to get away with keeping the same red carpet past its expiration date. Umm, how about no. Did he think I wouldn't notice?

Well, I did. The moment I stepped onto the carpet, my six-inch heels sank straight to the bottom and I could smell the filth. And I would not have it. After I threatened to call the alumni association, the board of directors, and the health department, he got his mind together. And promised me and my Richoids—a select few from my stable of fans—that the new carpet would be laid today and I could do the honors at the ribbon-cutting ceremony.

I couldn't wait! I had my publicist arrange the press coverage.

I had my Parisian stylist fly me in the flyest and the sleekest maple-brown Louis Vuitton stretch leather leggings and sleeveless A-line eggshell-colored blouse—that flowed with the L.A. breeze. The collar was a large, flimsy, chic bow that tied to the side and the loose hem stopped at my hip. My earrings were five-karat pink diamond studs, my stack of beaded bracelets were all pink and brown sapphires, and of course my handbag was an exclusive Louis Vuitton clutch. From the private collection. Don't hate. That's just how the gawds have blessed me to do it.

Fabulously.

I raced to my custom-made, crisp white Hennessey Venom Spyder, tossed my heels onto the passenger seat, floored the accelerator, and took off for the highway, never looking back. The Justice part of my life was behind me. Literally. Besides, I met this Latino cutie the other day at the Pink Lounge, and have mercy—sweet angel over sex appeal—this sugar pop was right and ripe. Ready for the plucking. We kicked it a little. He twirled a few curls in my hair. We tossed back a few shots of tequila. And with tequila being my weakness, I gave in to one of my damsel-in-distress fantasies and allowed this sweet butter-pecan Puerto Rican to melt all over me.

I placed the air conditioner on full blast as I felt a heated rush take over my body.

Mary, Joseph, and Raheem! After that night I had to say at least twenty Rosaries and go to three separate confessions—and I'm not even Catholic.

If only I remembered his name and had gotten his number, I could call him again. But I didn't. I told him my name was Sasha Fierce and that I was passing through on my way to Africa.

Needless to say, after that I was bored with Justice and realized that I needed to be a faithful virgin again. Which meant I needed to only be with my boyfriend, Knox. Well, Christian. But everyone called him by his last name, Knox.

And starting today—at this moment—that's exactly how things were going to be.

The electronic gates squeaked as I pulled onto the long, winding road that led to my parents' estate. My mother, an ex-groupie who was reared in the hood, had a thing for European charm—which explained the cobblestone driveway, English garden, the massive Greek fountains, and the fifty-room French château we lived in.

I pulled around to the servants' entrance. I had two minutes left to make a mad dash for my room. I eased in through the back door, skipped the elevator, tiptoed up the back stairs—taking two at a time—and made it to my room with a minute to spare.

My heart revved like a crackhead passing a collection plate. The last thing I needed was my mother, Logan Montgomery, known as Shakeesha Gatling when she doesn't take her medicine, walking up on me.

I leaned against the back of my closed door and my eyes scanned my suite, from the sitting area to the king-size canopy, to the crystal chandelier, to the balcony overlooking the very cliff my mother threatened to throw me off of if she ever caught me sneaking in the house again.

I ran over to my bed, pulled the sheets back, dived onto the mattress, and rolled from one side to the other and back again. I hopped up, flung off my clothes—leaving on my panties and bra—and walked toward the bathroom.

"Rich Gabrielle Montgomery."

I froze.

My heart fell out of my chest and my stomach went right behind it.

My mother's voice rose again. "I suggest you turn around slowly because any sudden moves will not work out for you."

Dear God...

I turned around and there she was—her face lit up on my computer screen!

What kind of...

I shifted my eyes from side to side. Was she serious? Maybe I was dreaming. Yeah, that's it. So I turned and took a step toward the bathroom. "I know you didn't just give me your back!"

Freeze!

I can't believe this! I had a minute to spare. What happened to my minute to spare? Was she doing digital rounds now? Why was she on my computer screen? I swear this woman was put on this Earth to drive me crazy!

Breathe. Breathe.

Okay. Okay... but breathe.

Dang!

How long has she been watching me? Has she been on my computer all night? Spying on me. Jesus! And to think when I went to confession the Father said prayer works. Yeah, right!

I pushed a plastic smile on my face and turned back toward the computer screen. "Ma, I would never disrespect you like that." *At least not to your face.* "But, umm, why are you on my computer?" I squinted. "Did you hack my system? Break and enter into my Skype account?

Really, Ma, who does that? I thought your life of crime was over."

"No, it's not," she said evenly. "I have one more murder to commit."

I swallowed. Hard. A vision of me rolling down the cliff to my death danced before my eyes and I did all I could to keep my knees from buckling. "I have to get to school."

"No. You have to stand right there. And you better not. Move. An inch."

A few wobbly seconds later, she was off of my computer screen and in my room, standing toe-to-toe with me. At any moment, I expected her to toss up gang signs and spit razor blades out of her mouth.

I was careful not to breathe too hard—because whenever she was *this* pissed off, everything that I did was a problem, including breathing. So I took light sips of air and smiled as I looked into her brown eyes.

Her glare shot a thousand bullets into me as she pushed an index finger into my forehead, forcing my neck to jerk with every move. "Where. Have. You. Been?"

Think. Okay, I got it. I'll cop to the truth. Yeah, that's it, she always tells me that if I tell her the truth she will be understanding.

"I was with Knox."

Bam!

My mother slung a fiery backhand across my cheek, forcing my rickety knees to give way and fling me to the floor. For a moment I thought about playing dead, but that would only aggravate her more.

I looked up at the dungeon dragon standing over me. "Ma!" I lifted my arms and crossed them over my face.

She shoved a hand through my shield, gripped my cheeks, and pressed her fingers into my dimples. "Lie again and you will be over that cliff! You were not with Knox because he called here looking for you. Now. Where. Were. You?"

"With London!"

Slam!

My cheek was scorching again.

"London's in Europe! Now, I suggest you tell the truth before I rip off your face!"

I could feel her flaying my skin with her eyes. "I was... I was..."

"You know what, Rich. You are two seconds from being cut off and disinherited. I don't know why you keep doing this to me! And it doesn't matter how hard I've worked for all that we have. You don't care! Why can't you just listen and be more like your brother? Instead, you'd rather piss on my accomplishments!"

"*Accomplishments?* Last I checked you were a hood rat groupie who stalked the locker rooms! What have *you* accomplished other than marrying my father and pumping out two kids and being all in my business?"

Whap! I expected that slap. But I didn't care. She knew I couldn't stand being compared to her RJ, her sick wonder boy! He may have been overseas at Oxford, but she was still express-mailing him her tittie so he could breastfeed. RJ this. RJ that. Eff RJ!

Nothing was ever about me! I take that back. Some things were about me—her slaps, her stress, her feeling unappreciated, her anger, her frustrations, her constant arguments with my father: all about me.

What. Ever.

All I needed to do was get up and off of this floor so that I could change my clothes and get back to being the boom-boom-bop of happy!

"I don't know why you hate your brother so much! But if you stopped hating him, maybe you could be more like him instead of being a Hollywood whore!"

"I'm not a whore!" I spat and scooted back, somehow making it out of her clutches. I quickly stood up.

She looked me over. "Oh, I know you're not trying to fight me!"

What? "Fight you?"

"You heard me!" She walked up close to me and I took a step back. She snatched me by my shoulder and I had no choice but to stand still. "I'm soooo sick of you. Sick. Of. You. You have everything you could ever want and all I ask is that you stop sneaking out of the house and doing God knows what! That's all I require. But noooo, you can't do that. You want to be in the street. Well, you're on punishment!"

Although my life was on the line, hearing the word *punishment* made me laugh. "Punishment." I all but flicked my wrist, twisted my neck, and said, *Girl, go sit down.* But since I knew better than to take it there, I said, "You can't punish me! What you need to do is back up and stop sweatin' me! I'm almost grown and you need to respect that!" She raised her hand and I flinched. "Ma!"

Wham! I was back on the floor with her elbow in my throat. She looked into my face, and as I struggled to breathe she whispered, "Make this the last time you say anything crazy to me. And make this the last time you sneak into my house. You better make sure it doesn't happen again because if it does, I'ma pack up all yo' things, Miss Almost Grown, and you gettin' outta here! Do I make myself clear? And you better say yes."

I nodded, still struggling to breathe.

"That's what I thought. I'm not playing with you. You are only sixteen, and that's what you need to act like! No more chances. After this, you're finished." She released her elbow and yanked me from the floor. "Now get in the shower because you smell like a cheap alleyway slut!" She forcefully turned me around and all but drop-kicked me into the bathroom.

I did all I could not to cry in the shower.

I am sick of her! She's going to kick me out? Really? Is that the game she wants to play? Ghetto wench!

I quickly dressed, got my face right and tight, covering the small bruise left behind by my mother's assault on me. I pulled my hair into a sexy fly ponytail and instead of stopping in the kitchen to eat breakfast with my parents and play my mother's game of the perfect Huxtable family—who always ate every meal together—I left her and my father sitting at the kitchen table. Looking stupid. I purposely nearly knocked over the butler, sending his silver tray of hot tea and cream to the floor. I shoved open the servants' door. Slammed it behind me. And took off, leaving er'body's face cracked!

I didn't have to be mistreated and called a whore in my own house. I was going to school, where they knew how to treat a lady of my caliber. Besides, I had a red carpet ceremony waiting for me.

I could hear my cell phone ringing, but I didn't dare answer it. Judging from the ring tone, it was Mother.

Trick, please!

I gunned the accelerator and twenty minutes later, as I made a left to go into the school's parking lot, a Honda Accord whipped from behind me and blocked my path.

"What the—!" I screamed, honking the horn and sticking my head out of the window. The driver tossed open his door and I could've died. This stalker had struck again!

It was official: This was the day from divafied hell.

4

Spencer

My Father who art in high fashion and luxury spas, I hope that gutter tramp learned her lesson…

With one hand on the trigger of a fresh can of Mace, and the other tightly clutching my Cesare Paciotti under my arm, I quickly slid behind the wheel of my dark sapphire Bentley Continental GT. Then I immediately locked the doors, slinging my handbag over onto the passenger seat. I reached up under my seat for my stun gun and laid it in my lap before revving the engine and screeching my wheels out of the parking lot and swerving west onto Century Boulevard. Away from the crack den my poor, ratchet friend Heather now called home.

Ugh! If she wanted to live among trash and squalor, she could have just crawled into the Dumpster on the side of the building. Or better yet, she could have simply moved in with the trash queen, London. At least she wouldn't have been living in some musty funk-box, but she would still be living in squalor. She didn't have to squander money she didn't really have on that ole nasty rattrap. It hurt my heart to see her living like some...some ole wild otter. Had she no dang shame?

And the chipped paint and graffiti on the walls were enough to make me want to toss my guts out. *Lord God!* The window curtain looked like an old raggedy bedspread someone just tossed up and tacked over a curtain rod with safety pins.

I'll have to toss these Louboutin heels into the Goodwill bin when I get home after standing on that filthy carpet, I thought, rolling my eyes and sucking my teeth.

"Oooh, I could spit fire! Hotjiggaboogaboo. I'm so goddangit pissed!" I banged a gloved hand on the steering wheel. "That sidewalk hostess knows I don't like wasting a good pair of heels in filth!"

It's a blessing I wore this disposable hazmat suit over my clothes before driving down to the slums. I wiped a lone tear that rolled down my cheek. *Heather had better wake up and smell the Pacific Ocean before the breeze blows her by. This is her last chance to get it right before they lock her away in some padded dungeon.*

"Thank YOU, mysweetLordandSaviorofallthingsrichand-wholesome!" I shouted, raising a hand in the air as I maneuvered through traffic with one hand on the wheel. "I give you praise, Lord God! Give you all the glory! You woke me up this morning and shined your penlight on me. You showed me the way to salvation...and a new shoe boutique. But right now, my prayer is for Heather. You are so kind and gracious. Please. I beg you. Smack the piss water out of her. Show her the error of her wicked ways. Keep her out of the whore barn so she doesn't have to scallywag for dollars. Punch the taste of skittles and black beauties out of her ratchet mouth. These things I beg of you..."

I hit a button on the steering wheel and waited for a little testimonial music to play low through the speakers while I journeyed down the boulevard. Stopping at a traffic light, I screamed at the top of my lungs. "Geezus-pleaseus...I need to exfoliate! I need a deep cleanse! Messing around with Heather's ole rancid behind, I don't even have enough time to stop for an Evian dip in the infinity tub at the spa."

I glanced at the digital clock. I only had thirty minutes to get to school before the homeroom bell rang. And I had no time for games. I took my education at Hollywood High very seriously. See, unlike those other Pampered Princesses of Hollywood High—Rich Montgomery; the fifty-foot, beetle-faced London Phillips; and Heather—I'm a straight-A, advanced honor student with perfect attendance. While the rest of those hookeroos spend their time trolling the halls, the cafeteria, the girls' lounges—and on occasion, the boys' locker room—I'm the *only* one at Hollywood High there for my education. Unlike those trampettes, I do all of my prowling during breaks and after school.

Mmph. Silly tricks.

See. Bubbles. He-he-he. I mean Rich, with her beautiful chestnut skin and those sparkling brown eyes of hers, was only good for one thing. Lying on her back. That ditch digger had more graveyards in her walk-in closets than a cemetery. Think I'm lying? Mmph. Open up those French doors of hers and see how many skeleton bones—or clinic receipts—fall out. All I'm saying is, she didn't keep her womb vacant for long before something was moving up in it. He-he-he.

And that Lorax, London. Not. A. Mumbling. Word! That snake! That lot lizard! That . . . that animal waste! That pile of rotted horse manure! She'd been nothing but problems ever since she got chased out of her Upper East Side New York penthouse and flopped her flippers into Hollywood High. She manipulated Rich. Then turned her against me. My dearest bestie, gone! Snatched away by a bunch of lies spewed out of the gullet of some whiskered mongoose in six-inch platform heels. And I wanted nothing more than to strap that roadkill to a concrete slab and torch her eyeballs out.

And then there was Heather. Now she wasn't the dumbest Pop-Tart in the toaster. And her GPA wasn't the lowest or anything like that. That award went to Rich Montgomery. No, Heather Stank Cummings was really, really smart. But she was broke. And she was too dumb to say no to drugs. She was weak! A nothing! And nobody liked her.

Except *me*, of course!

Yet that flat-back barracuda didn't even have the decency to be grateful for my generosity. She should have been on her knees bowing down to me. The Goddess of All Things Good to her! But she didn't! Then she had the nerve to eyeball me with them ole wiggly eyes of hers and act like I owed her more than what I was gracious enough to give her in the first place. Money I gave her. Not loaned her. Gave!

Mmph. Where they do that at?

Oh, wait. I knew where. Over on Century, in the Piss Motel where Miss Rank-A-Dank Crack-A-Lot had taken up residence. The gutter. The low-lowlands. Mmph. Lest we forget from whence the trash got dumped. Straight to the bottom!

But I couldn't even hate on Heather or say anything mean and nasty about her because I knew it was nothing but pride that kept her from showing her true feelings. I knew she appreciated my thoughtfulness. Underneath, she knew I'm the *only* one who'd ever be there for her. Yeah, okay, okay...I'd tear her panties down too. But I was still her only *real* friend. While everyone else talked about her behind her back, *I'm* the only one who had the decency to talk about her to her face. And I was the only one who visited her while she was in druggie jail. And I told her what her drunken mother wouldn't. I told her who her father is. Now, *that* was a true friend for you.

I glanced up in the rearview mirror as if I were looking at someone in the backseat, but I was thinking of Heather's appearance. "LordGodinallthingspureandtrue! Did you see what she had on? Oochiecoochieyahyahnoodledoodles, she had her cavernous boobs all bunched up in that itty-bitty tube thingy, looking like two tanks of stank-a-dank!"

Waaait! Pull over! Stop the tramp stamp! And those shorts she had on! Bendoverandspreadthetoejam! She had them things all twisted up in her lunchbox like she was ready for a stroll down Yeastville Central. Ugh!

And like I said, I wasn't going to hold that against her because I had a forgiving heart. And I didn't harbor ill feelings toward her. But I didn't forget. And I might remind you. But I wouldn't ever hold it against you. Well, uh, um, not *after* I did you in first. Which is why, *once again*, I had to thank the High Heavens for making me—*me*!

The kindest, most gracious, most fabulous beauty of them all.

Whew! With all of my giving and the charity work I did,

it took a lot of work to be me. I was loving to the lonely and shutout on Monday evenings. I was kind to the needy on Tuesdays and Thursdays. I was always sympathetic to the plight of the downtrodden. I was thoughtful. Generous. Humble. Pure. Sinless. Oh, wait...did I say fabulous? Yes, yes, he-he. I was obedient. Wait, wait...let me get back to you on that. Tee-hee.

I burst out laughing at myself, stopping at a traffic light. Whew, I crack myself up! Ha!

Another lone tear rolled down my cheek as I thought about Heather again. Sweetmercifulhandbagsandsixinchheels, she was one Hefty trash bag full of hot gutter wreckage. Pretty as a pickle, but Flatty Patty had no diggity-dang class whatsoever. Do you hear me?

None.

Nada.

Nooch.

And she couldn't find her way out of a sewer drain with the help of a GPS tracking device if it were hot-glued to her forehead. What a pathetic soul!

But I don't judge. No, no, no. Not Spencer Ellington. I might be the ace of spades of messy, but I was never trashy and gossipy with it. I'm too classy for that. I simply made my observations and kept my thoughts to myself. I threw Heather a lifeline because I was good like that. If I was your friend, I was your friend. Loyal to the end. Ride or die rodeo get-down style. The best friend you wish you had.

Yes, yes, yes, y'all! Mic check. Check-a-one, check-a-two...I'm the best friend you wish you had! But don't do me.

Don't. Do. Me.

Get out of order and watch *me*. Do. You.

You'd better check my credentials. Ugh! I rolled my eyes the second the music faded from the stereo and a call rang through. I sucked my teeth, glancing at the name flashing across the screen. I begrudgingly answered. "Yeah?"

"Spencer, darrrrling. This is your mother. Did you see Heather?"

I gave a blank stare at the console. I swear. As wealthy and successful as the multibillionaire media mogul Kitty Ellington was, she could be such a ditz-ball sometimes. I mean, ditzier than a bucket of truffles. Like, didn't she know I *knew* who the heck she was? Her name came up on the screen every time she called. Sea witch. And her name hadn't changed in the last fourteen of my sweet sixteen years of life. So what would make her think anything would be different now? I mean, really. What a Dumbo! And I was supposed to be the slow one in the room. Ha! Mirror, mirror on the wall, who was really the dumbest of them all? Miss Shitty Kitty! I mean, geesh! How could I forget who she was when she didn't stay her meddling behind out of my face *and* life long enough for me to?

Sweetjeezuz! Take the wheel! I needed a dang cigarette! "What do you think, Mother?" I snapped, sliding my hand down into my handbag, feeling around for my pack of ProVari Mini cigarettes. "Where do you think I've been *all-llll* morning? Jeezus! Did. I. Not. Tell. You. Last. Night. Where. I. Was. Going?"

Ohslutwagonsandhookertrains! *Now where are those cigarettes?*

I lifted up the console. *Oh. Here they are.* I pulled a sleek chrome cigarette out of the pack, then pressed the small button to spark up the blue LED. I cracked the window to keep the vapors from smelling up my car.

I took a deep pull. "Yes, sweetFatherGod!" I shouted, making a sharp left turn onto Crenshaw Boulevard. "I came through in the nick of time and saved Heather's wretched soul!"

"Spencer! Don't you hear me speaking to you? Sweet heavens. What in the world are you shouting and praising about? I asked you a question and I'm waiting for an intelligent response. One with some substance and meaning."

I took another pull on my cigarette. Rolled my eyes real slow in their sockets. *I am really, really trying to be nice. But this mugglyfuggin' sea monkey is really pressing me to get it stunk this morning and air her panties out real good!* I counted to ten in my head.

"Mother, brown bag it, okay! You ole wet mop! Don't you have some little boy-toy you can slog around with instead of badgering me? Jeezus! I don't know how many times I have to tell you, don't speak to me until noontime when I can stomach you."

"You will *not* use that tone with me, young lady. I am your mother. *Not* one of them little snot-nosed Pampered Princesses whom you can't seem to keep on a leash long enough to do as you're instructed. Now keep it up. You'll find yourself confined to your suite for the rest of the week if you don't watch your manners when speaking to me."

"And you can find yourself locked out of *my* house, Mother. Or have you forgotten that the estate I graciously let you board in is mine? Now you keep it up. How about that? Now before you get the dial tone, how can I help you? You're giving me cramps."

She huffed. "Spencer! Focus! I don't have time for your

histrionics, or any of your silly antics. Now get over yourself, my child, and tell me what's going on with that little
brat Heather. Did you give her the check?"

I blinked. "Yes, Mother."

"And the news about her new pilot show?"

I sucked my teeth. "Yes, Mother."

"Was Camille there drunk?"

I rolled my eyes. "Yes, Mother."

I took two angry pulls from my cigarette, feeling myself
about to swerve off the road and run down the nearest
telephone pole. As loving and kind as I was, this joy killer
had a way of bringing out the worst in me. I swear she did.
Mother or not, she was the epitome of a Messy Bessie. She
was slicker than a fox in a henhouse. She was cutthroat, vicious, and downright nasty! I had to always keep my blade
sharp and ready when dealing with the likes of Kitty
Ellington.

God, I hoped I didn't end up anything like her!

I gripped the steering wheel, flooring the accelerator,
zipping through traffic on the freeway, blowing the horn
for drivers to get out of the dang way.

"Have they found a place to live yet?" Kitty pressed, agi-
tating me even more. "You know that Camille siphoned
out all of Heather's measly savings while she was away in
rehab, for no other reason than simply being her old jealous, spiteful self. There was no reason for that conniving
bottom-feeder to do that when I'd given her a million-dollar
advance for those television and radio interviews I'd set up
for her. That dreadful—"

I yawned. "Okay, Mother, gotta go. You're boring me.
Night-night. Don't let the vampires bite. And you had *bet-*

ter have that three million dollars you had me give to Heather transferred *back* into my account."

I ended the call.

"Move out of my way!" I screamed, blowing the horn as I weaved in and out of traffic. "Goshdang you! I have to get to homeroom! If I had time, I'd stop in the middle of this highway and claw your eyeballs out! That'll stop you blind bats from slow-rolling your wheels, trying to make me late for school and ruin my perfect attendance!"

5

Spencer

I was late! Three minutes and forty-two seconds late! And now my mood was as sour as buttermilk. I wanted to beat the biscuits off of someone. That ding-dang Heather! Jeezus! I tried to be gracious and look where it'd gotten me. Stuck in traffic! Late for school! Why couldn't she find a sleaze Dumpster closer to school to stay at?

I kept my eyes focused on the road ahead. Traffic! Traffic! Trrrrrrrrrrrafffffic! I was dang tempted to swerve up on the tree-lined curb and burn these tire treads down the sidewalk, but I wasn't in the mood to run down pedestrians today.

I rolled my eyes, sucking my teeth, then commanded my car's Bluetooth, "Dial...Sweet Cheeks."

I glanced in my rearview mirror. Being late was going to screw my whole day up. First thing I liked to do when I got to school was go to my locker, gather my books for my first two classes, then go into the girls' lounge to freshen up my lip gloss, liner, and hair—even though everything always stayed flawless. I had to look fabulous.

Then in homeroom, while everyone else gossiped and cackled and plotted ditching their next periods, I sat up front and organized my morning. AP Latin was second period. AP Calculus was third period. Then lunch was fourth period.

"Hollywood High. How may I direct your call?"

"Mr. Westwick, please."

"I'm sorry. Mr. Westwick is in a meeting. May I take a message?"

I frowned. "No, *you* may *not* take a message," I mocked. "This is an emergency! Now get up off your pancakes and bang on Mr. Westwick's door. You and I both know he's in there painting his dang toenails! And probably in that god-awful fuchsia! Now be a dear and let that macho momma know Spencer Ellington's on the line. Please and thank you!"

"One moment . . ." she said blandly, placing me on hold. Classical music played in the background.

I glanced in my rearview mirror again. "I don't know why these old biz whiz grannies have to try me. They really want me messy." I slid a manicured finger over my arched brows. Then batted my lashes. "Not today! I'm staying loving and kind."

"Westwick here! Make it quick!"

I blinked. "Hi, Mr. Westwick." I started real sugary and sweet. "This is Spencer Ellington. I'm stuck in traffic."

"Okay? What do you want from me, a biscuit? A hand-clap? Should I call in the Coast Guard?"

My nose flared. "You wait one goshdangit minute, Mr.

Westwick! Don't you dare set it off on me, tootsie! Did you
forget to take your hormones or something, because I
don't like your tone. I will light your burgers! I called hoping we could discuss my being tardy today without messi-
ness. But I see you want—"

"Five thousand dollars."

"What?"

"You heard me, Miss Ellington. Five grand. I'm sick of
you spoiled little shits coming in and out of here, doing
whatever it is you want. There has to be some order
around here. I suggest you pull out your student hand-
book."

I slammed on my brakes, almost causing the SUV in
back of me to ram into me. The horn blared and I sped up.
Finally, the traffic was moving along.

"Sweet jeezus! You monster in a wig! You crumb licker!
You're trying to have me killed out here on the road. I will
sue you, Westwick! Drag your lipstick-stained drawz through
the wringer! You will not get one red cent out of..." My
voice trailed off as my eyes fluttered over to my left.

I slowed down. *Wait. Is that*—? I blinked. Squinted. "I
know that's not who I..." My eyes popped open. *"Oh, yes
it is!* And she's with...oh no! Oh no!" Across the two-lane
street, just a few feet down from the campus's entrance, I
spotted Rich's car. I eased over to the side of the road, riding the shoulder. Then stopped so I could get a better
look.

"Hello? Hello? Ellington? You dimwit! Are you there?
Hello?"

"Oh, shut up, Westwick! Go slide a ruler in it!"

I ended the call.

"What in the world is Rich doing standing out on the side of the road all gussied up like she's going to some award show for freakazoids? She's supposed to be up on the new carpet cutting ribbons and smiling for the cameras. So why is she out here with *him*? Pimp in Timbs?"

Rich and I still hadn't spoken since she'd sucker-snuck me in the face. And I wasn't going to let it go, or be over it, until I gave that five-foot-six pork roll in heels a taste of my wrath. *Putting her hands on me! Mmph!* I slid my hand into my bag and pulled out a pair of miniature brass and mother-of-pearl binoculars for a closer view of the spectacle before me. *Thinking she's going to get away with slapping me! Ha!*

I held the binoculars up to my eyes. *I'ma light her fire! Miss Crotch Rot! Ole pint-size hoochie!*

"Wait! Wait! Wait a dingdong minute! What is going on over there?"

They were arguing!

Oooh, this is juicy! London's lover boy and his side trick! Aww, gushy-gushy now!

I quickly reached for my iPhone and zoomed in, snapping pictures of the two jaybirds quarreling. I set my phone in my lap, looking through my binoculars again. He had his finger in Rich's face. Going off!

Mmph. Good for her … that's exactly what Rated-X gets for messing over a good man like Knox!

She was probably down here tricking along the highway! Ole monster slut …

Rich had one hand on her hip, snaking her neck, jabbing a finger in the air as she gave it right back to ole Mister Trick Daddy. Mister Hump Along. Mister No Good.

I rolled my window down, hoping to hear them yelling. But it was too noisy with all the cars going by. I couldn't hear a goshdang thing!

What the what? What the heeezyjeezy...?

"Aaah!"

He yanked Rich up by the collar. Pinned her up against the car. Jeezus! He was gutter! "Oh no! Oh no! No snatching by the collar! Unless it's a dog collar! Get your hairy mitts off of her!"

I snapped another picture. Then looked through my binoculars again.

"Oh no he didn't!"

He mushed Rich in the face!

Oh no! Oh no! He's over there tryna be the new Chris Beat 'Em Down Brown! I don't think so! Not with my bestie-boo-boo!

"Fight him, Rich! Tear his gullet out! Goshdangit!" I snapped, shutting off the engine then reaching up under my seat. "These tricks 'n' hoes stay keeping me messy! Now Godmomma has to pull out her goodie bag and take it to this boy's nugget!"

I pulled up my face mask. Removed my key from the ignition. Retrieved my black leather trick bag, pulled out a case and removed my two metal friends, Nun and Chucks, swung open my car door, got out, then slammed it shut. I was pissed! Some boy putting his hands on my dang friend! Oh, he had the wrong one, two, and three!

I raced across the highway in my hazmat suit and heels, zigzagging through traffic while swinging my nunchucks up and around over my head.

Horns blared. Tires screeched. Cars swerved.

I could hear him yelling at her. "I'm sick of you playin'

me, yo! You gonna have me eff you up, for real for real, yo! Keep playin' me for some sucka, Rich—"

I was light on my heels, swift in my hips, heavy in my swing when I pounced up on him and conked him in the center of his pumpkin.

He dropped.

"Aaaaaah! Clutching pearls!" Rich screamed. "Aaaaah! Martian gone wild! Somebody help! There's a killer in a space suit on the loose!"

I yanked my mask down. "Rich, shut it! It's me! Now, what the hell on fire are *you* doing out here?" I stamped my foot. "And why did that animal have his goddang hands on you, huh?"

Rich's eyes popped open. "Spencer, what the hell is wrong with you? Why aren't you in school? You have no business being in my damn business! You effen trickazoid! I'm sick of you all up in my business! I had this! I was handling it! I didn't need you all up in my mix somewhere, tryna save somebody! Don't nobody need you tryna save them! I'm a grown woman!"

I blinked. I just saved this roadside hooker from getting pimp-stomped and this was the thanks I got. Another thing I couldn't stand was an ungrateful trick!

I blinked again.

"I don't even like you, Spencer! I can't stand you! You effen intruder! You two-faced snake! You had no business coming over here after you tried to ruin me! This is illegal, Spencer!"

I narrowed my eyes. Tilted my head. Contemplated hitting her across her teeth with my metal friends. Counted to fifty instead.

"Stalking me! Tryna live through me! Everywhere I go,

there you go! Get your own life, Spencer! And stay the hell outta mine! I'll have you arrested. You murderer! You're so jealous and pathetic. You didn't have to kill him! Oh, you're going to pay for this! I'm going to make sure you get put away for the rest of—"

Slap!

I took my hand to Rich's face, causing her to stumble backward. "That's for slapping me in class, Jell-O guts! You thought I forgot, huh, stankalanka?!" I hit her again. "You want to be out here letting boys put their hands on you, huh?"

Rich charged me, swinging punches. "You dirty skank! You backstabbing—"

"Screw you, you slop mop!" I punched her back. "You adulteress!"

We wrestled. Yanked and pulled each other's hair. Swung fists.

"I'm going to kill you, Spencer!"

"Not if I kill you first!"

We tripped over Justice's body, crashing down on top of him then rolling over him. We rolled around on the ground, clawing and punching and choking each other until we heard the faint noise of what sounded like sirens in the distance.

"Tramp, you hear that? Is that the cops coming?"

Rich was breathing all heavy and hard, practically sounding like a grizzly. Her hot breath was curling my nose hairs. I held my breath for as long as I could.

We froze. Listened. It was.

I exhaled, gasping. "I think they're coming for us."

"Oh no, *bish*!" Rich yelled, hopping up off the ground.

"I am not going to jail! Not this time! Not for murder! You're on your own with this one!"

Justice was there on the ground, stone still.

"Jeezushavemercyonmysoul! I didn't mean to kill that boy! But he shouldn't be hitting on no girl!" Tears sprang from my eyes. "I can't go to jail! And be chained in a cage! Become some chick daddy's sex kitten! We gotta get out of here!"

We both started scurrying, grabbing up our broken heels.

I yanked her by the arm and ran-hopped in my one good pump, dragging Rich behind me. I yanked my keys out of my pocket, disarming the alarm.

"Hurry! Get in!"

I hopped behind the wheel, drenched. I glanced up in the rearview mirror and screamed. Steam was seeping from around my collar. I was on fire in this hazmat suit! I started the engine and floored the accelerator, peeling off.

"Where to?"

"Just drive, *bish*! Drive!"

6

Rich

Spencer was going down!

And I was going to make sure she spent the rest of her life on death row, being some butch queen's sex slave and washing her dirty drawls!

'Cause I *wasn't* going to jail!

I was turning state's evidence!

This chick was done!

I can't believe she ran up on me like the head of the coochie patrol, cock blocked and raided my moment! I didn't need her flying through the air in a hazmat suit and heels. This was real life. Not some twisted fantasy!

I knew how to handle Justice.

I didn't need her to kill him!

Ohmygod! She really tried to take his head off!

The bottom of my stomach had fallen out as I cried, "I can't believe you killed that boy!" I pointed to the street behind us. I could still see his body in the distance, lying there, motionless.

"Shut up!" she screamed, whipping the steering wheel to the right and making a sharp turn onto the highway. "Shut up!"

"I'ma shut up, all right. Right after I testify against you!" I pointed at the side of her face. "Right after I shut you down. Right after I tell the judge that something has always been wrong with you. After I demand they put you away for the rest of your life! You're a danger to the community. And a menace to my love life!"

"You know what, Rich?" Spencer zigzagged across two lanes, cutting two cars off and causing one to slam on its brakes. "If you keep talking, do you know what's going to happen next?"

My eyes popped out as she floored the accelerator and the speedometer spiked to a hundred and ten. *"What? What happens next? Whatchu mean?"*

"I'm going to take you to meet the grim reaper. So either shut your fox trap, or start writing your eulogy. It's about to be some slow singing and flower bringing."

Breathe in . . .

Breathe out . . .

This is not real! It's not!

I flipped the visor down and looked into the mirror.

"Ahhh!" I screamed in horror at the sight staring back at me. *My hair is a mess! My makeup looks like I've been to war! I'm supposed to be hot and pretty! This is a dream. Scratch that. This is a nightmare! I'm going to wake up at any moment and we will be at Hollywood High at my red carpet ceremony where the press is waiting and Miley Cyrus is giving us a first-class view of her cheap tongue wagging and her pink pleather twerk.*

"Rich!" Spencer snatched me out of my thoughts. "Get out the dang mirror and tell me where we are going!"

I slammed the visor up. "Excuse *you*! You're the reason my heel is broken off and now we're fugitives making a mad dash across county lines, hoping like hell the feds don't hunt us down, then shoot us on the spot. We're on the run and *you're* asking *me* where we're going? You should have had all this planned out before you went kung fu crazy and started dropping bodies. *I* should be going to school so that I can get my celebration on. *Not* riding shotgun with you, man-killah!"

"You know what? I'm getting ready to drive you off the nearest cliff!" She made a sharp pull to the left, cutting cars off.

I almost pissed my pants. "Stop it!" My heart felt like it had jumped into my esophagus. "You going to get us killed!"

"Exactly! NOW WHERE ARE *WE* GOoooooooING?"

"Go south! Go south! Toward San Diego! We'll escape to Chinatown and try to blend in!" I sniffed and did all I could not to lose myself in a crying fit. "You're dead wrong for this, Spencer!" Tears filled my eyes and wet my cheeks. "Why couldn't you just mind your business instead of being all up in mine? That's the same mess you pulled when you ran your damn mouth and told Knox that I had an abortion and almost broke us up! And now this! You're out of control!"

Her head snapped from the highway. "*What?* Don't get it wrong. I haven't spoken to Knox in like forever. So I didn't tell him a goshdang thing! Why would I do that to you?"

"You tell me! That's what I wanna know! *You* betrayed *me*!"

She swung the wheel to the right, almost sideswiping two cars. "I *didn't* betray you! I don't do that! You're the one who's always doing something all lopsided and crazy! Not me! And you know I worry about you, Rich." She tossed a glance over at me. "How dare you accuse me of trying to tear down your relationship? You're doing a good job of that on your own, Miss Cheater."

"I'm not a cheater! And after today, I don't need you looking my way! I'm done! Done! Done with you. Murderer! You left him for dead in the street. You have no shame. That wasn't Compton. That was Hollywood. It's illegal to walk around droppin' bodies over there!"

"Well, he shouldn't have put his grubby ole hands on you!" Spencer's voice trembled. "And don't even lie and say he didn't because I saw him. I zoomed in with my binoculars and everything!"

I could feel a drop of piss spread like a wet web in my panties as she screamed and drove like a maniac. All I kept seeing was my life flashing before my eyes. *This girl is going to kill me!* "Spencer, he didn't put his hands on me! Slow down! Please!"

She peeked back at the road and swerved, moments from slamming into the back of a tractor-trailer. "Then what is that bruise on your face?"

"My mother drop-kicked me in the jaw this morning, okay?"

"For what? Running your mouth?"

"No! For bad-mouthing RJ! Your once-upon-a-time G-spot lover! That's another reason why I can't stand him. First, he stole my parents. Then he skeeted on my friends!"

"Oh, Rich, please! You're just jealous because you know RJ is perfect!"

"RJ is a prick who keeps smoking weed and spreading his grimy seed. Screw RJ! And screw you! You're worried about RJ and he's over there in the United Kingdom with a set of twins straddling him! Girl, puhlease. You have bigger problems than RJ, like being on the run for murder and kidnapping me!"

"You're wrong for that!"

I huffed. "You just killed somebody in cold-water blood. And *I'm* wrong?"

I took two deep breaths to calm my rattled nerves. I wasn't about to boom-bop-drop it upside this nutty trick's head with her still behind the wheel driving way above the speed limit. No. I had to go into damage control to de-escalate the situation.

"Oh, you didn't think I had it in me, did you? I bust when I have to. Now tell me *why* we're heading to San Diego instead of across the border to Mexico."

"Mexico? Clutching pearls! I don't do that! Are you trying to have me boom-bop-drop and die? The last time I was in Mexico, I tossed back a bad batch of tequila, sucked down the worm, and woke up tied to the bed! No, ma'am, and no thank you! I'm staying right here in the good ole U.S. of California. Now, make a left into that parking lot. We're going into that building right there."

She eyed the deep purple–painted brick building that was Knox's on-campus apartment. It had gold shutters and a monstrous wooden bulldog bolted onto the flat roof. "Who lives here?"

"Knox."

"*Knox?*"

I raised a brow. "You know Knox. My man. My one and only. Don't get amnesia, Spencer!"

She rolled her eyes and sucked her teeth. "Sweetjigga-crazycatinthehat! And *whhhhy* have you dragged me down here to Knox's school?"

"Duh! We're on the run and we have nowhere else to go! We'll blend in here, right on campus. We'll be safe. This is a whole apartment building for the cuties. I mean, the Ques."

She grinned as we flipped our respective visors down and got ourselves together. Of course I had to borrow Spencer's makeup kit so I could put this face back together again. On the run or not, I still had to be fabulous! I pulled my hair back into a ponytail and slicked my edges with a fingertip.

Spencer glanced over at Knox's complex. "The whole building?"

"The. Whole. Building. *Yaaaas, Gawd!* Now you can have your choice of the cuties, but, um, I'm telling you now Knox's roommate is off-limits! He's dumb as a kick-plate and needs meds! All he does is eat, sleep, and hump around! That's it. Who can respect somebody like that? And he's dating some chick named Large Honey and that body of hers looks like one big food fight! Now come on. Let's go."

We eased out of the car, careful to look over our shoulders as we heel-hopped over toward the building, making sure no one was following us. We stepped onto the stoop and just as I placed my hand midair to ring the bell, Midnight yelled out the window, "BJ! Wassuup, Big Jawn! I told Knox you would smell this food. I got that hot goodness for ya lip smackers! Some honey-jerk-barbecue ribs, fried chicken, mac-and-cheese balls. Collard greens. Ham. And that bangin' sweet potato fight-er'body-and-their-mama pound cake. From scratch! All for five ninety-nine! We 'bout to bust a party up in here! And yo, who is that lil tender piece of neck bone behind you?"

"Her name is Off-Limits! Now buzz us in."

"He's kind of cute," Spencer whispered as we walked into the building and then stepped into the elevator.

"Yeah, cute if you're into dog piss."

Midnight held the apartment door open for us as we stepped off the elevator. I walked past him rolling my eyes. And just as Spencer went to step in behind me, he blocked her path. "Damn, baby cakes. I like your outfit." He looked Spencer over in her hazmat suit. "Can I call you Limits for short, huh? I promise you, you're so hot you've got me sizzling. Got me burning up all in my drawls! I feel it, girl. All through my bones. I'm on fire!"

"Is that why they call you STD?" I reached up and smacked him on the back of his head. "Now move and let my friend in!"

Of course Spencer was grinning like she'd just walked up on Mr. America. This girl was so easy. She must've forgotten she was on the run.

Anyhoo, I was doing my best to act like I didn't smell Midnight's food when the truth was I wanted to spread out at the table and get my eat on! After the morning I'd had, a plate of everything would have done me just right.

But I couldn't sink my teeth into a thing. Not without seeing my man first.

I walked over to Knox's room and pushed the door open. Empty. I turned around. "Midnight, where's Knox?"

"With Nikki," he said with ease, like this was a daily thing.

I felt like someone had put me in a chokehold. "What?"

"With Nikki," he repeated with the same level of ease, as if I was stupid to think he would be anywhere else.

"What the heck is he doing with her?"

"Why are you concerned?" came from the direction of the doorway. It was Knox and this chick. The same chick I'd seen him with before. The same girl he swore to me was just a friend. But, clearly, I could see—and Spencer, who had her mouth hanging open, could see—that this man-hungry bish, Nikki, was a little more—*maybe* a whole lot more—than a friend. If anything, she was a fraud trying to steal my man.

"Where are you coming from?" I asked Knox, but clashed gazes with Nikki.

"The question is: Where have *you* been?" Knox asked calmly.

All the places that I'd been appeared in short clips before me. I didn't know what to say. I couldn't even think of what lie to tell. All I knew is that I had to tell him something. Something that made sense. But what? "Um, baby, can I um, speak to you? *Now*?" I asked, my tone giving away that I was frightened he would refuse. "*Please*," I added for good measure.

I could see the hesitation on his face. He wanted to say no. I knew he did. And I was preparing myself to hear it. But instead he sighed deeply and turned to Nikki. "I'll call you later."

Call her later?
I don't think so!
For what?
And why would he want to call her later?
Relax.
Breathe.

Don't flip. You know be can't stand it when you go off.
I'm losing bim.
I can tell.

I eyed him as he walked Nikki to the door, then whispered something in her ear. She shook her head. And I felt like someone had taken a jagged edge and sliced my throat with it. I felt my blood run cold. I wanted to boom-bop-drop it on his head. But I willed my temper in check as he walked up on me, eyeballing me all crazy. He broke his gaze and looked over my head at Spencer and smiled. After she gave him a small wave, his eyes came back to me. He smirked and headed to his room.

I followed him and closed the door.

"What are you doing here and why aren't you in school?" he spat.

"What the fu—" *Relax. Breathe.* "What the heck was that about? What were you doing with that trick?"

"Don't question me. Don't call her names. And lower your voice."

I threw a hand up on my hip and my neck went into full swing. It took everything for me not to slap his face off. "Don't call *her* names? Really, Knox? So this is how you're dropping it now? This is why I haven't heard from you? Are you cheating on me? Is that why Nikki is always around?!"

Knox ran a hand over his shadow beard and looked over at me. "Let me tell you something. Check this. Don't come up in here questioning me. Demanding things. And now you wanna talk to me about cheating? Really? Maybe that's something I need to be checking *you* on since I haven't heard from you all week."

I scanned his face and wondered for a moment if he

knew. Justice's face flashed through my head and guilt suddenly ripped through me. Tears filled my eyes and my heart thundered. And just as I was about to run out the door, the look in Knox's eyes kept me planted still. I knew then that it was safe to say...

"I would *never* cheat on you! Never! I can't believe you would say that to me! I've been nothing but true to you! If you don't trust me then maybe we don't need to be together! I refuse to be with anyone who can't trust me."

"You know what? Maybe you're right. Bounce. I'm not gon' sweat you because either way, you're moving like you're single."

"I'm not moving like I'm single." My lips quivered. "I'm moving like a woman in love."

He shot me a look that said, "Bull."

"So you don't love me? Is that what you're saying?!"

"This is not about my love. That's not up for discussion. It's you and yo' ish I'm starting to side eye."

I don't believe this. I need to say something to make this better. Let me think... "You know I love you! You know I've always loved you."

"No. You've always expected me to sweat you."

"I'm not asking you to sweat me."

"Then what are you asking me? Because, on the real, I'm confused. All I know is, your mouth says one thing, then you turn around and do something else." He paused, keeping his eyes locked on mine, shaking his head. "Every time I turn around, Rich, it's something different with you. And it's getting real old, real fast. For real."

"Knox." I walked up on him and reached for his hand. He pulled away. And instead of me reaching for it again, I draped my arms around his neck and braided my fingers

together. He stood stiff, unimpressed. I went to kiss him
and he turned his head, my lips landing on his cheek. But
that was okay. I still had this under control. Now I knew
exactly what I had to do to make this all go away. "I'm
sorry," I whispered, my first step into turning this around.
Apologize.

"You're always sorry."

"You're right. I am. And I know I'm always doing something that makes you doubt my love for you." That was
step two. Acknowledging I'd done something wrong, even
if I thought I hadn't.

He narrowed his eyes. "Yeah. And it's getting tired."

"Can you forgive me?" I kissed him softly on the left
side of his neck. "I'm just going through so much at
home." I moved my kisses to the right side of his neck.
"My mother is always on me. Nothing I do is good
enough. You know how she is."

Silence.

"You know how hard I had to fight her just to be with
you. And now that she's finally given in, I'm not going to
let anything ruin that. I'm not tryna ruin it."

More silence.

I moved my kisses to his collarbone, working my way to
step three. "I'm not going to mess up again. I promise.
You're always on my mind. I won't ever go more than a
day without calling you." I lifted his T-shirt above his head.
I moved my kisses over his chest. "You're all I need."

He let out a deep sigh. He wasn't saying much. No, no...
he wasn't saying anything at all. But I could feel his body
starting to relax. That was all I needed. My magic kisses were
slowly working.

"I know you still love me."

Silence.

I unbuckled his pants, dipping down low and planting kisses around his waist. I gazed up at him. "Do you still love me?" I asked, my tongue teasing him to ecstasy. "I love you." Then I heard him groan as I eased back up, running my hands up his chest. "Tell me, Knox. Do you still love me?"

"Yeah." He moaned. Then, catching me by surprise, he scooped me up into his arms, walked over to the bed, and laid me on it. "I love you...maybe a little too much." His mouth covered mine and I closed my eyes, getting swept up in the heat of his kisses.

Step three, completed.

My work here was done.

7

London

Milan, Italy

Five a.m., I sat before the vanity table in my room, naked underneath my robe, gazing into the large mirror outlined with huge light bulbs. I'd just finished my mother-obsessed-weigh-in thirty minutes earlier. One hundred and ten pounds is what the digital scale read when I stepped on, holding my breath as she logged my weight into her leather-bound journal. I had passed with flying colors.

Mmmph. Whatever...

I wiped the remaining tears from my eyes, rubbing the side of my still-stinging face from where she had slapped me just fifteen minutes ago. I stared at the welt slowly spreading across my cheek; then closed my eyes...

"Look at you, my darling, London," my mother had gushed earlier, standing slightly behind me, her hand placed gently on my shoulder as we both stared at my naked reflection in the full-length triptych mirror. Full, firm breasts. Ultra small waist. Slightly curved hips. "Your face, gorgeous. Your neck, fabulous; so graceful and swan-like." She eyed my boobs, practically pushing out a sigh of disgust. "We'll keep taping your breasts as needed, for now." She turned me sideways for a side-view of my reflection. There sat two brown, rounded globes of all-natural goodness.

"Dear God! There is just *waaaay* too much of this." I cringed as she ran a manicured hand over the curve of my behind. "If we can just do away with this camel hump. I need to do damage control. The sooner we get all this removed, the more shows I'm sure you'll book."

I fought the urge to grimace. I was so tempted to smash an egg in her flawless face and tell her how I'd recently read in *Teen Runway Fashionista* that just as the days of thin, nearly nonexistent lips were long gone, so too were flat-back, invisible booties. Just as they looked for full, pouty, ethnic lips, designers were now craving models that had a little more junk in the trunk. But somehow I figured it didn't matter to her what the fashionistas in the teen world had to say about it. As far as she was concerned, my plump rump was a hindrance. A distraction. A liability.

And she wanted it gone!

I eyed her questioningly, shifting my weight from one foot to the other. I folded my arms.

Three years ago, she wanted to drag me off to Mexico to have me infected with a tapeworm—a procedure illegal in the U.S. The year after that, she wanted me to have my jaw wired. Then, last summer, she wanted to have a hard plastic mesh sewn onto my tongue for a month with fishing line as sutures—some crazy weight-loss procedure started somewhere over in Latin America that some nutty whack job cosmetic surgeon brought back to the States— knowing damn well it would be extremely painful if I tried to eat anything.

And now this!

I stepped away from her and the three-panel mirror, slipping back into my robe. "I'm doing *every*thing you ask of me, Mother. IV therapies. Colonics. Wheatgrass smoothies. Belly wraps. Master Cleanses. But surgeries..." I shook my head. "No. *That* is one of your crazy plans I am *not* doing. My butt *and* my breasts stay."

She huffed. "The breasts we can work around, but that backside of yours, not so much. I fear your work in the industry will be limited to print ads. And..." she paused, shaking her head. "At some point, plus-size fashions."

I rolled my eyes. "Well, what difference does it make if I'm modeling print ads or end up a plus-size model? It's still modeling, isn't it? That *is* what you've wanted, right? Me modeling?"

She frowned. "What kind of foolish question is that? Of course I want you modeling. As a high-fashion model, London, *not* traipsing around on some disastrous cattle circuit for Ashley Stewart or Lane Bryant."

"I am *not* doing it, Mother. And you can't make me." I eyed her sternly for emphasis, placing a hand on my hip. She might have been able to control my trust fund and dictate where I lived; she might have monitored my weight and bullied her way into my personal life and directed who I dated and stayed friends with. But she was *not* going to make me have plastic surgery. She'd taken enough away from me already!

It was too early in the morning for this. And I had a

mother I couldn't even talk to. All I wanted to do was stay curled up in bed with my head beneath my covers. I wanted to sleep away the rest of my time here on this earth. Pretending to be happy with my new forced life was beginning to wear the edges of my nerves thin.

And I wasn't up for being pinned and prodded and shouted at and shoved and critiqued by a group of bubble-head assistants and demanding designers. No. I wasn't up for it. Not today. The idea of keeping up with the farce for appearance's sake 24/7 was becoming too much to bear. I was homesick.

Lovesick.

And sick and tired of being sick.

Everything was slowly crashing down around me.

Ain't no body checkin' for ya...but me...and I don't even know why I eff wit' you...I feel sorry for you...

I blinked back tears, recalling my argument with my mother earlier this morning. "You say you love *all* of me? Yeah, okay. Whatever! I can't tell. And I can't wait to see just how much you and your uppity fashion houses *really* love me when these 34C's and this *camel hump* booty are bouncing down the catwalk! Or have you already told them that *you* planned on dragging *your property* into some plastic surgeon's office for reconstructive renovations?"

Slap!

My mother's hand landed on the side of my face, swift and hard. And a fresh gush of tears sprung from my already weeping eyes. I couldn't believe she'd slapped me. Stunned, I held the side of my face in my hand.

"I know this isn't the life *you* asked for! I *gave* it to you! And, make no mistake, London. Like it or not, *this* is your life! *This* is your world! Fashion! The lights, the cameras, and all of the glitz and glamour that come along with it, is *yours*! If I seem *harsh* to you, if I seem *cruel* to you, it's what I've been preparing you for from the moment you took your first step. Everything I have *taught* you, *told* you, *shown* you, has been to protect you! And hopefully prevent you from making some of the same mistakes I made.

"*You* have an advantage over the rest. *You* don't ever have to worry about being on the bottom, because I am one of the few on top of the fashion-industry's totem pole, still racking in millions without stepping a heel on a runway. *I've* paved the way for *you*! You don't want this life...?"

She glared at me. "Too goddamn bad! *Until* you are eighteen, *until* you are sufficiently able to take care of yourself without getting your hands on one damn dime of the trust fund that your father and I have so graciously entrusted to you, *this* is the only life you will have!"

She was about to turn to leave, then stopped. "I love you, London. You are my child—my only child. And the only reason I don't beat you senseless and have you rolled out of here on a gurney is that you have castings today. You had better *work* as if your life depended on it. Because it does!"

I watched my mother through furious slits of rage as she disappeared, her fashion glide still evident in each elegant step she took, slamming the door behind her.

I blinked, bringing myself back to the present. *Screw her!* I stared at my reflection in the mirror. *Putting her damn hands on me! You want me to be your protégé, your puppet? Then so be it!* I reached for a jar of Annick Goutal's face cream, removed the lid, and gingerly applied the multivitamin moisturizer to my face. *I'll give you exactly what you want and be the model you've always wanted me to be! Even if it kills me!*

I glanced at the itinerary my ever-so-efficient mother had set aside for me, feeling overwhelmed. How did she expect me to get through all of this crap with a wide smile when she'd practically slapped my face off and I had so many other things weighing heavy on my mind?

And right now, the thought of Justice possibly breaking up with me was all I could think about. That and the fact that Rich was blatantly avoiding me was pissing me off. I'd done nothing to that bed-hopping whale to warrant her opening my text messages and *not* replying back. How did I know this? Because we all had iPhones that indicated when someone opened a text you'd sent to them. And I knew she wasn't dead because she was constantly updating her Facebook status, tweeting, and Instagramming. So there was absolutely no excuse for this level of rudeness. None whatsoever!

Glancing at the time. I sighed, and reached for my cell. *I'm going to try this hooker one last time.* I dialed Rich's number. *Then I'm done calling her.* I'd decided late last night in between bouts of crying that I would wait until I got home to address her. What other choice did I have? It wasn't like she was breaking her neck to fly out here for the weekend like she'd promised.

Lying beeeeyotch!

"Heeey, Rich," I chirped into the phone, my tone seventy-eight percent sweet and twenty-two percent nasty. "The least you could do, heifer, is return my calls. And I *know* you've seen my texts. And you're all up on Facebook. Don't get cute. *Anyway*, whatever. It is what it is. I really wanted to talk. But I'll be home in two weeks. *Hopefully,* you'll find time to squeeze in a phone call or two between now and then." I ended the call, then tried Justice again. The phone rang once, and went straight to voice mail. I couldn't leave a message. The mailbox was full.

I stared into the mirror.

My life was in turmoil. And my mother had the audacity to want me to slay a bunch of fashion dragons. *Yeah, I'll work it all right!* I slung my call sheets to the floor. Then used my fingertips and began gently massaging the moisturizer into my face, glaring at my reflection. All I saw was my mother staring back at me.

I hated her!

I hated Justice!

And I hated me more!

I wiped my hands, sighing. *And Rich can't even be a friend when I need her to be! All that selfish ho ever thinks about is who she can lure next into some motel room. She's probably somewhere right now tricking with Spencer!*

I stared at my phone, checking for messages that I knew weren't there. *Damn you, Justice!*

I choked back more tears. *Nope, I said I wouldn't cry. Said I wasn't shedding another tear on that boy! If he doesn't want me, then I'm not going to beg him to be with me!* I swept my manicured fingertips over my eyes before tears fell.

Somewhere, buried between layers of *"I'm sick of you," "you're so stupid," "you're effen fat," "you're worthless,"* and *"ugly,"* I knew I was beautiful, even though I didn't always feel it or see it. Somewhere stuffed between all the lies and fights and sweaty body-tingling make-up sex, I knew I didn't deserve how Justice treated me. I knew I deserved someone who loved me and wanted to be with me. But how could I let go of Justice when, time after time, he'd reel me back in with empty promises, warm tantalizing kisses, and toe-curling sex?

Somewhere wedged in between broken promises and Justice's cold-shoulder treatment and deadening silence, he'd managed to consume me. He managed to turn me into a needy, obsessively jealous girl who constantly lied to and defied her parents and kept dirty secrets, all in the name of love.

A love that wasn't even my own. A love that I allowed to keep hurting me when I knew it was no good for me. How could I break away when Justice pulled me in with his charm and told me I was his universe, that I was all he ever wanted? How could I ever doubt him, when all I kept doing was holding onto hope?

"Nothing's gonna change with us, ya hear? We're in this together, thick as thieves, for life..."

"Lying bastard!" I spat, rummaging through my vanity drawer and digging out the crumpled up photos I'd received the other day. "If you were all mine, then why is your hand up on some naked whore? Why aren't you answering my calls, huh? Why?"

Our love was unstoppable. Unbreakable. That's what he'd always told me.

Then why the hell does he always keep breaking up with me? "Why does he keep hurting me?"

"Because you keep letting him," a sarcastic voice said, floating into the room behind me.

Startled, I jumped from my vanity, spinning around. My heart quickened. "Ohmygod! You scared the crap out of me! I didn't hear you come in."

Anderson smirked, shaking his head as he shut my bedroom door behind him.

"Well I guess you *wouldn't* hear me when you're all wrapped up in your one-woman pity monologue, again. Your door was ajar. I knocked. And once again, I walk in on you having another one of your emotional meltdown moments over...let me guess. That bum. Your secret hood lover."

He stepped further into the room.

I eyed him as he crossed over toward the chaise in the far right corner of the room, stretching his legs out, then crossing his feet at the ankles. He reached over, grabbing my *book*—the portfolio of my photographs.

"I don't need your lecture right now. And I'm not interested in one of your holier than thou sermons, Reverend Doctor Do Right."

"Oh, don't worry. No lectures. No sermons, Street Sweeper. I know you love it hood-ratchet, Mama," he said mockingly, flipping through the photos. "It's pathetic."

I swallowed. "You don't know what you're talking about," I said defensively, tightening my sash around my waist. I hated that he knew that I was so broken. I felt naked and exposed in front of him. "Why are you here?"

He looked up from my portfolio. "Isn't today your big day? Didn't your mother tell you I was coming? I wanted to see you. And be here with you when you went for your gatherings..."

I sucked my teeth. "They're *go-sees*," I corrected. "My go-sees."

"Yeah, those. By the way, you're beautiful." He cleared his throat. "I mean, these pictures of you are...beautiful." He allowed his gaze to penetrate me.

I shifted my eyes, swallowing back more tears along with a nervous energy I'd never experienced around him before. This was Anderson, for God's sake! Not some superstar jock I had a silly schoolgirl crush on.

Or did I?

"I bet you wish it was that leech sitting here instead of me, don't you?"

I frowned. "Well, he's *not* here. And I don't need you here, either."

Anderson stood and walked over to me. "When are you going to stop, huh?"

I cocked my head. "When am I going to stop what?"

He held me with his gaze, stepping in closer. His cologne wafted around me as I tried not to breathe him in. "Letting that punk play you. You know he's no good for you, London. I keep telling you that you deserve better."

I turned from him, holding my face in my hands, shaking my head. "Anderson, go. *Please.* I don't need this right now."

"You don't need *what*, London?" I could practically feel the heat from his body on me as he stood behind me, barely touching me as he spoke low in my ear. "Someone caring about you? Someone willing to love you? Someone wanting to build a life with you? Is *that* what you don't need?" My shoulders shook as I tried to keep my emotions in check, but I was spinning out of control.

Anderson turned me to face him. "Tell me. What is it you don't need, London?"

"This," I said, wiping my tears with my hands, and dry-

ing them on the sides of my robe. I tried not to look at
him. "You getting all up in my head, confusing me."

He *tsk*ed. "Confusing you? Me? And how am I doing
that? By being the man you wish your little fleabag
boyfriend could be? Nah, I'm not confusing you. You're already confused. All I'm trying to do, all I've ever been trying to do, is help you see the light."

I glanced up into Anderson's eyes and saw something
flickering in them. And the intensity of his gaze made me
uncomfortable. Nervous. Uncertain. I felt like I was seeing
him for the first time.

My lips quivered. I opened my mouth to say something,
but Anderson leaned in and kissed me on the lips—lightly
at first, then with more force, causing my lips to part. His
tongue slipped into my mouth. His mouth was warm and
familiar and tasting ever so slightly of peppermint.

I quickly pulled away before I got caught up in...him,
and in the strange feelings that were slowly growing inside of me and starting to heighten my guilt. My heart be-
longed to Justice, even if he had stomped on it a thousand
times over.

I swallowed hard.

Anderson wrapped his arms around me and held me
tight against his body. "I want you, London." He planted
slow wet kisses down my neck, and all the tension drained
from my body. "And I'm here for you. I've always been
here for you."

"I can't do this, Anderson."

He took a deep breath. He ran his hand over his
smooth-shaven face, and stepped back. "You know what?
You're right. You can't. And neither can I. I'm done throwing myself at your feet. I'm not going to exert any more of

my energy on to someone who doesn't want me the way I want them. Maybe you should try it."

"What are you saying?"

"Tell me you don't ever wanna see me again and I'll walk out of your life right now. For good, London. No more games. No more pretenses. No more drama. It's *all* of me or nothing at all."

I closed my eyes, feeling a piercing in what was left of my already shattered heart. I didn't want Anderson to not be in my life. But I didn't want him as a boyfriend. I mean, maybe a part of me did, but...I mean, maybe...No, I couldn't. Still, I'd come to rely on him in more ways than I'd ever imagined. He was the only one I didn't have to pretend around.

I swallowed, fought back more tears. "I-I can't. But I want for us to still be—"

"Still be *what*, London? *Friends?*" For a moment I thought I saw hurt in his eyes. He tsked. "I don't think so. I'm not signing up for that. Not this time. You want a friend; call the psychic hotline for one. Because I'm done being your advisor, your confidante, and the keeper of all of your lies and secrets. I'm taking off the superhero cape and moving on. I'm in love with you, London. But I'm not playing this game with you. Delete my number. And I'll do the same. I'll let you off the hook and tell your parents that I've ended our so-called relationship because I'm no longer interested in being with a girl I could never love."

My chest tightened as he turned to leave. I choked back tears. Suddenly I heard my mother's voice in my head, haunting me. *"Anderson is a real thoughtful young man... he'll make a fine husband..."*

I heard myself countering her. *"Anderson isn't who I want..."*

"You will learn to love him..."

Dear God, it's too late! I think I already do...

I swallowed. "Anderson...wait."

He kept walking toward the door.

"Anderson, *please.*"

He stopped in his tracks and turned to me. "What is it, London? Because when I walk out of this door, it's for good. I'm done trying to be your savior. I'm done *playing* boyfriend with you. You don't even realize what you have in front of you." He shook his head. "You either want a man who is ready to love you and accept you for everything that you are and aren't. Or you want to keep being with some idiot who keeps disrespecting you. The choice is yours. Now what do you want?"

My lips quivered.

I didn't know what I wanted. All I knew is, I didn't want to keep hurting. I didn't want to keep feeling empty. I didn't want to keep feeling unloved. I didn't want to keep feeling unwanted. And I didn't want to be left alone.

Not now. Not ever.

I opened my robe and let it drop to the floor.

8

London

Milan, Italy

"**L**ondon, daaaaarling," my mother said, sounding overly excited as she whisked through the door of my suite. "Wake up! Up! Up! Up! I just received some fabulous news, my darling! Jason Wu has his eye on you!"

She has got to be frickin' kidding me! She's barging into my room, disrupting my misery-inspired pity party God, she's so obnoxious!

"London, my love, I can see it now: Teen sensation London Elona Phillips takes Milan by storm. You'll be booked incessantly with shoots for magazines, including *Vogue Italia* and *British Vogue*. You'll be casting for the Paris, Milan, and New York fashion shows. Oh, London, darling, you are on your way!"

God, lay my weary soul to rest, not now...right now!

I'd lain perfectly still, pretending to be comatose. Hoping my mother would get the hint and leave me the hell alone. I wanted to die in peace. But when I heard her shuffling around my room, snatching open the draperies, I knew, once again, withering away wasn't going to happen. Not today.

I held my breath as my mother whizzed through the details of which fashion designers vied for me to hit the catwalk in their couture. Like I gave a damn!

"After Jason designed that fabulous inauguration ball gown for Michelle Obama, he's been to die for, darling. And Valentino and Miu Miu, darling!" she added gleefully. "They both want you for Fashion Week! Oh, London... wake up! We must celebrate!"

Celebrate?

Lady, beat it! I'm dying inside!

I am mourning!

And the idea of being trapped in the *mwah-mwah* ritual of the fashion industry and cutthroat cattiness while being chained to its grueling schedule of late-night fittings, six a.m. starts, layers of makeup, endless hair changes, and three shows with three-hour advance call times for hair, makeup, and rehearsals every day for a week was not cause for celebration.

Talking to my man was!

My head was buried deep beneath the charmeuse silk of my Kumi Kookoon blanket, along with my aching heart and swollen eyes. I'd cried most of the night until I was finally able to drift off to sleep for a few hours before waking up drenched in sweat from a horrible dream I'd had. My man was somewhere out there laid up with some ole nasty, mysterious big-booty skankazoid! And I was here! Helpless!

Who would let someone take naked pictures of her like that? A skid-row troll doll would! That's who!

Receiving those photos yesterday coupled with my mother's constant badgering about the upcoming fashion show premieres and the multitude of demands from an annoying fashion photographer, then not being able to reach Justice, only heightened my anxiety and had me on edge. I called his phone over a gazillion times and each time he kept sending me straight to voice mail. And all of my text messages have gone unanswered.

Something had to be terribly wrong! He'd never gone this long without at least responding to one of my text messages—even if it was to argue. Justice never went more than two or three days without returning my calls. Okay, okay...one time he ignored me for two whole torturous weeks. But that was because I'd upset him really bad—although I'm still not sure exactly what I'd said or done. But he said I was getting on his nerves. That I was suffocating him and that he needed space and time to think.

In the past, I'd been mindful to do everything right to keep Justice happy. Give him sex whenever he wanted it. Drop whatever I was doing when he felt like making time for me. Not question him. Not stress him. Not be all up under him. Except for not successfully hooking him and Rich up, I'd been the perfect girlfriend. Even if it had been initially my idea to hook the two of them up so he could use her. I played and replayed the plan in my head over and over. Rewinding it. Fast-forwarding it.

I'd introduce Justice to Rich. Rich would play hard to get—wishful thinking, of course, because we all knew how she turned into a vamp at the sight and sound and smell of a fine boy. Any boy, for that matter.

Still...

I'd play my part. Encourage the nightwalker to give Justice a chance. Pretend to be his best friend, instead of his girlfriend then sit back and watch him weasel his way into Rich's father's recording studio, ultimately landing him a record deal. And a bright future on top of the billboard charts as R & B's hottest crooner.

Photographers from various newspapers, tabloids, and magazines would surround him, wanting exclusives. He'd have tons of drooling, panty-tossing groupies who I'd have to Taser and beat off of him with a stun baton.

Justice would become an overnight sensation. He'd dump Rich. And he and I would finally run off and get married and live happily ever after. But first, I'd have to find *happy* and figure out a way to get to *ever after*.

In the meantime, I'd have to be stressed out wondering, worrying, how Justice would be able to stay out of Rich's lair. Yes, the original plan was to use Rich to get him a record deal. But the thought of him falling into bed with her, let alone in love with her, was too much to bear. She was like a black widow spider—lethal, hanging upside down in her web waiting to sink her teeth into her next prey. Slowly sucking the life out of him while seducing him to death.

I closed my eyes for just a moment and the photos popped in my head. The thought of Justice being with some slore, holed up in some seedy motel room making hot, sweaty love was a smarting pain. The kind of stinging hurt I'd liken to slicing into skin with a rusty razor blade, zigzagging open the flesh, then gliding a sliced lemon over the skin, squeezing its juices into the wound.

Justice Banks was my life. Without him in it, I ached. I

throbbed. I agonized. Just the thought alone was enough to throw me into a full-fledged panic attack. Every time he ignored me, made me invisible, he'd slice me. Right now, I felt like I'd been pushed into a sea of lemon juice.

I croaked back tears as my mother snatched the Chinese raw mulberry silk comforter away. "I've booked us a day of luxuriated splendor at Boscolo Milano, darling, for five-star spa pampering. We'll get you waxed, plucked, and ready for this afternoon's shoot with Hermès. Hermès, darling! Can you believe it? And since it's right in the heart of the fashion district, we can shop, then dine at one of our favorite *ristoranti*."

Can't you see I'm in distress, lady? I don't care about eating at some damn Italian restaurant or shopping! I heard myself screaming in my head.

I felt a lump swelling in my throat as I remained stone still. I dared not utter a word as I heard my mother flit about my room. All I wanted to do was remain tucked between my Egyptian cotton sheets until it was time for the coroner to come in and announce my time of death. I'd had more mother-daughter bonding than I could stomach in this lifetime. I just wanted to croak, breathe in my last breath, meet my dressmaker, then be reincarnated.

Into my own woman.

With my own voice.

With my man beside me.

I adjusted the silken mask over my eyes and turned to face away from her annoying voice. *Dear God, where are You when I need You the most?*

"London, why are you lying there unresponsive? Do you not hear me talking to you?"

I nodded reluctantly.

"Oh, and...by the way, we'll be flying to New York in the next week..."

The minute I heard New York, it was like music to my ears. I missed New York terribly. With trying to acclimate to living on the West Coast since the end of last school term, my parents thought it best I not go back unless it was absolutely necessary. They'd thought it best I leave my old life behind and start anew. And I hadn't been back since the end of last school year.

The idea of heading back to the East Coast was divine. I felt my pulse quicken. Although I needed to get back to L.A., I needed to get back to the States more. And New York was a start. My mind was already spinning out my escape. I'd slip out of my suite in the still of the night wearing some hideous biker chick disguise, then hail a taxi to JFK or LaGuardia airport. *No. Scratch that. No airports. That'll be the first place they'd look.*

Lord God, I'd have to travel cross-country some other way. Hmm. I wonder if they have first-class service on those Greyhound buses. Ugh. I can't do bus service. I'd rather hitchhike and ride on the back of some farm boy's pickup truck. Hmph. If Rich was any kind of friend, I'd be able to call her and have her send her family's private jet. Screw Rich!

My mother's voice cut into my thoughts. "We'll fly out to New York, spend a few days there so you can rest, then be back in time for Fashion Week."

Rest? Yeah, right. How about you get out and let me rest now?

I silently rolled my eyes up in my head behind my mask.

"We're scheduled for a consultation with Doctor Nona

Grupalanna…she's a renowned plastic surgeon who comes highly…"

Wait a minute! Did I hear her correctly? Consultation?

I shot up in bed, yanking the mask from my eyes. *"Whaaaat?!"* I shrieked. "Consultation for what?"

My mother stepped out of my walk-in closet holding up a pink, knee-length wrap dress. I frowned. After my shoot yesterday for Pink Heat, I didn't want to look at anything else *pink* for a long while. "For your breast reduction," she said in a matter-of-fact tone as if she were talking about the weather. "We have to get you down to an A-cup."

I frowned, swinging my feet over the edge of the bed, reaching for my cell sitting on my nightstand. "Mother, you can't be serious! I'm *not* having my breasts reduced to an A-cup."

There were no calls! I glanced over at the clock. Eight a.m. *Okay, that means it's eleven p.m. back home.* I sent Justice a quick text: GM, BABE. I MISS U & NEED U! PLZ CALL ME WEN U GET THIS.

"Oh, you most certainly will. Aside from binding them down, there's no other option. I thought with the diet your breasts and that big jungle-bouncing rear end of yours would have shrunk to match your gorgeous waistline. But they didn't. I need you hanger thin. Not voluptuous. You are too curvy, London. I have to be proactive to keep you working, darling. One day you'll wake up and those C-cups will have ballooned into double Ds and that colossal derrière of yours will start to drag to the ground. I can't have that. *No, mia cara Londra. Sei troppo bella per essere grasso.*"

I rolled my eyes at her. I hated when she spoke English and Italian in the same sentence. Oh my darling London, nothing! I didn't give a damn about her thinking I was too beautiful to be fat. I wasn't fat—although sometimes I felt like I was, because *she* made me feel fat. Because Justice would tell me I was fat. They both had a way of making me feel like a hippo. Still, I wasn't interested in surgery. I'd starve myself first before I let anyone slice, suction, or staple anything on me.

I stood up and huffed indignantly. I was ready to have it out with her. "I'm not having anyone cut out any parts of my body, period. If the Italians don't want me on their runways, then so be it."

Before I knew what was happening, my mother was up in my face lightning fast. "You will *not* use that tone with me, London. You almost ruined everything once with your weight gain." She glared at me. "I. Will. *Not*. Risk. You. Becoming some cheesy model who catwalks bedsheets or some god-awful, ill-fitted potato sack down a runway."

She stroked my cheek. "I love you, my darling. One day, you will appreciate everything I'm doing for you…"

In that moment, I floated back to my childhood. I was five again. From charm school to being shuffled from casting call after casting call, to spending hours walking up and down a red carpet rolled out in the middle of our foyer, while balancing phone books on my head and walking in custom-designed heels way too big and high for my small feet, to being expected to stand like a mannequin, changing poses every fifteen minutes until I'd perfected the pose, the walk, the pivots, the hip thrusts. From go-sees to cattle calls and callbacks, my life has been a whirlwind of flashing lights, thick matte satins and frilly tulles.

"And you will thank me. But for now…*you* can show

your gratitude by *acting* like you appreciate all of the wonderful opportunities being placed at your feet."

Opportunities?

Really?

I let out a deep breath.

My man was ignoring me. My mother wanted to have me gutted and disfigured just so I could fit into her crazy mold of what beautiful was, or wasn't. My so-called bestie still hadn't had the decency to return any of my calls. And my mother expected me to happily embrace staged chances. The life she wanted for me.

She was delusional.

Rich was ignoring me.

Justice was avoiding me.

Was everyone back at home that absorbed in their own little worlds that they couldn't take a minute, or two, or three, to reach out and touch? What was going on back in L.A. that had me feeling as though I was missing out?

My phone finally vibrated, causing my heart to jump. I quickly glanced at the screen. It was a text from Justice.

My knees buckled as I read: WTF?!!!! WHY IZ U ALL UP ON ME? STOP SWEATIN' ME!!!! WORD IZ BOND YO! FALL BACK! LET ME BREATHE. U ACTIN 2 EFFN THIRSTY YO! IM NOT DIGGIN IT N IM OVER U. DO U LONDON N LET ME DO ME.

I blinked. Reread his text. Thirsty. Fall back. Stop sweatin' me. Let me breathe. *I'm over you. I'm over you. I'm over you...*

I felt like I was losing my mind. Felt like the world was falling apart. My world, my life...over!

I dropped to the floor and screamed.

9

Heather

Governador Celso Ramos, Brazil

Your favorite actress is officially hot.
Posted up in a cushioned and canopied hammock.
Gettin' my beauty rest on beneath the tawny afternoon sun.
Surrounded by the exclusive and private white sands of Ponta dos Ganchos.
Eyes shielded by mirrored aviators.
Hair blown wild and free in the heated breeze.
Metallic gold knit bikini painted on me.
Fresh blunt pressed between my Mac Cotton Candy glazed lips.
Yak on ice.
iPod on Snoop.
Body now servin' you:
36-24-38.
Brick.

House.

Fiyah.

Bam!

The new Buffy.

The slayer.

The mayor of All Things Fly and Fabulous.

Don't hate.

Bow down and celebrate.

I pulled in a long toke and pushed out a thick cloud of smoke as round and gracious hips sauntered across the beach and slithered into the water.

I did my all to keep my eyes from smiling and my lips from lifting at the corners, but the beautiful bronze bodies strewn across the beach sent taboo chills through me.

Stop it.

"Where the hell are you?" Kitty's voice barged through my head as thoughts of her out-of-order wake-up call pissed me off, again.

Calling me at seven a.m. Screaming like she'd gone crazy. She'd been calling me practically every day since I'd been here over the last two weeks, stressing me out, badgering me. So what if she was really the one behind the three million dollars Spencer had delivered to me? I didn't owe her anything. I wasn't her slave. And so what if I'd slipped out on the escort she'd sent with me? I was tired of granny sweatin' me. Following me. And hawkin' me like I was on an invisible leash.

Therefore, I did what I had to do: spiked that trick's morning cup of orange juice with three Ambien. And as soon as she was comatose, I boarded a flight for this sexy, sophisticated, and chic beach.

I pulled in another toke and this time slowly let out the

smoke, as more luscious bronzed sweetness strolled past me, forcing me to trade in thoughts of Kitty for the wonderment of how my soft, plush, and luscious skin would feel pressed up against...

Stop it!

"Listen up, trashy." Kitty's voice haunted me again. *"Let me inform you of what I will and will not tolerate! You will not go anywhere without my permission."*

My eyes scanned the beautiful beach. From the towering palm trees, to the snow-colored sand, to the crystal-blue ocean.

"You will not drug people!"

I smiled at the thought of my escort being nowhere around.

"You will not get high!"

I flicked my blunt's ashes into the breeze.

"You will not drink."

I poured more Yak in my glass and sipped.

"I want you drier than the Sahara! Your mother's already an unmanageable drunk. The world doesn't need two."

I didn't know who she thought she was talking to. She needed to worry about her daughter. Jizzle mouth. Queen of the Kneel Down. No shade. Spencer was my girl and all, but I'm just calling it how I see it.

"You will not hang out with Co-Co."

Bish, please! Kill yourself! Bite me! Crawl over my perfected butt cheeks and get lost in my new crack! Yeah, you paid for this booty. And yeah, it was everything. But you do not own me. And for real for real, after Spencer disrespected me with that three-million-dollar check, you're lucky I'm even taking your calls. Mmmph. Don't do me. I choose my own friends. And yeah, he dropped out of Hollywood High to sell drugs, but that didn't make him a bad person. It simply made him misunderstood. So Kitty Ellington needed to get her life. And worry that dizzy broad she gave birth to.

"You will learn discretion."

I am discreet. You can't find me. And in a minute you won't be able to reach me either because I'm having my number changed.

"And to help you build a new image, you are now happily involved with R & B sensation Haneef. I have e-mailed you a glossy 8-by-10 head shot and full body shot of him."

Was she serious with this?

Did she really expect me to be the new Selena Gomez? Rihanna?

I'm not thirsty.

I'm not playin' those games.

I'ma be with who I wanna be with! How I wanna be with 'em! And wherever I wanna be with 'em!

"Heather?"

I looked to my left and spotted an over-tanned, short white man, dressed in green-and-yellow Bermuda shorts, a white tank top, a pencil behind his left ear and a camera hanging around his neck.

The paparazzi! Oh my God!

I'd forgotten that I called TMZ anonymously—three hours ago—and told them that I spotted Heather Cummings on an exclusive beach.

I quickly mashed my blunt in the ashtray and knocked it behind the table and into the sand.

"Heather Cummings?" He was now standing alongside the hammock.

I side-eyed him. And yeah, I may have called the paparazzi, but at this moment I was pissed. How dare he show up here three hours late like I was some *Celebrity Rehab* D-lister?

I twisted my lips, slid my aviators down the bridge of my nose, and said, "Who wants to know?"

"The world." He tossed in a smile. "And in addition to the world, *Teen Enquirer* wants to know."

Teen Enquirer? Teen Enquirer?! I called TMZ! Not these lonely, low-totem-pole, don't-move-off-the-newsstands-ever magazines! Where the heck is TMZ?!

Okay, okay, breathe. Breathe. Relax. You're queen. And apparently they need this interview! "Yes, I'm Heather Cummings."

"Great! Do you mind—"

"Mind what? If you take some pictures of me? Of course not." I jumped out of the hammock and the first shot I served him was a camera full of butt cheeks, my delicious thong bikini lost like dental floss in the crack of newfangled booty. I was bent over with my hands on my toes, my head tossed to the left, looking back over my shoulder.

The next pose I handed him was a sexy squat—from the back, of course.

And last, I took my sunglasses off and blessed him with a full-face shot. Lips tooted and manicured hands on my newly expanded 38s.

"Wow, great shots! Real classy!" he said, a little too excited. "Now, do you mind if I ask you some questions?"

I sat back on the hammock, crossed my legs, and batted my lashes. "Of course not."

"Great." He pointed his iPhone toward me and pressed record. "How does it feel to be fresh out of rehab?" Before I could answer, he continued on. "And have you given any thought to being the spokesperson for the Say No campaign?" He looked over at my drink, then at the bottle of Yak that I'd forgotten was on the table, then at the blunt half buried in the sand, and back over at me. "Or will you be following in the steps of Lindsay Lohan?"

My heart thundered in my chest. *Should I punch him in the face now or later?*

Relax.

I batted my lashes again before sliding my aviators back on. "No. And no. I don't think so. Now, I just graced you with exclusive pics of me. So the last thing you need to do is try to play me."

"I would never do that. Nor would the folks at *Teen Enquirer*. We're big fans of yours. Now, let me ask you this: Now that Wu-Wu's dead, what's new on the horizon for you?"

I felt like he'd just gripped me by the throat. "First and forevermore: Wu-Wu is not dead."

"Well, the show was recently canceled."

"Because the imposter Wu-Wu killed it."

"So what you're basically saying is that you ruined your career?"

"You motherfu—" I paused. My eyes took in this short and orange-looking mofo. I was doing all I could to be the gracious star that I am, but he was pushing me. "How. Dare. You. Try to blame me? If anything, it was the producer being an idiot. Throwing chairs around. Having mangina tantrums. Acting like he had a period. That's the problem in Hollywood. The ones who should have balls are on their period, and the ones who are supposed to have a period got their feet stuck in Timbos. Spaghetti and meatballs in the producers' and directors' chairs!" I reached for my drink and then shot him a nasty smile as he clicked his camera.

"What are you drinking?" he asked.

"Fruit punch."

"Nonalcoholic?"

I sucked my teeth. "Of course."

"So I hear love is on the horizon?"

Breathe. "Yes, me loving my new body."

"Not just your new body, but a source close to you says that you are also loving R & B superstar Haneef. Is that so?"

"Really?" I looked up at him over my sunglasses. "If that's your story, then run with it." I flicked him a dismissive wrist.

"So would that be a yes?"

I took a deep breath and forced it out through my nose. In a minute, I was about to pop off! For one: I called TMZ and this bottom-scraper showed up, turning this interview into a circus. Two: I didn't like him coming out the side of his neck, questioning me about my drink. Drinking was never a problem for me. That's Camille's issue. Not mine. And as far as Haneef goes, I don't know that East Coast hood bugger. And don't wanna know him!

This freak continued running his mouth. "So your boyfriend, Haneef, is number one on *Billboard*. Two-time Grammy Award winner. And an all-around ladies' man. He was recently linked to Rihanna. What do you think she'll think of the two of you? Do you think she'll come after you?"

I slid off the hammock and stood with my bare feet planted in the sand. I pointed. "Let me get you together real quick. Rihanna and her big-ass forehead better behave and have a seat. Because I don't want Haneef. I don't like him. Or his whack music! Auto-Tune king. Pst, please. I'm not about to be another one of his beards!"

"And how would you know all of this? Do you know him or don't you?"

I pushed a finger into this sucker's face and snapped, "Know what? I know what I'm not about to do. And that's you and your interview!" I picked up my drink to leave.

"So are you still homeless?"

I felt like he'd kicked me in my chest. I spun around toward him and dashed my drink in his face.

He smiled as he wiped his face with the back of his hand. "Thought you said it was nonalcoholic." He smacked his lips. "Tastes like cognac to me."

I screamed. "Whack ninja! Eff you and your lowlife magazine!"

10

London

Milan, Italy

Two a.m. I was awakened from a restless sleep, heart pounding, chest heaving. Eyes wide and crazed. I'd been dreaming. No. Having a nightmare was more like it. I was locked away in a small room with white padded walls and a white floor. I was wearing a white paper-thin hospital gown, sitting in a large wheelbarrow. On the other side of the room was a sign—no, a banner—that read: FAT GIRLS RULE. Beneath it was a huge bariatric scale with a four-hundred-pound capacity.

I sat up in bed, blinking back tears. I reached over and grabbed my cell off the nightstand. There were no calls. No texts. Nothing!

Justice, how could you do this to me?

I sent him a text: JUSTICE WHAT HV I DONE 2 U?! Y WOULD U BREAK UP W/ME? PLEASE CALL OR TEXT ME.

I wiped at my tears. *This is fricking ridiculous! I'm so*

effen stupid to keep sweating this boy! I flopped back in bed, resting my cell up on my chest, holding it against my trembling heart. I shut my eyes, my mind drifting back to my nightmare.

My face and hands were covered with different types of frosting: lemon, strawberry, chocolate, and cream cheese. In my lap was a boxed assortment of three dozen mini cupcakes. In my nightmare, I was popping them into my mouth one by one, stuffing my jowls with the moist cakes and delicious whipped frosting. I devoured the entire box.

I could hear keys clanking on the other side of the steel door. Panicked, I started stuffing the cupcake foils into my mouth, gobbling up all evidence, just as the double locks clicked and Justice walked in. Stalking over to me. Grinning. Maybe he was sneering. And I was happy to see him. He didn't speak. Just leaned in. Then with his finger, he swiped a fleck of chocolate frosting off my nose, brought it back to his own mouth, and licked. And I could feel myself melting, melting, melting all over my-self as he leaned in farther and licked the lemon frosting off my chin. I went to reach for him with my pudgy little hands and he slapped them down, inching his face closer to mine.

His gaze met mine. In anticipation, I had closed my eyes and puckered my cream-frosted lips and waited with bated breath to feel his soft kisses against my lips. Instead, I am greeted with laughter. "You're a fat nasty slob...I don't know why I ever effed wit' you...stank hippo...Look at you..." He kept shaking his head over and over. "Pathetic, yo...You crazy, London...I hope they put you outta ya misery, yo..."

*Then I was being violently rolled over toward the scale.
"Get up, Miss Piggy! Time for your weigh-in!" The gown rus-
tled and swished as I lifted up on legs that stuck and
rubbed together as I wobbled up on the scale. Gas passed
from between two wide cheeks, dimpled and cratered and
exposed. As I shut my eyes, held my breath, tears leaked
from my eyes, staining the front of my paper gown as I
waited for the verdict.*

I weighed 357 pounds.

My eyes snapped open. I lay in the dark, crying, aching
in silence. Contemplating my demise until I heard the
stash of snacks I'd discreetly packed and hidden inside
various handbags calling out to me, taunting me, from inside my Louis Vuitton trunk.

"Lonnnnndon! Ohhh, Lonnnnnndon!"

"Eat me, London. Eat me!"

"Come sink your teeth into me . . . !"

I glanced over at the time: 2:33 a.m. I shut my eyes.
Willed myself still. *Don't do it. Do not give in to temptation. It's way too late. You're going to be weighed in
three-and-a-half hours.*

*"You know you wanna wrap your lips around me.
Sink your teeth into my cream-filled goodness . . ."*

Lead me not into temptation . . .

*"C'mon, you greedy cow . . . you pig . . . you ugly moose
head . . ."*

I bit the inside of my lip.

Deliver me from this evil . . .

*"Come gobble me up, Lonnnndon . . . Come stuff your
mouth, jabber jaws . . . you beached whale . . . You know
you want it . . ."*

Ohmygod! Will you pleeease shut up! Leave me alone! Get out of my head!

The taunting wouldn't stop. The voices kept getting louder and louder until I could no longer take it. I flung back my comforter, throwing my feet over the edge of the bed. My feet hit the floor with a heavy purpose. My head swooning, tears sprang from my eyes as I knelt down and slid my hand up under the edge of my Persian area rug and retrieved a small key.

Walking over to my travel chest, my hands shook as I quietly slid the key in and unlocked the latch, flipping open the trunk. My hand slipped in and pulled out a red Valentino tote bag.

I raced over and locked the door to my bedroom, then positioned myself on my bed. My heart raced as I opened my bag and dumped its contents in the center of the bed.

"Yeah, that's it, greedy..."

I tore open two small packs of honey-roasted peanuts, then tossed my head back and emptied them into my mouth, chewing and swallowing as the voices kicked my brain around like a soccer ball.

"Peanuts, London? Really? You can do better than that, Chunky Monkey..."

I blinked back tears, ripped open two oatmeal cream pies. Smashed them together, then bit into the sweet double-decker as if it were a Big Mac.

"Yeah, that's it...gobble, gobble..."

Justice dumped me! And with the snap of a finger, expected me to forget about him, about us! How could I forget, when I couldn't stop feeling his fingertips dancing along the curve of my hip every time he'd spoon himself behind me. How could I forget when I'd risked everything to be with him?

Damn you, Justice! You bastard! I gave you every damn part of me!

The rush of sugar burned through me, dissolving in my mouth, clinging to my tongue. My stomach heaved a little as I sent Justice another text.

U DIDN'T HAVE TO HURT ME LIKE THIS!

I was rocking, my knees pulled up to my chest, my arms wrapped around them. Then I was crying—hard and without control. I needed to get out of my own way. But my mind wouldn't shut off.

"That boy is not to be trusted, London, do you hear me...? He's troubled and from the wrong side of the tracks! I don't want him sniffing around here trying to manipulate his way into your life...He will do nothing but ruin you! I do not want you anywhere near him...!"

Waves of anger surged upward, crashing into view the memory of Justice taking my hand and placing it over his heart. *"Feel that?"* I'd nodded, feeling the galloping beat of his heart against his chest. *"That's us, baby. One heart, one beat...one love. Nothing can ever change that...I'm all yours in mind, heart, and body."*

"Liar!" I hissed. "Then why is there a picture of your hand down some skank's shirt?!"

"I forbid you to see him, London!"

I reached for a Capri Sun, stabbed into it with the pointed tip of its straw, then slurped the wild cherry–flavored drink in thick, greedy gulps and swallows. I opened another, did the same thing. I coughed and spit, gasping and choking as juice went down the wrong pipe.

Justice wanted me to forget him. But I couldn't stop remembering. Remembering the first time he'd pulled me into his grown-man-like body and boldly kissed me under the light of a streetlamp. *"See. You stay playin'. Stay teasin'."* He grabbed my hand. *"You feel all this?"* He pulled me back into him. Started kissing me again, his lips trailing along my neck; his hand slipping into places where I'd never allowed any other boy to venture.

I couldn't escape it. The memories. The emptiness. The craving. The hurt. The guilt. My mother kept my passport and bankbook hostage so I was trapped in this cage. Couldn't flee without money or documentation. But it didn't matter because regardless of where I ran off to, she'd eventually find me. And when she did, she'd be standing there, sneering, with her trusted tape measure in one hand and her electronic scale close by. Narrowing her eyes, foot tapping, waiting for me to undress—to strip down to the naked truth—and step onto the scale, just so she could remind me of what I was, of what I'd always be... a beached whale stuffed in a sardine can.

My stomach burned. I was almost at the end. My end. Not quite there yet. But I felt it as I crawled back up under the covers, unconcerned with the empty wrappers, cake crumbs, empty boxes, and half-eaten sleeves of cookies that lay scattered all over the bed. I clutched my stomach and wept into my pillow as honey-roasted-nut gas and loads of sugar bubbled up from my insides, then burst out in loud, angry rumbles.

No. There was no escape. There was no hiding from this, or from her. I was sentenced to a life of suffering. This was my death row. A fat, three-hundred-and-fifty-seven pound girl stuffed in a skinny girl's body, waiting for execution.

London Phillips... we hereby sentence you to death by way of lethal ingestion.

I closed my eyes... and waited.

11

Rich

For twenty-four hours I'd been wrapped in a fairy tale and for once, dreaming about the right knight.

Knox.

But.

In the whistle of a text message, it all ended.

I was lying naked in the center of Knox's bed in his dorm in San Diego, next to the warm spot he'd left behind. My iPhone clutched in my right hand, my brown gaze locked on the screen and my thoughts racing alongside my thunderous heartbeat, I was trying to figure out what Justice was tripping about.

Instead of being thankful he wasn't dead, and paying homage to the Second Chance gods, he was on my phone and coming at me all shades of crazy. Yeah, I dumped him. And, yeah, we left him for dead. But still. Don't disrespect me.

U MAD FOUL, SON! WORD IZ BOND, YO. U LET YA PUNK DUDE SNEAK ME, YO? DAT WAZ SUM REAL SUCKA ISH YO! ITZ COOL THO. I C U. U REAL GRIMY! THEN U

GONNA LEAVE UR WHIP TRYNA GET ME ALL HEMMED UP. ITZ ALL GOOD. I GOT U. REAL SPIT.

What. Is. He. Talking. About?

I read the text again.

And again.

And again.

Mad foul?

Who's mad foul?

Me?

And dude?

What dude?

That was Spencer.

There was no dude.

Tired of his dumb riddle, I texted him back. HUH? BOY, BYE! DON'T COME 4 ME! WHAT U NEED 2 DO IS STOP BEING SO PRESSED. AND FOUL? U MUST BE CALLING URSELF OUT! WHACK NINJA!

He texted back, 4REAL, LIL HOMIE. RUN ALONG N GO PLAY WIT' OLE BOY. LIKE U SAID THIS IS DONE. NOW STEP!

I blinked. Suddenly, the air was stale. No, no, actually there was no air in here. All of the oxygen had fled the scene. But somehow I pulled in a deep breath. Inhaled it through my nostrils and forced a gush of it through my lips.

I gathered the white sheet over my bare breasts and sat up. I pressed my back against Knox's wall and just as my eyes scanned the texts from the top again, another text binged in. U AIN'T SHYYT, YO!

What? I squinted. Blinked. And before I could read the rest of his text I had to go back and read the first line again: *U ain't shyyt, yo!* A raging dropkick landed in my gut. I swallowed, cleared my throat and continued to read about how he'd parked my car across the street from where I'd left it. That my purse and the five hundred dollars I'd left on the nightstand were in the glove compartment. And how I was lucky my car wasn't set on fire and floating in the bay somewhere.

Screech!

He got me all the way twisted!

I hopped off the bed and paced from one end of the room to the next.

I need a cigarette. And I don't even smoke.

Calm down.

Eff calming down! This howling mofo came straight for my throat! Spraying bullets out of his mouth like a drive-by! He ain't no ole G, he better watch how he's comin' for me!

I'm 'bout to read this Piru for blood, honey!

I stopped in my tracks as the thought of what he'd said played around in my head.

"So he wanna get it crunked?!" I laughed in disbelief. "Oh, okay. Well let's do this then."

I raced over to Knox's bedroom door and locked it. Leaning against the door, I called Justice, held my breath and chewed the corner of my bottom lip as I waited for the phone to ring. It didn't. Instead I was greeted by his voice mail.

My eyes bucked and my heart tried to claw its way out of my throat.

Ten...nine...eight...

I pulled in another deep breath and called this jank again.

The phone rang.

I let out a sigh of relief. I could feel my mouth about to burst into flames. I couldn't wait to aim and mouth-piss

on this silly loser! The ringing stopped and just as I was
about to let loose, a recorded operator said, "You have
been blocked. This user does not desire to speak with you
at this time."

I blinked.

Reeeewind!

I called again. "You have been..."

"Ahhhhh!" I flung my phone across the room.

I don't believe this.

Really, Justice?

Are you serious with this?

Chill... Chill... Relax.

He ain't mean ish to you anyway!

What you sweatin' it for?

I stormed over to the window and placed my forehead
up against the thick pane, the sheer purple curtains
shielding my naked silhouette.

I stared out into the courtyard and watched an ener-
getic line of pledges stomp their loosely tied combat
boots, lift their chins and howl into the early morning
breeze. I caught the reflection of my face in the glass and
saw tears dancing in my eyes.

What the hell are you crying for?

He ain't your man.

You dumped him, remember?

He was just a toy.

A thing.

I turned back from the window and my eyes landed on
my phone.

Call him again.

I yanked the phone off the floor and noticed my screen
was cracked.

WTF?!

I swear on everything I love, I hate this mofo!

I dialed his number and again the same robotic trick delivered the same message. I'd been blocked.

"Screw this!" I scrambled around the room trying to find something to wear. I found an old pair of jeans, snatched one of Knox's hoodies out of his drawer, stuffed my feet into an old pair of sneakers, then pulled my hair into a messy bun and charged out the door.

I swung open Midnight's bedroom door, startling Spencer, who lay alone on the bed. She sat up as I eased her car keys from off of the nightstand.

"Rich?" she asked, half asleep.

"I need to use your car. I'll be right back," I said abruptly as I walked back toward the door.

"Where are you going?"

I didn't have time to respond. All I had time to do was get out of here!

No purse.

No license.

Nothing.

But a tank of gas to get to my destination.

A road trip that usually took me two hours, took me an hour and fifteen minutes to be at this mofo's building and ringing every bell until somebody finally buzzed me in.

Once I was in the white tiled lobby, everything moved in fast-forward motion. I was so focused on bashing Justice's face in for talking to me slick and crazy that in a flash, I'd covered four flights of stairs and was now pounding on the door to his studio apartment.

"Justice!" I kicked and banged over and over again. "Open this damn door!"

Every door on the floor opened with the exception of his.

"Justice! I know you're in there! Open up this door! Right now! You gon' talk slick to me and then block me?! Don't hide! Open up this motherfuckin' door!"

I took six steps back and just as I was prepared to sprint down the hall and kick in his door, one of the neighbors two doors down stepped into the hallway with her phone to her ear. "Hello, police," she said. "Yes, yes, a black girl. Long hair. Jeans. Hoodie. Threatening to burn down the building!" She squinted and then whispered into the phone, "She looks like that crazy girl Rich Montgomery. You know. The one who was on the front page of *Gossip and Stars*. Page twenty-four. Showing her bare beaver. Yeah, uh-huh . . . that one. I don't know what this world is coming to! We're in the last days! These rich kids today are out of control. Too much money on their hands. Please hurry up and get here!"

A wave of nervousness and defeat washed over me as that nosy bird kept whispering into her phone. I shot her a nasty look. "For your information, granny, my name is *not* Rich Montgomery! It's Shakeesha Gatling! Get it right!"

I pulled the hoodie over my head and made a mad dash for the stairs, brushing roughly against her shoulder as I fled. I couldn't afford the cops coming after me. And at this moment I didn't want any part of the media! I shook my head, doing all I could to find a thought . . . any thought that would calm me because I was clearly out of my zone. I couldn't believe I was playing myself in some low-budget hallway. Sweatin' some broke dude and chasin' him down like some desperate needy chick.

Psst, please!

Eff him!

This was my world!

I was queen!

I reigned supreme!

And *yeah*, Justice made love to me like the best there ever was.

And *yeah*, if I really kept it one hundred, I didn't leave him alone because I wanted to be faithful to Knox. I left him alone because I felt myself being captured by his smile. His laugh. His eyes. The feel of his hands. His corny jokes.

Too many times I found myself drifting off to a place beyond space where I envisioned being with him all the time. Calling him mine. And me his. Doodling his name.

Getting butterflies.

And all kinds of corny, mushy, and silly little-girl ish.

I didn't have time for that.

I couldn't get caught up in any man. Ever. Not even Knox. And definitely not Justice. I knew by watching my mother that you could be the baddest chick in the world and you could love your man more than you loved yourself. But no matter what, he would never love you back.

I tried hard as I could to fight them back, but a rush of hot, blinding tears erupted from my eyes and covered the sides of my face. I felt myself starting to heave as I raced out of the building and into the parking lot.

I froze when I spotted his car.

So he was up there! Like I thought he was!

Oh, you wanna play! Oh, you wanna disrespect me!
You wanna say I ain't shyyt! Oh, I'ma show you!

I gripped the car key in my hand, slid it in between my middle and ring finger and clutched it real tight as I clawed up the entire driver's side of his car.

Oh, I ain't shyyt! I ain't shyyt! You gon' talk sideways to me? Oh, you gon' block me? You wanna come for me? Pop all kinds of craziness in text! I got your lil homie, punk! I'm about to give it to you real good!

I looked around the parking lot until I spotted what I needed to leave my last mark. I ran over, picked it up, then hurled it through the air with all my might and watched it kiss his windshield, sending an explosion of glass into the air.

12

Heather

Two weeks later

Showtime...
I took two deep breaths in an effort to calm my racing nerves as Jackson, my new driver, rounded the corner in my brand new silver Mercedes limo, bringing Club Noir Kiss into view. People were everywhere and the line to get inside was roped off and stretched for blocks.

I was back home. This was the first time I was rocking my new look and I didn't know what to expect, given that paparazzi had already tried to slay me after that Brazil fiasco. I lifted *Teen Enquirer* and scanned through the headlines:

FROM BRONZING TO BRAWLING
"A heated war of words turned vicious when teen actress Heather Cummings, known for her eccentric style and over-the-

top sass as the once-upon-a-time star of *The Wu-Wu Tanner Show* tossed her drink in a reporter's face, then burned him with the tip of what sources identified as a blunt, before attacking him with the shell of a coconut…"

Lies!

I tossed the magazine across the backseat and blinked my eyes.

And he has the nerve to be suing me.

I took in another deep breath and noticed that standing outside of the club's blue glass entrance was Co-Co—voguing. In electric-pink kitten heels, silky hot-pink boy shorts, a vintage striped beige suit jacket, an iridescent pink tie, and a leopard bra wrapped around his flat and hairy pecs.

My heartbeat matched the thumping bass in the club's music as Jackson parked alongside the red carpet. "Make room! Make room!" he shouted—in the exact way that I'd told him to—as he walked around the limo and opened my door. The crowd standing in line gasped and shrieked as I swung one black five-inch pencil heel onto the red carpet and then the other. Cameras flashed and shouts of, "We love you, Wu-Wu!" filled the air.

Co-Co slowly looked me over. Stopped dancing. Placed his hands up on his narrow hips. Posed. And served me his best high-end mannequin.

A few seconds after giving me frozen fever, Co-Co broke his trance and said, "Geisha. Black girl. Goddess." He did a ballet twirl. Stopped. And snapped his long fingers with every word. "You. Better. Work! Bow down, bishes!" He dropped to one knee. "You have slayed every fish in the place." He popped back up and smiled. "Now gimme love. Miss Co-Co needs a royal hug."

I couldn't help but smile as Co-Co and I melted into each other's embrace. "Queen Mother, you are servin' 'em like a sex slave. Look at that hair." He ran his hands through my thick sun-blond wisps that draped an inch past the small of my back.

"This hair is giving me magic carpet realness." Co-Co fluttered his extended lashes. "Bish, when you step up in here, every five-for-ten weave trick will lay. Down. And. Die."

"Awww, Co-Co, you think so?"

"Fierce recognize fierce." He wagged an index finger as his narrow black eyes worked their way over my black, ultra mini, painted-on stretch leather dress that made love to every one of my new and bursting curves.

Co-Co slanted his neck and continued his inspection. His heels clicked against the concrete as he walked around me and stopped at my ten-thousand-dollar behind. He ran his hands over both sides and slapped both cheeks. "Gurrrrl, this booty has refreshed my life! White-girl booty has been Blackarized and Brazilianized! Somebody send for the guards!"

I was doing all I could to feel Co-Co's excitement and not worry about what people were really thinking, given that debacle in Brazil where the paparazzo that I called turned on me.

Relax.

Breathe.

You are queen.

No, I'm not.

I'm a mess.

You are fierce. Just like Co-Co said.
Then why don't I feel it?
Because you need something to take the edge off.
No, I don't.

"This is all for you, bish." Co-Co interrupted my thoughts, waving his hand over the crowd.

"Are you serious?" *I couldn't believe it.* "You did this for me?!"

"All day, baby. You know I'm your number-one fan." He locked arms with me. "Now, let's get ready to live and let have."

We stepped inside of the club and the crowd erupted into applause and screams of, "Surprise! Welcome home, Wu-Wu!"

There were so many people in there that I couldn't even begin to guess how many. All I knew is that the club looked filled to capacity.

My favorite beat from "Put You on the Game" blasted through the speakers and twirling rays of indigo lights streamed from the balcony and shone over the massive crowd like a blue sun.

Faces of all shapes and sizes looked at me in amazement and their eyes danced in delight. Some people flashed their cameras from a distance while others ran over and anxiously asked to take pictures with me. This was incredible! People were practically begging for autographs while confessing their love and admiration. And all of this would have been the bomb had I felt like these people were truly there for me.

But they weren't.

They were there for Wu-Wu. The party girl. The funtime chick. The turn-it-up queen. The girl who I would give anything to truly be...again...

But I wasn't.

I was Heather Suzanne Cummings. The black-and-white pissed-off mutt. The Mexican-looking chick who wasn't Mexican and hated being mistaken for it. The girl with the drunk-all-day-every-day mother and the sperm-donating-question mark for a father.

Get it together.

My eyes scanned the cheering crowd once more and I pushed out a smile so wide that my almond-shaped eyes sank into my cheeks.

Co-Co released my arm and danced his way to the stage. "I feel a freestyle coming on!" He looked down at me and I knew that was my cue to get my mind right.

"One time for your mind!" Co-Co rapped into the mic. "Two times for your shine! Ah, Wu-Wu's in the house! Ah, Wu-Wu's in the house!"

I did all I could to push away and bury any feelings of insecurity. I had to kick Heather's ridiculousness out of my head and force myself to become Wu-Wu again.

I blew Co-Co a kiss, tossed my arms in the air and acted as if all that mattered in the world was a hot beat and a dope lyric. "Turn it up! Turn it up! Turn it up!" I shouted, working my way to the stage. "How y'all feeling out there?!"

"It's all love, Wu-Wu!" the crowd chanted.

"A'ight, A'ight. Somebody get their phone out and record this. 'Cause we 'bout to get right up in here! I got something for y'all called Put Your Diamonds Up!"

They cheered.

"Now I'ma show y'all a dance, and once we got the moves on deck, I want you to bust 'em while I rap!" I turned toward the DJ. "Drop that 'Put You on the Game' beat again!"

The crowd cheered as I showed them a freestyle dance where I lifted my hands over my head, pretended to be patting the world's biggest Afro wig, criss-crossed my legs, swung my hips from left to right, slid an invisible ring off my index finger and flung it on the floor. Crushed it. And then broke out into a twerk. Co-Co and the crowd picked up the dance instantly.

"Put your diamonds up!" I rapped, " 'Cause Wu-Wu's back! Back on top but guess who's not? The Hollywood trolls!"

"Put 'em up! Put 'em up!" Co-Co rapped into the mic.

"I'm in my own zone! And the next time you see me I'ma be sittin' on the fame of thrones!"

"Put 'em up! Put 'em up!" Co-Co rapped as the crowd cheered and danced.

I repeated my rhyme and for the next ten minutes we danced, rapped, and waved our arms in the air.

I'd killed it! Straight slayed it! And there was no doubt in my mind that by morning Co-Co and I would have a craze on our hands.

By the time I got off the stage I felt great. Almost as if I'd taken a black beauty. Well . . . almost . . .

You looked stupid.

I sat down at the bar and refused to let Heather's self-doubts sneak up on me and blast defeating thoughts through my head.

"What are you having?" the bartender asked.

I smiled. "Let me get a trash can with a double shot of Cirôc."

He nodded. "Coming right up."

While I waited for my drink, a few people rushed over and showered me with compliments, snapped more pics, and asked if I'd traded in acting for rapping. "Never," I told them. "As a matter of fact, I have a few things lined up. You'll be checking me out soon as Luda Tutor." I winked.

The bartender set my drink in front of me. I quickly took out my phone, snapped a pic, and Instagrammed it.

"Girl, you killed it!" A smiling chick walked up from behind me and slid onto the stool next to me.

"Thank you."

"You're welcome. And this dress! You're wearing the hell out of it." Her eyes drank me in, working their way from my hair to my spilling cleavage to the outline of my hips. "Girl, you are beautiful." She said it more to herself than to me, as she boldly tucked some of my hair behind my right ear and smoothly slid a single fingertip down my blushing cheek. "Heather, you did your thing out there, for real."

I didn't know what surprised me more: her touching me; her calling me Heather, when everyone in here, including Co-Co, called me Wu-Wu; or that her eyes were drinking me in again.

I didn't know what to say so I fell back on, "Thank you." While struggling like hell not to soak up the beauty of her smooth chestnut skin and short bob—one side cropped, the other side asymmetrical and shoulder length. Her makeup was laid to Barbie doll perfection: soft pink eye shadow, lashes that curled at the ends, and hot-pink lips.

By the time my eyes drifted to her thighs I realized what I was doing. I quickly snatched my glance away and turned back toward the bar, sipping my drink again.

"Heather, what are you drinking? Let me buy you another one."

I did my best to resist the blush I felt creeping back onto my face. "No. Thank you. But no." *Why am I nervous?* "I can barely get through this."

"Okay." She smiled, her beautiful teeth gleaming. "I won't hold you." She swept up and twirled the end of a lone curl of her hair before winking and sashaying away.

I refused to let my eyes follow her and instead, as unwanted butterflies danced in my stomach, I sank my smile into my trash can.

This was crazy. I knew she wasn't a guy but I still couldn't stop my throat from being dry, or my knees from feeling too weak to stand up. Or my heart from rushing through its beats...

Stop it!

"I just thought about something," poured over my shoulder. I knew it was her and I didn't have to turn around to confirm it. She reached for my phone, which was next to my drink, clicked on my camera, and surprised me by taking a picture of us. Then she punched in a few numbers and placed my phone back on the bar.

She leaned into my ear and whispered, her heated breath making a trail of goose bumps along the side of my neck, "I programmed my number in your phone, and the picture is so you won't forget me." She turned to leave and then quickly turned back. "And by the way, I'm Nikki."

13

Spencer

*O*h *no...oh no...oh no...! Where they do that at?
Calling someone at this ungodly hour. Disrupting
my delicious dream! The cows aren't even up with the
roosters yet! Have they no shame?*

I was right in the middle of sliding red-hot skewers into
London's broiler once and for all for being the fraud she
was. And I was sautéing Heather's face for spitting on my
kindness. I had a mallet in my hand getting ready to season Heather's forehead up real good when the annoying
buzz of my phone pulled me away from what was turning
into a scrumptious dream.

Now I had no idea how things ended, thanks to the in-
considerate person who was calling me.

Imbecile!

My phone finally stopped buzzing. I sighed, sinking
deeper into the crisp sheets and warmth of my comforter.
Jeezus. Now I can't get back to my dream. I angrily flopped

around on my plush mattress for several moments trying to find the right spot to settle into. And just when I closed my eyes behind the silken cloth of my mask, my phone buzzed again and again and again, slicing into my feather play. Now I was madder than a bucket of bees dipped in hot butter. I pulled my mask up over one eye, lifting my head just enough to see the glow of the clock. One o'clock in the morning. *Oh, this is goshdangit ridiculous! Who the heck called at this sluttish time?*

I groped at the nightstand until my hand found my iPhone. A number with a 619 area code flashed up on the screen. "Muggafugga!" I snapped into the phone. "Whoever you are calling *me* this time of hour, you had better make it good, or get crushed into a meat grinder, goshdangit!"

"What's good, sweet roll?" the voice on the other end said real low and deep. There was a song by Ekco playing in the background. *Picture me on top of you...Legs up. Body down...*

"Grind me, baby. I love it when my meat is grinded, 'specially when you do it right."

I blinked, then frowned. "*Whaaat? Sweet roll?* The number you have dialed has been disconnected! This is not a bakery! And I am not serving up pastries, you ole nasty pervert! Now who is this?"

I could hear the singer singing about having the munchies wanting to eat me up. Mmmph. The voice on the other end chuckled. "It's Midnight."

I glanced at the time. "*Midnight?* You idiot! You better do a time check! It's waaaaay after midnight! I need my beauty sleep. I don't know what kind of freaky mess you got going on over in your time zone, Mister Kink Daddy, but this Pacific-Standard-Time-zone girl is not playing those kinds of reindeer games."

He cracked up laughing. And that irritated me even more. The nerve of this debauched heathen! "And I don't see a dang thing funny! Let me find out who you are… you, you, you dream killer, and I'm going to fillet your guts! You woke the wrong one, you sleep thief!"

"Daaaaayum! You go in hard like a leg of lamb and come out falling off the bone; all mouthwatering and juicy." He made smacking noises through the phone, causing a chill to shoot through my spine. "This is Midnight, Knox's roommate."

"Oh." I giggled. I'd forgotten I'd given this tall, sexy, dark chocolate hunk of man muscle my number on the low-low just as Rich and I were finally—after two days of being fugitives—swaying our hips out the door of their frat-house apartment. And even though Rich had stepped out grinning and smiling, smelling like powder-scented baby wipes and sardines, I had managed to catch him winking his eye and licking his lips. Then he jutted out his pelvis and gyrated his hips. And my knees almost buckled.

Still, I played it off as he flicked his tongue, shaking my caboose to the left, to the right, then booty bouncing it just enough to let him see how these hotcakes were stacked.

"Well, why didn't you say that in the first place? I don't play phone games. I don't do booty calls at this time of night. I'm not into whispering sweet nothings. I don't do phone sex on the first phone call. And I don't like it *dirty* unless it's in my martini."

"Daayum, you got me harder than a frozen sausage right now."

"Hmmph." I batted my lashes. "Oh really? What kind of sausage? I hope it's not those little bitty links. 'Cause I don't do those. I'm hanging up right now."

"The thick, juicy, succulent kind, baby-boo. The kind you wanna smother with a buncha onions and green peppers, then slide into a nice, soft potato roll. Daayum, you got me feelin' some kinda way."

My mouth watered. And I felt my juice box getting juicy. I smacked my lips. "Umph, umph. Well, I don't eat meat." I giggled. "Not *that* kind anyway."

"Aaaargh! Aaarrrgggh!" he barked. "Woof, woof...!"

"Who opened the cage and let the dogs out?" I said, getting caught up in the hype for a moment.

"Aaaargh! Aaarrgggh! You let the dogs out! Eat. Me. Baby-boo. Come get up on this bone."

"*Whaaat?* You dirty dog! You even think about wagging your bone up in me and I'ma put a muzzle on it. I don't play that. Now what do you want?"

"Yeah, a'ight. Talk dirty, baby. I think I gotta sweet tooth for you, honey glaze. All I keep thinking about is how I wanna roll you up in some cake batter, sprinkle powdered sugar all over you then lick you up. I wanna paint ya toes with peach jam 'n' suck 'em one by one."

I pressed my thighs shut. Ooh. He was my kind of freak. I felt electricity shoot through my good & plenty. And if I wasn't a classy type, I would have told him to meet me across the border so I could run my hands all through his meat basket, then nibble on his giblets. But I didn't believe in opening up the buffet to just any ole body.

No. You had to earn your way into my snack shack.

"I wanna get freaky with you and make you my nasty girl. I'm sayin', sweet biscuit, you got me goin' through it.

There's something about you, girl. You're sexier than a fresh batch of pipin' hot blueberry muffins with sweet melted butter."

"Mmph. Well, I'm not that kind of girl, boy. So you need to go wreck yourself before you check yourself. Wait. I mean before you get checked. I'm not giving up none of this cake batter until—"

"I can't get you off my mind, baby boo-boo. I just wanna lay all my meat out on your grill 'n' let you marinate it. I ain't never felt like this before so I know you some kinda special rice pudding treat. Let me take you out somewhere real nice, Spencer. Let a man show you a real good time. I know this fly spot out here. Muddy Waters."

I blinked. "Muddy whaaat? Oh no, oh no...I don't do *nothing* muddy; well, except for that one time when me and Rich mud wrestled topless at this ho-down in Texas."

"Daaaayum. I know you were looking real sexy with your boobs all muddied up. I gotta box of chocolate I'd like to melt and pour all over you. I got the munchies for you, but I'm not even gonna do you like that. I'ma wine 'n' dine you first, before I lavish you with this tonguefest."

"Mmph. And what about Big Nasty? I know you love your petting time at the zoo with that wide-back girlfriend of yours. But I don't do triple-chin drama. So if you even *think* you're taking me anywhere, you have another think coming. That bearzilla has gotta go *first*. I don't want to have to pull out my tranquilizer gun and harpoon to take her down because I *will* if she tries to step to me."

I shuddered at the horror of seeing all the 8-by-10 portraits he had of her in gold frames plastered up on his purple walls in his bedroom. In one, she was holding a huge turkey drumstick up to her gold-painted lips with her tongue hanging out. In another, she had her big face hovering over a whole ham garnished with pineapples and cherries. Her beautifully lashed eyes were looking up at the camera while she held her wide mouth open over the meat, like she was ready to take a humongous bite into it.

Then there was a 16-by-20—hanging in the middle of two huge wooden paddles—of her wearing some ultra-short, black see-through and lace, tablecloth-type thingy with a pair of two-inch heels that leaned over to the sides. Although her knees looked stuck together, her chocolate skin was smooth and shiny. She was holding up a huge bucket overflowing with chicken from some chicken shack called Wings-N-Things.

Ugh, just looking at all of those pictures of Big Nasty up on his wall posing with food gave me indigestion and massive gas. And it had me needing a deep cleanse, pronto!

He chuckled. "Oh, nah, baby boo-boo, you good, ma. It's over between me 'n' Lil Bit. She's back in jail again..."

I gasped. Jail? Again?

"I can't keep doing no bids wit' her like that, feel me? The last bid she did, she was down for six months for attacking one of the cashiers at her father's Dairy Queen. Now she's on lock for attacking a cashier and the manager at KFC for giving her all dark meat instead of the twenty breasts 'n' wings she ordered. One thing 'bout Lil Bit. She doesn't play when it comes to food. Mess over her food 'n' the beast comes out."

I blinked as he described how Big Nasty snatched the poor little cashier from over the counter and gave her a beat-down with them big paws of hers. And when the manager tried to break them up, Big Nasty grabbed her in a headlock, pulled her weave out, then threw her across the counter. Wildebeest gone wild!

"Lil Bit done went too far this time. She's really broken my heart." He sniffled. "They saying she might get two years this time. I'm done. I can't keep holdin' on to WWE wrestlers with state numbers. I need me a lil sweet thing-thing with some class and style who I can seed 'n' breed. I'm tryna be a family man one day."

I stifled a yawn, glancing over at the time. I wanted to scream. I couldn't believe that I'd been on the phone with him for almost an hour already. *Ooh, sinful!* I liked him. He was different from all the other boys I'd talked to, or snuck off with. After spending two days in hiding and getting to know him, Midnight talked my talk. And for the first time, I felt like I might have met a man who'd appreciate good sexual energy. I felt like I might be able to unleash my inner sex goddess and behold the purple and gold.

Mmmph. Heat shot through me as I closed my eyes and envisioned his long athletic legs wrapped in his long johns with one leg purple and the other leg gold. Sweetjeezus! It took everything in me to stay a lady and keep the tramp in the box.

I know he was all manly and rugged. He was an ole horny corndog with oodles of noodles of sex appeal, who liked lots and lots of hot nastiness. But after my disastrous two-week fling with Anderson, I wasn't about to chance investing a lot of time and energy and good lingerie and panty sets on another confused trash-licker. Before I made any commitments to go anywhere with him, I had to know, "Are you one of those tri-sexuals who likes to drop the soap in the shower? I mean. It's okay if you are. But I don't go that way. I don't bump purses or rub kitty-kitty meow-meows."

He laughed. "Oh, nah, nah, ma. I'm all man, lamb chop. And the only kitty I'm tryna hear meow-meow is yours. Arf! Arf! Woof, woof, woof, aroooooo . . ."

I giggled at all of his silly barking sounds. Then kindly told him, "Heel, boy. Roll over. If you want to get a treat out of me, then you need to call me at a decent hour and ask me properly."

"Daayum. That's how you gonna—"

"Goooood niiiiiight, Midniiiiight," I said in a singsong voice. "Get your thoughts right. And call me in the daylight." I giggled, ending the call. I smiled. Pulled down my night mask, laid my head back on one of my fluffy pillows, closed my eyes, then this time instead of counting all of Rich's dusty pigeon moments in my head, I counted the number of freaky ways I was going to rock, bounce, and roll the purple and gold off of that long-legged stud daddy.

14

Heather

"**A**re you ready to serve the rest of them tricks sweet-fishrealness?" Co-Co spoke into the early morning breeze as we sat parked along the edge of the Royal Palms cliff, silhouetted by the rising sun.

"Trying to be," I said with my head back and eyes closed, soaking in the feel of my new hot-pink '57 Chevy convertible—top down, hydraulics up. I gave that old lady tin can crap of a car Spencer gave me to my new landlord as part of my security deposit.

I could feel Co-Co turn toward me. "Tryin' to be?"

I opened my eyes and the corners of his gloss-covered lips curled as he repeated while snapping his fingers, "Tryin' to be? What kind of business is tryin', *bish*? You 'bout to be Luda Comin'-for-Throats Tutor! Better get your life, honey! We don't have no time for tryin'. You better snatch, slay and lay them pampered trolls. The same way you did on that stage!" He flipped down the visor, looked at himself in the mirror, and fluffed the blond curls in his lace front. "Tryin'? Mmph, you better live." He ran his hands down the sides of his black beard.

"Things are not that easy for me, Co-Co."

Co-Co's deep brown gaze drank me in. His press-on lashes batted rapidly. "What's not easy for you? Or are those code words for 'I'ma slice my wrists'? How about you spare me the suicide speech and save us all the trouble now, jump off the cliff, and leave me this new whip." He ran his hands across the dashboard. " 'Cause I'm not doin' this. And as a representative of the Fierce Nation, I'm here to tell you that that ain't hot. At. All." He looked me over. "That new body has no room for you to be Miss Dumb-azz. Miss Dull-azz Sunshine. Major fail."

Oh no he didn't! Not Mister Near-Dead himself! What? Did he see the light and now he was trying to give me advice? Oh, I don't think so.

I was pissed. And it had crossed my mind to read this queen for filth, but I didn't. The only thing we didn't do together was panty drop. Still. That didn't give this boy the right to come at me crazy. Slow down, low-down.

I picked up my sixteen-ounce bottle of vodka-spiked Coke and my eyes combed him slowly.

He grunted. "Don't do it, bish. Don't tell me you have crossed over the line and are now a sensitive fish. Oh honey, see this is what I can't do: feelings on the sleeve. Look, I just need you to get in order. Your fans need you to make a comeback. And right now you are scaring me. What happened to my Wu-Wu? What happened to last night? Bring her back. Seems like you might be the one puttin' your diamonds up 'cause you're about to lose it!"

Spencer's and everyone else's voice rang in my head. "She's dead. D-E-A-D."

Co-Co gasped. "Who told you that? Wu-Wu is not dead! I don't know where you got that news from, but you've been misinformed. Wu-Wu is back. B-A-C-K. New body. New rack. New stack!"

"Wu-Wu is not coming back, Co-Co. I was fired. I was in rehab for thirty days. Went away. Came back. And they are still coming for me and talking about I was the reason for Wu-Wu being canceled—"

"Lies, fairy tales, and fallacies. Oh no. The only thing we're going to cancel is this conversation. Now if they're talking then let 'em talk. As long as they're talking it means you're droppin' heat. You need to snap out of it. Toss your drink back and tell me what else is going on. I need to know where you got that new behind, that new driver, and this ride. 'Cause last I checked you were two steps from skid row."

My eyes fluttered up and then dropped over at him. "Spencer gave me three million for my troubles."

A shadow of shock covered his face but as quickly as it came, it left. "Mmph, that's the least that sloppy fish could do! Bottom scraper. Condom eater! Jealous trick. I can't stand her."

I chuckled. "Down, girl. Down. Relax. Put the claws back. Spencer's been on her best behavior."

He pursed his lips. "For now."

"Exactly. For now." I smiled, enjoying the irritation gleaming in his eyes and the hate causing his lips to curl. "Did I ever tell you about Spencer and one of your ex–lil daddies?" I tossed it out there for no other reason than to be messy—oh, and to add to his misery.

He gasped. "What?"

I smiled and rocked a little in my seat. "Well, let me tell you who ole gutter-mouth Spencer was suckin' down."

"Who, bish, who?"

"Your old boo. You know the one you tried to turn out but failed."

"Girl, give me a name. You know those straight boys be taking me through changes."

I twisted my body toward him and said, "Anderson Ford."

"Chile, boo!" A gust of air rushed from between his lips. He paused. Raked over his thoughts and did his best to reel himself back in. "Do you really think I give a damn? Spare me. That trashy fish can have that closet queen. Movin' on. I don't even wanna talk about him, her, or it."

I blinked my eyes. "So are you over him? Remember, he's the reason why you wanted to cross over to the dark side and instead you ended up in the hospital with your liver practically burst open and your stomach practically gutted out."

Don't do me, bish!

He jumped up and down in his seat. "Don't do it. Don't do it, *bish*! You being a raunchy twat right now. You tryin' to serve me sour sushi. Attention, shoppers: clean up in aisle three 'cause this bish is tryna do me. I did not try to kill myself over him. Now next story. Movin' on. Shall we talk about the articles written about you? 'Cause there's quite a few."

He pulled out his iPhone, tapped the screen, and read, "'BRONZED & BARE: Heather Cummings, who gained stardom in 2010 playing the rambunctious and very mischievous teenager Wu-Wu Tanner on the once-popular comedy series *The Wu-Wu Tanner Show*, slung a string of profanity at paparazzi after an interview turned nasty. She then bent over and flashed her newly implanted assets after becoming angered by paparazzi for questioning her on her drinking, drugging, and rumors of dating R & B sensation Haneef. Although the once adored teen star denied being under the influence of alcohol, a source who staffed the bar on the day of the incident confirmed Heather's drink of choice was a bottle of Cognac...'"

Co-Co cleared his throat. "So it looks to me like somebody needs to stay the eff outta my boxers and dig up in their own panties."

"Why are you being all sensitive?"

"I'm a man. And I am *not* sensitive, but I will slice you down. Now I'm done with this. You will not turn my party out, down, or around!" Co-Co bounced as he turned on the radio and T.I.'s *In Da Streets* filled the car and floated out into the new day. "You have got me all worked up." He reached in his Hermès clutch and pulled out a pale blue velvet pouch. "And I need something to help keep this party alive."

Co-Co placed the pouch on the dashboard and pounded it twice.

Saliva filled my mouth and drowned my tongue. My teeth pinched the corner of my lips as the sound of crackling foil made me squirm in my seat and practically gave me an orgasm.

You can't eff with that.

Yes I can.

No you can't.

He tossed his eyes over at me. "You know you want some."

"No, I don't." I stirred my Coke. "I'm good." I sipped, nodding my head to the music.

Co-Co rolled his eyes and then looked back to the smashed pills. He dipped his long acrylic pinky nail into the powdery pile and as he inhaled it through his left nostril I eased in a deep breath and released it into my drink.

Co-Co snorted, clearing his passageways for more. "This is that good ish, bish. Black beauty mixed with Vicodin. The streets call it 'murder.'"

I salivated. *Damn, I wanna die. Murder me.* "Nah, I'm straight." I sucked up the last of my Coke and swallowed hard. I did all I could to shake off the sharp pricks of jealousy shooting through my skin.

"You better get you some and stop acting stupid." Co-Co dug in for a sophomore round. He looked back up at me and his eyes hung half-mast. "Wu-Wu"—he flicked his nose—"I hope you didn't go into druggy hell and come out a saint. I hope you ain't let it change you."

"Change me? What? I'm still the same. I just pop bottles and party."

Co-Co laughed and went in for another round. "Whew." He patted his chest and my stomach churned. "You better get into it. All you need is a pinch. That should be good enough to take the edge off. Besides, you just got out of rehab—You can't go all junkie throttle. No need in you relapsing."

No.

Whatchu scared for?

I ain't never scared.

"You say the streets call it what?" I smirked.

"Murder." Co-Co wiggled his nose, passing me the foil. "Get ready to die, bish."

Sweet beads of sweat gathered in my palms as I held my way to heaven. I took in a deep breath, dipped my finger in, and a few minutes later I could've sworn that Co-Co was God. I felt like...like my chest had opened up and I could feel my heart beat. I felt the warm blood rushing through my veins. And I could see angels smiling down on me. "Co-Co, I think I'm dead."

Co-Co laughed. "Yes, gawd. Along with your career. Now come on and get you another pinch."

I dipped my finger into the powdery pile, going back for more. "I feel like...like..."

"Like what?"

"Like I could go and eff Camille up." I handed him back the foil. "I ain't been home in two weeks."

"What home, girl?" He held one nostril closed and snorted the last of the murderous snow. "You live in a motel. Mmph, what you need to be doing is yankin' your mother up for runnin' all through your money."

I shook my head and pushed out a breath. "I can't believe I came out of rehab and she has us homeless."

"And to think I paid the rent for y'all. And now y'all up in some Sleazy Eight. I don't even know how you stayed up in there."

"Why do you think I've been gone for two weeks? And why do you think I'm not going back? I celebrated my welcome home last night. And today I'm moving into my new property."

"Is it yours, or are you renting?"

"Renting."

"Chile, cheese. You frontin' again, huh? And how did you rent a place and you're not even eighteen?"

"Money talks. And when I slapped the landlord with a half a mil for one year's rent—cold cash—he proudly handed me the keys. Beverly Hills."

Co-Co's neck flung into action. "Oh really? That's cute..."

"Is that a breeze I feel or is that shade you're throwing my way?"

"Shade. Never. You got me confused with Camille. Instead of worrying about me you need to be worrying about running up in Sleazy Eight to claim your lil boxes and your knockoffs."

15

Spencer

A week later

Sweet fashion gods of glory, thank you for laying me and slaying me in this Valentino jumpsuit and seven-inch red bottoms. Thank you for making me anti-back-fat and stomach-roll-free. Thank you for keeping my shimmy-shimmy under control. Now all I need you to do is give me patience and keep me from slaughtering this five-six, broad back wildebeest as she gets out of her car and stampedes over to me.

"How's my hair?" Rich's version of *hello*. Before I could answer, she whipped out her gold compact. "Oh, never mind!" She took a quick left-to-right peek at the flawless weave draped over her shoulders. Then blew herself a kiss and slammed her compact shut. She tossed a glance at me. "Trick, you already know I need some face time, honey. Now smile, Spencer." As if on cue, we flashed middle fingers at the not-so-well-hidden paparazzo who hung upside down in a tree and zoomed his camera in on us.

We locked arms and proceeded up the red carpet. "Why didn't you call me last night?" she demanded as the doorman tipped his hat and welcomed us into Hollywood High. Never one to take a breath, she continued running her motor. "See, Spencer. This is what I'm talking about. I keep *trying* to be nice to you. *Trying* to be a good bff to you, but you are wearing me out, honey!" She fanned her face. "You stay trying to bring it. And *you know* I'm having man problems. And *you know* you need to be on my phone for support. And *you know* I'm the only one who hasn't turned on you, not once! But did you call me? *Noooo*, you didn't. And this would be why I don't do slores."

I blinked.

She continued, holding a finger up in my face as our heels clicked against the gleaming marble. "Don't get defensive. Just apologize for being rude and non-supportive, I'll forgive you, and we can move on."

I stopped in my tracks and bit my tongue to keep from taking it to Rich's blemish-free face. I lifted my chin and waved my hand to the high heavens. I was *not* about to let Hogetha set my liner on fire with the slop that was drooling out of her gullet. Oh, no. I was going to be sweeter than a mud pie today, even if I had to choke to death on it.

Rich rolled her eyes. "Know what? You can keep your apology. But don't keep trying me, okay? Make that your last time..." Her voice drifted off as her eyes locked on Mister Lick Him Up Fine, the permanent substitute teacher, Mr. Sanchez Velasquez. He swagged his way up the hall in our direction.

Rich sucked in a breath and her eyes popped open. Mr. Lick Him Up blinked. Then his eyes zigzagged from Rich to me, then nervously back to Rich, before quickly making a beeline down the west hall.

"Ohmygod! I need an asthma pump!"

I furrowed a brow and eyed her suspiciously. "For what?" Her eyes scanned my face and I could tell she was contemplating spilling a secret, or trying to come up with a lie. I pressed on. "What do you need an asthma pump for, huh, Rich?"

She shot me a plastic grin, placing a hand up over her chest. "Girl, it's just that he was so fine I forgot to breathe. Revive me." She took my hand and fanned it lightly over her face. "Whew, girl. Thanks."

I yanked my hand back. Twisted my lips. Then tilted my head. "Yup. He's fine. Reeeal sexy fine. Puerto Rican give-it-to-me-one-time-fine."

"Yes, he is!" She did a quick twerk, dropped down to the floor, and snaked back up.

"He's also Mr. Sanchez Velasquez. A *teacher*."

"Oh," she said absentmindedly, blinking her lashes as if she were fluttering out a memory. "So *that* was his name, Sanchez. I knew it was something like that." She popped her fingers and mumbled, "I knew it started with a Z."

I narrowed my eyes at her. Then snapped them open. "Oh *nooo*!" I choked back a scream. "You dirty tramp! You trickasaurus! You *didn't*? Did you?"

Rich plastered another fake smile on her face. "Did I what?" she said as we walked up to our mahogany lockers. "*Forget* how rude you've been to me? Of course not."

I punched in the code to my combination, then opened

my locker. I shot Rich another look. "Uh-huh. You slept with him. Didn't you?"

Rich's brown eyes met mine and then quickly flicked away. "Clutching pearls! Do I look like my coochie is marked *trashy* to you?"

"Nooo! You *look* like it's marked *used goods*!"

"Don't do me! And *don't* play me, bish! I don't sleep with teachers. Okay. Get it straight. I am—"

"In denial."

She cocked her neck to the right and placed her left hand on her hip. "What? Excuse you. Didn't I tell you not to do me? I see I'ma have to get you together real quick! First off, you need to check your geography. I'm not in or on the Nile. I'm in Hollywood, California, honey. So get it right. You *know* I don't do Mexico."

I heard crickets. But I was determined to overlook her dumbness even if it sent me to an early grave. I blinked, then sniffed the air. "You know what I smell?"

She frowned. "What?"

"I smell a whore. A low-down, man-eating, no-panty-wearing, dirty, skank-a-dank-a-dank whore who's added freaky teachers to her roster!"

"*Lies!* Never!"

I lowered my voice, eyeing her. "I *know* you. And you slept with him. So where were you when you sucked in his bones? The steam room or the janitors' closet? Pour me the man juice, sweetness! And let me get my drink on!"

Rich gave me an incredulous look. "Janitors? *Whaaat?* Clutching pearls! I don't do janitors. And I *don't* do closets. I *do* one man only. Four nights a week! Knox. My boo, you've got me confused with you, Miss Down On Your

Knees, making videos in bathroom stalls! Don't try to project your tricks 'n' dirty treats over on me, swamp ho!"

I clucked my tongue and rolled my eyes. "I wasn't in a stall, for your information. When I unsnapped Corey's jeans and his belt buckle hit the floor, I was out in the open. With the door locked. So get it right, Trixie."

"No, you get it right. Tryna call me out like I'm some loose woman! I'm a vixen." She tilted her head. "See, you need to stay up off your knees and be more like me. I proudly label myself Miss HPV. Miss High Property Value. Let a boy get up on these curves and watch how his net worth shoots to the roof."

Sweetjeezusinsixinchheels. She. Is. So. Dirtfloordumb! Where are the brain gods when you need them? "Okay, Miss *HPV*, Miss Human Pressure Vent, are you ready to *finally* tell me where you raced off to when we were at Knox's? You left me in that campus apartment for hours, alone with them. I could have been molested. Now do you mind explaining yourself?"

"Nope. I had an emergency and that's all I'm saying." Her diamond bangles clanked together as she walked up the hallway and pushed open the door to the girls' lounge. I shut my locker and followed behind her.

She slammed her YSL clutch on the counter and looked into the mirror. "And don't ask me again." She lifted her eyes and clashed gazes with my reflection.

I locked the door and checked each stall. I was determined that this outdoor roadkill tramp was going to tell me the truth today or I was going to reach down into her esophagus and snatch it out of her.

"Oh, I see we need an intervention, pronto."

"Clutching pearls! I don't do that! I don't need *you* entering a thing in me!"

Jeezuskeepmechainedtothebedsheets! This girl's brain was filled with dust balls. "Would you shut up?! I'm not here to give you a pap smear. Although I'm sure you'd enjoy that. All I want to know is what the heck is going on with you now. Right now. And don't lie. Does this have something to do with that boy, *Justice*? Please don't tell me he's dead!" My heart skipped four beats. "You told me he was alive. Did he die? Do we need to live on the run? Did you turn state's evidence against me? Because I know you're a wet snitch!"

She rolled her eyes up in her head, then dropped them back over me. "No, he didn't die. But I wish he had!"

"What? Why?" I asked anxiously.

She turned around and leaned against the soapstone counter. "Spencer, I *swear* if I tell you something you had better not open your slut-bucket and go back and repeat it to Knox *or* Heather. That's what got your face slapped to the floor the last time, running your mouth. For trying to do me in with my man by backstabbing me."

"*Whaat?!*" I slammed my purse down on the counter. "Rich, do me a favor, sweetness. Drink bleach and rinse slowly! I already *told* you I *didn't* tell Knox anything. So for the last time, drop it! And anyway, you already know I don't *backstab*. I front stab! I tell you to your face what I'm going to do. Then I do it. Now what is wrong with you? Are you pregnant? Ohmygod! Not again!" I stomped my foot and wiped my brow as if I were about to faint. "I can't with you. How many times will somebody have to scrape your insides out before you learn? What is wrong with you?"

"I'm not pregnant!"

"Thank goodness! Miracles do happen. Then what is it?"

"Justice." She eyed me. "No judgment."

This trifling ho-bag keeps her legs spread wider than an all-night buffet! How dare she accuse me of being judgmental! Whatever. I swallowed my attitude. "No judgment."

"God, Spencer. I want to be pissed off with him. I want to hate him. I want to never think about him again. But I can't seem to do that. I can't get him out of my thoughts. I thought when I dumped him that would be it. But it's not." Tears filled her eyes. "He's in everything that I do. My thoughts. My dreams. My everything. I close my eyes and I see him. I hear him. I feel him. I taste him. His hands. His kisses. His voice. Everything about him is stamped into my brain. And I can't shake him, Spencer. I swear I'm trippin'."

I chewed on my tongue like it was a piece of cherry bubblegum to keep from blowing a blood vessel. I stared at her, chomping away on my tongue.

"And believe me, I have tried everything to shake him. Platters and platters of hot wings. I've bought two hundred pairs of shoes in the last week. Had my stylist do me a new wardrobe. The other night, I flew to Paris for dinner. Ate up a bunch of snails. Alone. Only to come back home the next day with this mofo *still* on my mind! I need to be free of these thoughts, of him, but they are consuming me! And it's killing me because I don't know why."

I kept chomping on my tongue, staring at her, wondering what was wrong with this dumb trick. That boy was a hood roach! No good! And from what Anderson had told me, capital T-R-O-U-B-L-E. *Hmm. I wonder if she knows*

that her little dusty thug-muffin waxes London's dinosaur.
Well, if she doesn't, she won't hear it from me. I don't gossip. And I don't do judgment. I thought to ask her who she
thought took that blind-item picture of her that was scattered all over the internet, but decided to take a deep
breath instead. I stopped tongue chomping long enough
to ask her if she was in love with him. I held my breath,
waiting to see if I would have to Mace her down real good.

"Never. I don't do love. Ever."

I pushed out a sigh of relief. "Thankyoujeezus! Now
what about Knox?"

She paused. "I love Knox. I really do."

I narrowed my eyes. *And his only flaw is that he loves
you. But noooo, you don't care. You'd rather dog him
with your lying and cheating. Like he's some plaything.
He's a boy with feelings; you obviously don't give a flim-
flam about him.*

"Rich, your mouth is saying you love Knox, but you just
confessed that you were about to kill yourself over Justice."

"Whaaat? Clutching pearls! I *never* said that."

Where is my dang gavel? She is guilty as charged!
"Then what are you saying, huh? I'm trying to keep my
mouth closed, trying to stay loving and kind. But you are
really working the one nerve I have reserved for you."

Rich sighed. "Spencer, I try so hard to do right. But I'm
a magnet for swag..."

And fleas...

"I can't help it if this thick shake keeps all the boys barking in the yard. It's like they see all this thickalicious goodness and go crazy. Is it my fault I'm beautiful...?"

And ratchet.

"Rich, you *are* beautiful, sweetness. That isn't the problem." *But your lies are going to ruin you.* "Knox is one of the few good ones left."

Tears rolled down Rich's cheeks. "Don't you think I know that, Spencer? You're so hateful! I asked you not to be judgmental! This is why we can't ever be friends for longer than"—she glanced at her Harry Winston Rosebud—"twelve minutes and forty-seven-point-three seconds. My *real* friend, who shall be nameless because she's too busy trying to make a comeback on the runway, would *never* do me like this. Never. I'm sitting here pouring my heart out to you. And you know I don't do tears and drama. I just really hate you right now."

I frowned, placing a hand up on my hip and tilting my head. "Don't you *dare* throw that cougar in Chanel up in my face. I heard you. You said you *loved* Knox but *missed* Justice. You said you knew Knox was a good guy. That the bad one is who turns you on. You don't want judgment, then fine. But know this"—I pointed a finger at her—"I'm not about to stand here and babysit your foolishness. I've been practically chewing my dang tongue off trying to keep from taking a lighter to your weave.

"You need to stop being so goshdangit selfish, Rich. Stop being a greedy man-eater! I'm not trying to tell you what to do, but you need to seal it up. If you *can't* be faithful to Knox, then break up with him. Let that boy go! All of this leading him on while you stop, drop, and roll from stroll to stroll is *c-c-craaazy!* He doesn't deserve that!

"And Justice?" I tsked. "He's a nothing. A mess. A menace! And all he can do for you is bring you a bunch of problems. You are too good for that leech! What, are you bored, Rich? You need something to do? Well how about you learn to keep your legs shut and either do your so-called man, or break up with him. But that Justice..." I shook my head. "Uh-uh. He's bad news and you need to leave him alone! Now!"

Rich rolled her eyes, then put a hand up in my face. "Scrrrrreech! Let me read you for blood real quick. You don't come at me all crazy like that. Trying to tell me what to do. Not this grown woman over here. I got this! So stay in your little crooked lane, and let me handle mine. Obviously you're still a little girl trying to be in a grown woman's world. Relationships are not that cut-and-dried. And they're not that black-and-white..."

I huffed. "Rich, this has nothing to do with race."

"You know what, Spencer? You are such an anti-genius."

Blank stare.

She continued, pulling out a Chanel hanky and dabbing her eyes. "I'm trying to get my life right. I'm trying to settle down with one man. And the only advice you can think to give me is for me to leave my man? So what if I had a few moments of not being perfect. Why would you want to see me a struggling single? You are such a damn hater!"

I stared at her. Blinked. Stared some more. Not. A. Word.

Rich sucked her teeth. "Ugh! So now you wanna stand there looking lost? Selfish!" She slung her handkerchief at me. "I'm in full-fledged crisis mode and all you care about is being your mean, catty self. How dare you! God, Spencer!" She dabbed under her eyes with the back of her two pointer fingers. "You're so despicable sometimes. I don't need your judgment! I need a friend!"

I raised a brow, tapping my fingernails on the counter.

"Ohhhhhhhh, *now* I'm your friend, huh? The otter is over in Milan waddling through the Alps. Stay away from that Justice creep!"

She slid back onto the counter. "No shade. But, girl, *bye*. I can't do you right now. I'm not looking for a lecture. And I'm damn sure not looking for a sermon. I can sit in class for that. Why are you all in my life, trying to be someone's counselor? This isn't church. I'm sixteen. I'm tryna live."

I stared at her. "You forget. I know the *real* you. Okay, sugar dumpling? Do I need to pull out those pictures of you before—"

She gasped. "Clutching pearls! Clutching pearls! Don't you dare! I will peel your face off if you do! Why you always digging in graves for the dead? Are you lonely?"

I sighed, dismissing her lonely dig. Yeah, I was lonely. But that wasn't her business. "Rich, shut. Up. I'm trying to stay loving and kind. Now"—I scooted onto the counter beside her—"I know you suffer from slutarexia. But your weekly relapses are going to destroy a good thing. I mean, really, Rich. Why do you keep doing what you do when Knox is already yours?"

Rich waved a hand in the air. "Girl, you went there. You just had to go there, didn't you? You didn't have to go in that deep, Spencer. That's way too much to think about right now. You wanna go have a drink somewhere so I can get my mind right?"

I blinked. I gave that one-stop slop the best advice I could. I. Did. That. Goshdangit! And the only thing she could think about was going out for drinks to wet her guzzler. Was this big basket of dumbness *serious*? "What?

Drinks? You are out of control, Rich, which is why you're in the mess you're in. Now, before we get out of here, I'm going to ask you one more time. Did you do the teacher?"

Rich hopped off the counter. Turned toward the mirror to fix her face. "You know what, Spencer. You're crossing the line. That is a private question, and a personal matter that I'm not going to discuss today, tomorrow, or ever. You know there are four things I don't do: Drama. Personal talk. Old men. And I don't ever kiss and tell. Now, what I did or didn't do is between *me* and the Hispanic Stallion, and that cute little mole on his gigantic love pole."

I giggled, snatching my things up and shaking my head. This girl was a walking crotch fire. "Come on, trickamosis. Let's talk about his love pole on the way to homeroom."

16

London

God, I beg of you. Please let my first day back at Holly-wood High be without a lot of gas and a bunch of drama. Amen.

After a month of being away, I was finally back in L.A. for a brief moment before I had to fly back to Milan for Fashion Week. And, yes, I was back without my mother dragging me to New York to be put under a knife. There was not going to be any plastic surgery done on me.

My stomach grumbled as I drove down Wilshire Boulevard. I clutched my abdomen, feeling queasy from my late-night carb binge on Nutella and vanilla crullers from Spudnuts, one of my favorite L.A. doughnut shops—snuck in through the back stairwell by one of our security staff as a special favor to me. Now I was nauseous. I felt bloated. And sooo fat. I'd have to drink gallons of water to flush out my guilt, then spend my whole third and fourth periods getting sweaty on the treadmill, running myself into the

ground to ward off any ugly pounds of fat cells that might
be lurking around in my body.

My stomach rumbled again.

Oh God no!

A roar of gas passed through me. I started coughing and
gagging, turning the car's AC on high and rolling all the
windows down. Yes, this bout of gas was the end result
and punishment for being up at 2:38 this morning *bing-
ing*. My guilty indulgence; my dirty little secret brought on
by stress.

Thanks to Justice. He tended to be—no, he *was*—my
biggest stress trigger; especially whenever he'd go days or
weeks not returning any of my calls. Or when he'd finally
decide to bless me with his greatness, then start verbally
attacking me, talking to me as if I were last night's trash.
And last night was no exception when he finally felt chari-
table. That's exactly how he made me feel—more often
than not—like I was some afflicted charity case. As if he
were making enormous contributions to the Pitiful London In Distress Foundation. I suppose he was contributing
to my cause every time he'd toss me a bone of kindness.
Every time he'd whisper sweet nothings in my ear after
having cursed me out like some Lower East Side projects
tramp. Every time he'd mush me in the face, or flick me in
the head with angry fingers for not attending to his needs
to his liking. He'd contribute to my cause—my cause of
stress, distress...and being one big mess.

Mmph.

I guess I *was* afflicted.

By him!

He was my plague.

Justice ate away at my heart, like acid.

And still...I hung on. I refused to let go. Didn't know how to let go. He was my past. My present. And the only boy I could see in my future. Everything I was was tied up into him.

And last night he'd finally driven the stake straight into my heart then twisted it when he hung up on me, right after telling me he wished I'd go somewhere and drop dead. He said I was *useless* to him or anyone else...*alive.*

Okay, okay...so what if I'd called him twenty-seven times before he finally decided to return my call. That still didn't give him the right to tell me I was *useless*. And, yeah, okay, maybe I shouldn't have screamed at him for not returning *any* of my calls the whole time I was away. And maybe I shouldn't have questioned him about the photos I'd received. That still didn't give him the right to tell me he wished I were *dead.*

I felt myself tearing up as I sat behind the wheel of my Aston Martin at a traffic light, replaying bits and pieces of our phone conversation.

"Yeah, what up?" he'd answered nonchalantly. "Who's this?"

I had blinked, glancing at the screen to make sure I'd called the right number. "It's me. London."

"Oh word? What you want wit' me?"

I blinked again. "I'm back."

"Back where?"

"In L.A."

"Good for you."

"I wanna see you. I've missed you. Can you come see me?"

"Mmph. Nah, I'm good. I ain't beat for none a that underground railroad crap. I'm not wit' sneakin into ya crib like I'm some runaway slave. That BS's mad whack. I'm done wit' all that. And I'm done wit' you, yo."

"Justice, please. I need to see you." I felt myself sinking into a dark hole. Since my parents moved us out to California, I still hadn't seen the inside of wherever Justice lived. And anytime I'd ask him about it, he'd always give me some kind of excuse as to why I couldn't. It was being renovated. It was being redecorated. It was being exterminated. And his last excuse to me was, no, I couldn't come to his place because I kept sweating him too much about going. So it was all my fault that I wasn't allowed over. "I can leave now."

"Nah, I'm good, yo."

A car in back of me blew its horn. I glanced up into my rearview mirror at the silver Jag, snatching me from my thoughts.

I groaned as my stomach knotted. More gas seeped out. *Ohgodohgod!*

I quickly swerved over to the side of the road, swung open my car door, then leaned my head out and tossed up my guts.

God, please get me through these cramps and gas. I promise I won't stuff myself with so many doughnuts the next time. I'll only eat ten instead of the twelve I scarfed down. And no more Nutella.

I coughed. Then spit out the rest of the sugary guilt rising up in the back of my throat. I reached for my bottle of Tasmanian Rain water and took a swig, swishing it around in my mouth, then spitting it out.

"You so effen worthless, yo..." Justice's voice stomped its way back into my thoughts as I wiped my mouth with a

handful of tissues. *"Just look at you. Pig. Hog. No wonder you're so fat..."*

My cell phone buzzed, bringing me back into the moment as I shut the car door. I quickly pulled my cell from the console, hoping it was Justice. But it wasn't. It was my father.

"Hey, baby girl. Welcome home. Your old man missed you."

In spite of my current dark mood, Daddy still managed to pull a smile out of me. "Hi, Daddy. I missed you too."

And Justice more...

"I'm sorry I wasn't home to greet you and your mother last night. I'm flying in from London today. My flight should arrive at LAX around four."

"Oh, that's great, Daddy. I can't wait to see you."

And Rich too...

"I was thinking you and me could go somewhere special for a bite to eat. Would you like that?"

"I'd love that," I told him, pulling back out onto Wilshire, heading toward school. "What about Mother? Is she going to be joining us?"

There was a brief silence before Daddy finally spoke. "No. Not this time. This is our night, just you and me. Your mom and I will do something later on in the week." He wanted to know how it felt being back in front of all the flashing lights and all of the pomp and circumstance that went along with being a model. I was careful to not push the envelope too far and tell him how much I hated being around all those snotty models. Or how I hated being unable to keep tabs on Justice—who I was convinced, after receiving those photos with his tattooed hand on that girl's butt, was cheating on me.

"What?" Justice had snapped when I confronted him last night. "Are you serious right now, yo? I'm *waaaay* over here 'cross the water. In Cali, yo. Where *you* should be. Wit' ya man, yo. But you ain't. You somewhere tryna get ya shine on. Yet, you comin' at me 'bout some flicks of some naked chick, like I'm s'posed to know what you talkin' 'bout. You dumber than dumb, yo. Real spit, London. You mad silly. Why you think I'm no longer beat to rock wit' you, huh? You still a lil girl. You ain't ready for no real man, lil girl. How you gonna blast me 'bout some flicks, yo, when you ain't even on ya J-O-B handlin' ya man right? What, London? You want me sittin' 'round on rock, mad horny, twiddlin' my thumbs while you overseeeeeeas somewhere, huh, L-Boogie..."

My lips quivered. "Justice, why are you being so mean to me? I only asked you a simple question. And you're taking it way to the left. I do nothing but love you, Justice, and all you want to do is treat me like I'm nothing..."

"*Juuuuuustiiiice,*" he mocked. "W-w-whyyyyy you bein' so mean to poor lil London? All she's tryna do is love you, *Juuuuuustiiiice.* Boo-hoo, boo-hoo. Poor lil baby's feelings are hurt." He grunted. "Yo, get over ya'self, lil girl. You don't love me. You don't even love ya'self. If you loved me, you'd be here when I needed you to be. I was laid up in the hospital for two days wit' a concussion..."

I gasped. "Ohmygod, nooo! What happened? How'd you get a concussion?"

He snorted. "What, now you care 'bout what happened to me? Just a few minutes ago all you cared 'bout is some chick's naked flicks and some cat's hand down her shirt."

"But it's your hand, Justice."

He started yelling. "ARE you hearin' how dumb you

sound, yo, huh? STOP bein' so retarded, yo! I tol' ya that somebody prolly photoshopped them flicks. Think, London, think! I just tol' you I was hit in the head 'n' you still tryna beat me in the skull 'bout some flicks that I already tol' you I don't know jack about.

"See, that's ya mutha-effen problem, yo. You don't listen. You never listen. Because you too effen busy bein' selfish, only thinkin' 'bout London. You don't care 'bout me, yo. I was practically bandaged from feet to head; just one second from bein' dead 'n' I ain't get no flowers, no visit, no phone calls, no cards, no nothin' from you. But I'm s'posed to believe you love me. Yeah, right. You can go suck a—"

I cut him off. "I do love you, Justice."

He laughed. "Yeah, whatever. I ain't beat. What's up wit' ya peoples?"

I frowned. "My *peoples*? my peoples *who*?"

He sucked his teeth. "Ya girl, Rich, who else? Why you so stupid, yo? Ain't nobody else effen wit' you. You was s'posed to be hookin' that up for me 'n' you couldn't even handle that right."

"I tried. But then I had to—"

"Save it, yo. I'm not tryna hear none a ya BS. I don't need no lil silly girl tryna make moves for me. I got this. I already put work in. So go do you."

"What are you saying, Justice? You already hooked up with her? Is that why you haven't had time for me? Is that why you broke up with me? Because you're giving all of your time to Rich?"

"See. That's what I'm talkin' 'bout, lil girl. That dumbness you be on. That silly lil girl jealousy crap you stuck on. I already said it. I'm baggin' that." He clucked his tongue. "Move on, yo. It's over. For real, yo. You straight up worthless. I don't know why I ever wasted my time effen wit' you."

The tears fell unchecked down my face as Justice stabbed me over and over and over with his harsh words.

I sniffled.

"You all right, baby girl?" Daddy asked, pulling me out of my casket before the lid slammed shut.

I swiped my tears. "Y-yes. I'm fine. I think my allergies are flaring up, and I'm sort of jet-lagged from the flight. I didn't sleep well last night."

I guess you didn't, piglet.

"I understand. It can definitely take some getting used to. If you want, we can have dinner tomorrow night."

I shook my head, swiping more tears. Told him no. That it was okay. That I wanted to have dinner with him. Truth was, I needed a distraction, anything to keep me out of the house, anything to keep Justice's cruel words from lurking in the shadows of my already cluttered mind. And I needed to be away from my hidden arsenal of snacks. We talked a few minutes more, then ended the call as I slowly pulled up to the entrance of Hollywood High with less than ten minutes to spare before the homeroom bell rang. I was anxious to confront Rich and get to the bottom of her attitude toward me. I needed to know why she had been acting funny and ignoring me. And, on top of that, I needed to know whether or not she was messing with my man.

I took a few deep breaths, flipping down the visor and fixing my face. Hollywood High was all about pretense. I might have been half a breath short of death, but I'd be damned if I was going to hand the grim reaper my eulogy.

* * *

"Well, well, if it isn't America's Next Top Flop," the headmaster, Mr. Westwick, said in his nasal, annoying singsong voice as I walked through the glass doors. "Welcome back. I see you're still on the runway thinking you can flounce up in here"—he glanced down at the time, tapping the face of his watch—"with less than six minutes before homeroom. Be late if you want, and it'll cost you…"

My stomach rumbled again. I clenched my booty cheeks to keep gas from easing out. "I know, I know…it'll be five grand, or two days detention."

God, please let me make it to the bathroom in time.

He batted his thick eyelids. "Oh, you Miss Fancy now, huh?" A stumpy hand went up on his hip. "Should I ask for your autograph now or later?"

"No, later will be fine," I snidely replied, parting a tight, phony smile. "Now, if you'll excuse me. I have to get to my locker."

"Yes. You do that. Oh, and London…"

I stopped moving but didn't turn back to look at him. I didn't need to. He'd walked up on me, practically charring the back of my neck with his hot breath. "It's been real quiet around here since you've been overseas. I hope you left the ratchet at Customs. I won't stand for any more of your Big Apple shenanigans. I expect you to follow the Hollywood High Academy protocol or be escorted off the grounds in handcuffs. You New Yorkers come here and really bring down the school's reputation and property value with all of your hoodilicious antics."

I blinked. My nose flared. But instead of going off, I slowly unclenched my booty cheeks and gently eased out a puff of gas, then quickly stepped off, leaving Mr. West-wick coughing and wheezing.

"Someone bring me my oxygen tank," he called out, gagging. "Hurry! Hurry! I think my emphysema is flaring up..."

I smirked, pulling out my buzzing cell. *Choke on that! Calling me ratchet!* I glanced at the screen, sighing. It was a text from my mother. NO CARBS.

I rolled my eyes. *Ugh! If you only knew!* I replied back as I headed to my locker. I KNOW.

Next, I decided to send Rich a text as well. HEY BESTIE-BOO. C U @ LUNCH. WE HAVE LOTS 2 GET CAUGHT UP ON. *Yeah, like what the hell is up with you and Justice.*

My mother sent another text. DID U DRINK ALL OF UR SEAWEED SMOOTHIE?

I huffed. *God! Disappear already! No, I didn't drink that slimy ish!* I deleted the message, tossing my phone back into my bag. I reached my locker and quickly grabbed my books for my first three classes, then slammed the door shut.

I almost slid out of my six-thousand-dollar Italian be-jeweled heels when some low-life banshee walked up into my space, pulling an issue of *Gutz & Glam* from her last season's Bottega bag.

I blinked. *"Umm, really?* Can I help you?" I said, eyeing her over the rim of my diamond-studded Luxuriator shades.

She tossed the magazine at me. "Page three. Read it and weep." And as quickly as she'd intruded in my space, she was already gone. Ghost. Missing amongst a throng of Louis Vuitton, Gucci, and Mulholland deerskin backpackers.

FROM RICHES TO RATTY...HAVE THE PAMPERED PRINCESSES OF HOLLYWOOD HIGH FINALLY GONE ROGUE? blared the headline. I blinked as my insides twisted and knotted. First Justice dismissing me, like I was last year's trash. Then seeing Mr. Westwick's face first thing in the morning. And now this trash rag being tossed at me! I didn't know how much more I could take before I snapped. I felt myself swoon as I looked on. The story read:

Looks like Hollywood High's pampered princesses have laid down their crowns and gone ratchet for good. From mud slinging to fist swinging, these four teen divas have rolled up the red carpets and taken to the boxing mat.

In round one, socialite and scandalous sex kitten Spencer Ellington dropped down and got her bobble on as she brazenly super-soaked her bestie Rich's then-boyfriend, the son of Senator Corey Othello Marshall Sr. And how deliciously convenient that some-one would leak footage of the rising teen-porn-star's stellar performance. Can you say tongue tricks that'll put any Hello Kitty fan to shame? Is it safe to wonder how many licks it takes the teen sex-muffin to get to the center of a Tootsie Pop?

Ding, ding, ding! Round two kicked off with party vixen Rich Montgomery, daughter of entertainment royalty Richard Montgomery Sr. of Grand Records, along with New York socialite London Phillips—the daughter of renowned international supermodel Jade Obi Phillips. In tag-team pizazz, the two molly-whopped and stomped Spencer down in a ditch, then—from aerial footage we uncovered compliments of TMZ—turned on each other and cat-clawed and tiger-mauled one another up in a lily pond. Shall we say, "No tea, no shade?" *Meeeeow!*

But the grand-slam finale goes to teen star Heather Cummings, who slayed her bad girl counterparts by boldly firing rhymes of venom about the clique's snobbery, denouncing her allegiance to Hollywood High's royal court. Soon after, she threw the last punch, drugging her own mother, then landing herself in jail...thanks to the reigning queen of messy, Spencer Ellington, who dropped dime and got her bestie-boo serving time. So who's saving the stitches for the snitches? Looks like someone's gonna need their plastic surgeon on speed dial.

And now, there are rumors of a rematch bout. A source close to the teen actress reports that the heavyweight, Heather Cummings, is in the lab working on some fire tracks to set the exquisite heels of her three frenenemies ablaze...

I blinked. *Dear God! These tabloid slores are atrocious. They'll stop at nothing!* My eyes traveled to the last paragraph of the article.

And most recently, in a botched carjack-kidnapping ploy, media-crazed Rich Montgomery and Spencer Ellington have dropped to an all-time low, becoming the new Thelma and Louise of Hollywood as the two thugettes in baguettes allegedly fled the scene of an assault on an unidentified man.

Can we say, what's goodie in the hoodie?

I blinked. Blinked again. Then reread the paragraph again. *Oh dear God, no! Please don't tell me Rich is back chopping it up with Spencer. So that's why the hell I haven't heard from her. I knew it!*

I heard a scream bubbling up in my throat just as I locked eyes on Rich and Spencer walking out of the girls' lounge arm in arm, cackling like hyenas. Then my worst fear was realized when I called out to Rich and she tossed me a quick wave, flipping her hair over her shoulder and shaking her tail feathers down the marble-lined hall, not once looking back.

17

Heather

Here was the plan: get my ish and bounce. No words. Walk straight past Camille—like the nothing she is—and be out. Finished. Never to see her drawn-up white face again.

I pulled into Sleazy Eight's parking lot and parked diagonally across the two spaces in front of the door to our room. I raised my car's leopard-print ragtop roof and looked at a shocked Co-Co.

"Oh bish." He wiped invisible sweat from his brow. "You need to ferociously snatch Camille by her throat and lay her dead in the hills for doing you like this! Do it for the *gawds* if not for yourself, *honey*!" He looked around; his eyes seeming to take in the entire trash-littered, two-story complex, from the short-circuited Twenty-four Hour Vacancies sign, to the torn blinds in the windows, to the tractor-trailers parked everywhere. "This is vile!"

I sighed. We'd been together too long. He'd been living with me at my new spot for the last week but no more, because I was putting him out. I was done. I was getting tired of Co-Co and his slick mouth. I was not in the mood and today was the last day I was going to let his balls swing freely in his panties.

I *already* knew this place was a dreadful and run-down crack den where greasy truckers and Hollywood's low-level drunks and junkies congregated. But I didn't need Mister and Missus Co-Co tossing it in my face and killing my high. 'Cause God knows his empty bra would get real twisted if I went in on the tumbledown K-town he lived in.

I gave Co-Co a look that clearly said, "Don't do me." I took a deep breath and turned on the radio. "You can sit here until I come back."

"*Whaaaaaat?* Bish, are you serious? You are not about to have me molested by some hood-hoein' beast! You're trying to set me up to be raped! Have all my chestnuts laid out over an open fire!"

I was two seconds from tearing out what was left of his Adam's apple. "If you come in here with me then you better not say a thing to Camille. Nothing. We walk up in here. I get my stuff and we bounce."

"Fine with me." He paused and refreshed his lip gloss. "As long as she doesn't come for Co-Co then Co-Co will be as quiet as a down-low freak."

We eased out of the car and walked up to the door of room 111. I slid the card key into the lock and was greeted by thick clouds of cigarette smoke and a nicotine breeze as I walked in.

Camille sat at a small round card table facing the window. She took long, deliberate pulls off of her Newport before mashing it into the overflowing crystal ashtray.

She tossed back her glass of scotch and faced me. Our

eyes locked. She gave me a dark stare and for a moment her brow looked creased with worry. But just as quickly as I spotted it, it dissolved and melted into her usual look of disappointment and disgust.

Eff her! I broke our gaze by waving a hand in dismissal, then I gave her my new behind to look at as I turned my back and grabbed my empty suitcase from the far right corner of the room.

I walked over to the 1970s dresser, the one Camille forced me to stuff my clothes into, and wrestled with the handles, snatching the broken-down drawers open.

"Where. Have. You. Been?" Camille asked, tight lipped—like she owned me.

It took everything in me—or out of me, depending on how you looked at it—not to laugh. I shot a glare over my shoulder at Camille. My eyes strolled from her pink matted bedroom slippers to the murky whites of her blue eyes, and I hoped my blazing gaze delivered the message that this trick was out of line.

Waaaaay out of line.

Especially if she thought I owed her an explanation of where I'd been.

Beyotch, puhlease!

I've been doing me! That's where I've been. Spending *my* money. *My* money. Doing me.

That's where I've been.

Popping bottles. Shopping it and dropping it.

Camille's hot breath landed on the nape of my neck but I simply flicked a few fingers and dusted her repulsion off of me; 'cause one thing I couldn't care less about was this mad ex-starlet and her temper tantrums. Not!

"*And why* are you looking at me like that, Norma

Marie?" I heard Co-Co say from behind me, calling Camille by her government.

`Didn't I tell him to keep his mouth shut?` I turned my head and lifted an eye up at Co-Co, yet before I could say anything Camille spat, "Let me tell you something, trans-confusion. Don't come for Norma Marie unless Norma Marie sends for you."

"Trans-confusion?" Co-Co grimaced. "Ya see, Wu-Wu, Co-Co is trying to be nice. You do see this, right? But you better get mama-fish 'cause she just tried it!"

Camille's gaze drank Co-Co in and then turned back to me. I rolled my eyes "You know how trash do, Co-Co. That's why I'm out of here! Because the only thing I can do for trash is burn it."

Camille batted her lashes and pulled out a full bottle of scotch from beneath the mattress. She walked over to the mini-fridge, took out a frosted glass, and poured her liquid crack into it. "Let me wet my tongue real good." She gave her glass a light stir before taking a sip. "'Cause I'm not sure what's going on here." She took another sip. "All I know is that this here heifer's been missing for far too long. Ever since she got back from Brazil."

Camille carried on, speaking to her invisible sounding-board. "And then she stepped up in here like she doesn't owe me an explanation. Not to mention she ran off with the last three weeks' rent money!"

"Touché! 'Cause you ran off with all my money! Now you know how it feels!"

"Heather, where have you been?"

"Last I checked, I didn't have to answer to you!" I fanned my fingers as if I were counting on them. "I pay my own bills. I take care of myself! Mmph, I'm grown. And I don't owe you jack! Now fall back or get slapped back because you're not getting a dime out of me! And if ya broke, that's not my problem! It's a wide track out there so get ta strollin', baby."

Camille stared at me and took two steps into my personal space. All the color left her face, but the purple veins in her neck glowed and her eyes shrank to two icy blue slits. "Miss Pill Popper, let's take this from the top. Where have you been? And where do you think you're going? And how much money do you have left? Because I smell nothing."

I looked over at Co-Co and said, "Are you ready to get out of here? Because I feel myself getting—"

Whack! Whack! Bap! Slap!

I fell over my suitcase, hitting my head on the floor.

I'ma have to kill her.

Camille grabbed me by my ponytail and bashed my face into my suitcase!

"Co-Co, help me!" I screamed as I tried my best to get a handle on Camille but failed.

"Get off of her, Camille!" Co-Co screamed, wrapping his arms around himself.

Whack! Whack! Bap! Slap!

Camille tossed me into the wall and I heard my nose crack before I felt it. Blood spritzed everywhere.

"You ungrateful pill junkie!" Camille yelled.

Whack! Whack! Bap! Slap!

"Co-Co! Get her off of me!" I screamed as Camille flung me across the room and I slammed into the nightstand—stomach first.

Sharp jabs shot through my chest cavity and suddenly it was hard for me to breathe. "Co-Co!" No matter how hard

I tried to fight back, I was no match for this crazy trick! She'd lost her mind and I'd be dead before anyone knew it.

Whack! Whack! Bap! Slap!

"Ahhhhhh!" I screamed as Camille's rage grew.

"You took it too far, Heather Suzanne! You disrespect me? And then you bring his showtime Suzie up here and watch you show out!" She kicked me in my behind and I swore I felt the silicone burst.

"Help!" I screamed. "Somebody help me!"

"Yes! Please! God!" Co-Co yelled. "Somebody help her!"

Camille carried on, "I will kill you in here!"

Whack! Whack! Bap! Slap!

"And then I'll slice Co-Co's damn throat!"

Whack! Whack! Bap! Slap!

Camille gripped my hair and dragged me around the room, the carpet burning my calves and the backs of my thighs. "You've been missing for three weeks!"

Whack! Whack! Bap! Slap!

"Three weeks!"

Whack! Whack! Bap! Slap!

"And *nooooow* you think you can come back here!"

Whack! Whack! Bap! Slap!

"And not tell me where you've been?"

Whack! Whack! Bap! Slap!

"Ahhhh!"

"Shut the hell up!"

Whack! Whack! Bap!

"Did you really think you could come in here and leave me stranded? You stole my rent money and now you want to leave me, your mother, with nothing! Never! I would never let that happen! I'd kill you first!"

"Ahhhh!" I could see stars flashing before me as Camille did her best to dislodge my head from my shoulders and take my face off!

"All the sacrifices I made for you!"

Whack! Whack! Bap! Slap!

"And to think I was the best mother I could be to a no-good, rotten daughter like you! Maybe your daddy had the right idea! I should've flushed you out on the gurney. But I didn't! And now I have to live with my choice, and like it or not, we're stuck together until you're eighteen! Now it's my way or get dragged!"

Whack! Whack! Bap! Slap!

I knew I was screaming, but I couldn't hear a sound escape my lips. And I knew I was swinging my arms, trying to fight myself free of Camille. But none of my hits seemed to help me. She was killing me! I knew it! As I've always known she would. She's always hated me; and her gripping me tighter by the roots of my hair and flinging me back into the wall was proof of it.

Blood was everywhere. My head felt like an electric chisel was buried inside and my chest cavity had caved in on itself.

Camille huffed, and sweat had pasted her white cotton gown to her skin. She took a step back and looked down at me. "From here on out you'll watch your mouth!" She took a cigarette butt out of the ashtray, lit it, and took a pull as the door flew off the hinges.

18

Spencer

Everyone had a price at Hollywood High. From the headmaster to the muscled, spray-tanned janitors, if you wanted to get out of something—or, in my case, *into* something, all you had to do was write a check or slide a few dollars deep down into someone's front pants pocket. And *voilà*! You had whatever you needed.

Heeheehee. Like the master key card to the locked girls' lounge on the third floor, where London raced when she thought no one else was looking.

I'd been waiting for this coyote to hunt. And the minute I saw her ease her horns into the lounge during last period, I accessed one of the master key cards, slid it down into the door slot, then crept in smooth as silk and as easy breezy as Rich spreading her thighs when she sees a boy, locking the door behind me.

I could hear her grunting and groaning and a whole lot of plop-plop-plopping. I frowned, throwing a hand up over my nose and mouth. It smelled like something had crawled up inside of her, got lost then died trying to find its way out. And now she was delivering it to its final resting place.

Thank the heebie-jeebies I had a surgical mask down in my bag. I fished it out, placing it over my nose and mouth, then pulled out my iPhone. I waited a few seconds, listening to Beast Creature growling and gnashing her teeth as she delivered funk baby after funk baby. I kicked in the bathroom stall door, snapping a picture. "Say cheese, you gutter rat! You ole funky turd mama!"

London's face cracked in horror as her head shot up and she saw me. "Aaah! Ohmygod! *What the hell!* Do you *not* see me on the toilet? Get out!" She quickly held her purse up, shielding her face as I snapped another picture.

"I'm not going anywhere, dixie doodle, until you and I have a little chat." I dropped the camera back into my bag.

She let loose a string of bullets and gas bombs.

I gagged, waving a hand in front of me. "You septic tank! If you think for one minute that you're gonna chase me up out of here with all of your funk, you have another think coming."

She leaned over, clutching her stomach. "Biotch! N-n-not. N-n-now. Ohgodohgod...get out!"

She fired off more rounds of funk grenades.

"Plop, plop, fizz, fizz. You can try to hide all you want, drag racer. But make no mistake. Eventually the truth will show its pretty face. And when it does, you filthy, stinky, lying, troll doll, I'll be right there to greet it in the face and set you free. You're a fraud. A fake. A phony. You might have Rich fooled with your little Miss Perfect Patty sham, but I know better. I know what you are, Miss Beetle Juice. You're a three-dollar dream in a sandbag! And know this:

I'm not going to rest until I find every pair of your raggedy drawers. Then I'm going to air your filth for all to see and chase you up out of Hollywood High once and for all."

She grunted again, practically breaking out into a sweat. "Screw you, Spencer! I'm not going anywhere, so you might as well get used to seeing this face. On billboards! On Jumbotrons! On banner ads! I'm here to stay! I hate you! So go roll off a cliff. I don't care about you or your threats. Now get out so I can use the bathroom! Wait until I'm off the toilet then step to me, you lonely, pathetic leech!"

I stood there and eyed her as her face twisted as if she were being gutted and filleted. Her stomach grumbled. I almost felt sorry for Miss Loose Stools. Almost.

I rolled my eyes, then said reeeeeeeal slllllllllow, "I. Don't. Like. You. I never have. And I never will."

She grunted. "Good, heifer. Uhh…because I don't like… uhh…you either. Now get…uhh…the hell out and let me use the bathroom in peace, you wretched…" She grunted again.

I laughed. "Oh, stinky-stink London. Poopty-doopty-doo-dah. You thought you were so slick when you talked Rich into attacking me in finance class; thought you were going to come in between me and my As, too, didn't you? But guess what? No one gets in the middle of my grades and me. I still have an A average. And the highest GPA in the school. And Rich and I are stronger than two pit bulls mating, thanks to *you*."

"Well, good for you," she snapped, grunting and almost toppling over as she leaned forward, holding her stomach. "Now get out!"

"Oh, no no no, Miss London, London, London…I

should broil your drawers right here. But I need you in one piece." Her eyes popped open. "Oh yes. One. Piece. You crossed the wrong one, Little Miss Muppet..."

Someone banged on the door.

"Help!" London yelled, letting out another string of gunfire. "I'm trapped in a stall with a—!"

I quickly yanked my can of Mace out of my handbag, pointing it in her face. "You shut your flytrap," I hissed. "Or I will seal your eyes shut."

She shut her mouth. The person on the other side of the lounge's door kept knocking a few more times before finally deciding to take her business elsewhere.

I leaned up against the side of the doorframe.

She glared at me. "You're crazy, Spencer! A Looney Tune! A psycho! A nut!"

I curled my lips, twirling the end of a curl through my fingers. "Yup, I sure am, trashy-dot-com. I'm a crazy Looney Tune...the psycho nut who *you* shoulda did your homework on *first*, before you tried to turn Rich against me. I *warned* you. I *told* you"—I pulled a bottle of Nair hair remover and a mini blowtorch from my oversized handbag and pressed the torch on—"that the next time you tried to come between Rich and me that I was going to Nair your lashes off..."

Miss Fright Night gasped, her face filled with dread. She fumbled through her handbag, pulling out her phone. "Ohmygod! I'm calling—"

I giggled, shutting off the torch's fiery blue flame. "Oh, shut it up, you goat! I'm not going to burn you here. When I Nair those long, luscious lashes off your lids, it'll be when I catch you with your eyes shut." I dropped the hair remover back into my bag. "So the *only* thing you're calling, you gargoyle, is the help line for Uglies Anonymous. Now put the phone down or I'm going to singe your eyeballs out."

My nose flared as I thought back to the first time I'd met this skankazoid and how this bougie ghetto-tramp turned her nose up at me like I was hot trash, giving me the tips of her fingers to shake when Rich introduced us over the summer prior to her transferring to Hollywood High. That was strike one for the beaver.

You don't snub *me*. *Not* when I'm being wholesome and pure toward you. I was nothing but gracious to this little snot. I didn't give her attitude or an ounce of stank-a-dank. And *she*, Miss Low-Money East Side, had the gall to look down at me. Oh, I don't think so. Don't matter how many times she had her face plastered on the side of a trash Dumpster for some designer's couture. Trash was still trash. And London Phillips's garbage bags were about to get dumped.

Strike two was her making faces at Heather when she waltzed in wearing a pink onesie that was cut real low in the front and rrrrrrreal low in the back to her butt crack, and a pair of six-inch leopard-print gladiator sandals. I overheard Dogzilla ask Rich, "Where'd you find that crack whore? She looks like she stinks."

Ole two-faced Rich laughed. But I didn't find it funny one diggity-dang bit. And I wrecker-checked her on it. I slid an icepick right up to the center of her throat and told her she was out of line for calling Heather a stank crack-whore. Heather might not take up for herself, but I could, would, and goshdangit did. Heather came from meager earnings. It wasn't her fault she was a part of the one-stop 'n' drop back-to-work program and her mother was a drunk. She didn't deserve to be talked about by some outsider; some long-legged, big-faced nobody with big feet, big hands, and a big, wide mouth. No. Heather was only allowed to be dragged by Rich and me. Not by some sneaking, conniving trick.

Strike three was the queen of dust monkeys coming to Hollywood High *thinking* she could sandbag and pony her way in between Rich and me. I *knew* Rich. She didn't. I *knew* London. And, unfortunately, Rich didn't. But then again, she wouldn't, because Rich is gullible like that. She wore her blinders on backwards and was only able to see the forest through the peephole of a pair of boy's boxers. She was totally delusional when it came to London, who smiled in your face while plotting behind your back.

At least I was woman enough to tell you to your face what I was going to do to you. Not this half man, half creature. She was the worst kind of dirty, low-down, good-for-nothing freak in a sardine can.

Strikes four, five, six, seven, eight, and nine came when she continued to test my gangster. But she had the right one, baby. This rat snake was going up against a mongoose. There'd be no win for her. And when I was done striking her down, *snake* would be on the menu.

She grunted. "L-l-look, Spencer. Do you...uhh...mind backing the hell up and closing...uhhh...ohgod...the damn door...so I can have a little *privacy*? Whatever else you need to jibber, you can do it on the other side of the door."

I shook a finger at her. "Oh no. Oh no. So you can call the po-po and try to have me hauled off in some cheap silver wristlets? No deal, snickerdoodle. The only way I'm getting dragged out of here in handcuffs is for humpback-U-crooked letter-D-E-crooked letter." She gave me a look glazed in dumbness. Like really? Did this hoof-foot gorilla think I was going to spell M-U-R-D-E-R out for her and have her have it recorded? I might have been a hundred and ninety-nine things, but dumb wasn't one.

"Oh no. We're going to have it out with me standing right here. So if you want to use the bathroom, use it. Or hold it until you explode. Either way, I'm not leaving until I'm done."

She huffed. "Then say what you have to say, you dumb Beanie Baby, then get. OUT! What is your problem with me anyway, huh, Spencer?"

"Your whole existence is the problem, Little Miss Flake-A-Bake. You're a scheming, lying, phony waste of air and space."

The hate in her eyes was blinding. I lowered my shades from the top of my head, shielding my eyes from the rays. "How desperate," she said, curling her lips up. "You can call me all the names you want. Are you that insecure of someone else being Rich's friend? Are you that jealous of me that you have to take to kicking in bathroom stalls?"

She leaned over, clutching her stomach again. I felt myself becoming light-headed from all the toxic fumes coming out of her. If I had cared, I would have asked her what the hell was wrong with her guts. Then graciously offered her the number to a fabulous plumber I know who'd flush her insides.

But she could suffer for all I cared.

I guffawed. *"Jealous?* Hahaha! Oh, London, London, London...hahaha...*not!* You're lucky I'm not kicking in your teeth for filling Rich's head up with your lies and having her put her paws on me. But I'm going to tell you like I told your *play* boyfriend, Anderson Ford..."

Her eyes bucked. "*Anderson?*"

"Yessss, sweetie. Anderson. That very wealthy, hard-bodied *pretend* boyfriend of yours."

"Ohmygod, you're such a pathetic cow," London snarled, clearly trying to keep it together. But I could see her eyeballs popping around in her head like pinballs as she scrambled to keep her little playhouse from crumbling down around her. "You keep Anderson's name out of your filthy mouth! Once again, you're down on your knees rustling through the trash for someone else's scraps. How Spencer!"

I smirked. "Like I told Anderson, before I was rudely cut off, I don't do *jealous*, funkalina. I do revenge. And I mean that. You might have Rich all discombobulated believing there's a wizard in Oz, but you can save the pig feet and pickle juice act, because I know your kind."

"And I know yours." She sneered. "A little lonely, spoiled, rich girl with a mother who never wanted her and a prehistoric father related to dirt. Your own mother would rather spend her life chasing young boys than being a mother to *you*. And your father would rather sleep in jungles and chase the world's greatest wonders than be around either of you. God, it must hurt to be you. Unwanted. Unloved. No wonder you're so mean-spirited and miserable. Nobody loves you."

"You shut your sewer hole!" I screeched, jabbing a finger at her. She had struck a nerve. And I was ready to spit-shine her cuckoo clock. It took everything in me not to lunge at her and drag her off the toilet.

Lucky for her, the angel in me knew how to dance with the devil. And the switch in my head that kept me from going to prison clicked on and my wings didn't flap and my heels stayed planted in place. "And you have parents who don't even like each other. Your supermodel mother is an old ice queen who can't even keep her man satisfied in the sheets because she's too busy licking catwalks. But it doesn't matter, because your perfect lawyer daddy is getting his meat and potatoes marinated somewhere else. Ooh, how scandalicious."

"Shut your trap with your lies, you smutty tramp! You don't know a damn thing about *me*, or my parents."

"Oh, really? You think? Well, let's try this heel on for size: I know all about your sham of a relationship with Anderson."

I folded my arms. Tilted my head.

She took two deep breaths. "Spencer, I don't know what fireflies you have flapping around in that little empty skull of yours, but you don't know nothing about me and Anderson. And if I wasn't on this toilet, I'd stomp your face in."

I laughed. "Ha! Leap! Jump! Make my day, slutisha..."

Out of nowhere Anderson's voice floated around in my head. *"I don't like it when you call her names, gumdrop. Actually, you shouldn't call anyone names..."*

I hadn't given that no-good man-tart, that...that purse bumper a thought since he turned on me weeks ago. Well, okay, okay...he didn't really turn on me. He just dumped me to be with this boar-faced dog. But it felt like he'd turned on me at that moment. Anyway, I'm over that. I didn't really want him; just what was in his goodie bag. And now he was in my ear.

*"London doesn't want me...we have an arrangement...
she uses me as a cover...she keeps her dirty little secret
well hidden..."*

I blinked. Shook his voice out of my head. Wellsweet-
jigglymanbiscuits! That was it! Why hadn't I thought of
this sooner? I had my priorities all screwed on backwards.
If I wanted to get rid of a snake, I had to chop off its head,
then sling it into the fire. Yes, that's what I was going to do
to London. I was going to use the biggest and sharpest ax
I could find, then...

I tapped a manicured finger up against my lips. "I know
all about you and your secret boo, too..."

She blinked.

"How's *Justice*? Mmph. All that fine, deep, delicious,
thugalicious man kept locked away in your secret chest of
lies all because your parents don't approve of him. They
want to make believe you're perfect. But you and I both
know you're pathetic."

I watched as her chest heaved in and out. Her eyes
widened beyond what was humanly possible. Oh yes. I
had struck ET's nerve. I went in for the final dig as my
phone buzzed. "If it ain't rough, it ain't right, huh, rough
rider? You like it hood, don't you, ooga-booga. You like it
when he treats you like crap, don't you? No wonder
you're such an ugly mess. He uses your face as a doormat
to stomp all over you. And you sit up all night crying and
begging and feeling sorry for yourself. How pathetic. Desperate."

I remembered something Rich said to me one day, after
sliding me a note in Mr. Dante's finance class, asking me
to meet her in the girls' lounge. *"Remember Justice from*

the Kit-Kat Lounge? He's. Crazy…Justice has been sweating me for the last two weeks…"

Ooh, how tempted I was to let her know that I was the one who'd sent her the text message that had her stalking the Kit-Kat Lounge's parking lot waiting on her dirty little secret to come out from his sweaty night of raunchy playtime with Hot Drawz herself, the queen of easy sleazy, Rich Gabrielle Montgomery. I'd waited and watched in the hotel's lobby as they stepped into the elevator, groping and grinding and lip-locking it up. I watched until the elevator closed and stopped on the twenty-first floor, then graciously sent this subway rat a text letting her know there was a freak on the loose doing her man.

Ha!

I couldn't show my full hand, but I wanted so, so, so badly to smear it in Boo-Boo the Fool's face that her so-called wannabe bestie had slept with her boo. And probably still was if he had enough energy and kept her interest long enough. Mmph.

Humpback stared at me. Her eyes were filled with anger. I'm sure she was wondering how I knew so much about her boo-thing. I decided not to tell her it was Anderson who'd first whispered that little piece of information into my ear in between whispering a bunch of sweet lies to me, getting me all juicy and wasting my dang time. But that was neither here nor there. Anderson wasn't my issue, or problem. This barracuda was.

"Ummm. What were you saying, London? You're mighty quiet. Not now, but right now. Oh, this is going to be delish. First, I'll send those luscious photos I have of you sitting here on the toilet with those ugly faces you were making, then I'll expose your filthy backside for the world to see. Oh yes. *Glamdalicious* and *Teen Gossip* will love an exclusive, I'm sure."

"You wouldn't dare!"

"Oh, of course *I* wouldn't. I'm not desperate for money, silly. I'll give the photos to Heather or some homeless person and let them be the ones to auction them off to the highest bidder for a few dollars. I'm sure the gossip rags will pay quite a penny for these photo gems."

She blinked.

"Be lucky I don't give you a makeover beforehand. The only reason I don't slice your face from ear to ear, from forehead to chin then peel the skin off, is because I want you to be able to keep modeling. I want you out of Hollywood High and out of Rich's life."

She glared at me. Her nostrils flared. "Screw you, *bitch*! Do and say whatever you want. But be clear. I'm *not* going anywhere! So get used to seeing this beautiful face, because everywhere you are, it's going to be . . ."

My phone buzzed again. "We'll see, queen of the desert," I warned as I quickly dug my cell out of my bag, keeping my eyes on London. "We'll definitely see. Trust me. You'll be going in a burning handbasket straight to hell. And I'll be the one tossing the gasoline on you. When I'm done exposing you for the fraud you are, London, you're going to curse the day your mother fished you out of that swamp she found you in."

London's eyes bulged. "*Exxxcuuuse* you?"

I sneered at her, sliding my hand down in my bag. "Don't get all Helen Keller on me, you trash bucket. You heard what I said. You've been trouble from the moment you arrived. Well, put your diamonds up. It's about to get real messy. And I'm going to be the one to sweep you up, you dirty birdie."

I spun off on my heel, answering my phone as I shook my bouncy cakes out of the bathroom, leaving ole Miss Slumdog with her jaws askew, and her lace panties wrapped around her ankles.

19

London

As I sipped my apple martini—knowing I shouldn't have been drinking *anything* except sparkling water laced with antacids after spending most of the day slumped over, on a toilet—I crossed my legs and eyed Rich over the rim of my frosted glass. I'd been watching the clock slow-tick all day at school, counting the hours until the last-period bell rang. My first day back at school was H-E-double L. I tried everything I could to get back into the groove of things, but to no avail.

I tried to block out Justice's voice jarring and jabbing away at me. *"I got this. I'm baggin' that wit'out you... it's over between us. I'm done wit' you, London..."* There was a hundred-and-sixty-pound weight crushing my heart and I needed help lifting it from my chest. And the only way to do that was by confronting the root of my anxiety. I needed to know just how much of a lying whore Rich really was.

It was a little after four o'clock and Rich and I were sitting at Club Tantrum—a swanky martini bar on Sunset Boulevard—having cocktails. And for it to be early in the day, it was already swirling with some of Hollywood's youngest who's who.

After Rich's icy greeting this morning, then acting all shady during lunch, being her messy self, I decided to take the high road and extend an olive branch by inviting this borderline alcoholic out for drinks. It took a little...okay, a whole lot of prodding to get this moo-moo to finally agree to fit me into her life schedule.

So here we sat...

Rich frowned, tucking her hair behind her ears. "So what, you have no conversation, London? You invited me here and you haven't said a word. Like, really? Seriously? I'm busy and I have other things to do, like ensuring my house manager oversees the organizing of my shoe closet, or she will be fired. I can't sit here in silence with you. So you know what?" She pulled a hundred-dollar bill from her purse. "I've had two martinis, and unless you can find something to say, I'm out of here." She flicked her wrist and the money floated onto the table.

I blinked.

She carried on. "Staring at me like I have hair between my teeth. Is that what they're doing on the runways these days? Cat walking rudeness?"

I tilted my head, taking a deep breath. I didn't come out to argue with this drama queen. My nerves were already rattled after my encounter with that Looney Tune psycho Spencer, kicking in the bathroom stall while I was using the bathroom, snapping photos of me, then threatening to expose me. I was exhausted. Drained. And I was not in the mood for this. Not today.

"So, what's new?" I forced myself to smile. "Give me all the dirt on what's been going on since I've been gone."

Rich waved me off. "Dirt? Girl, bye. Had *you* stayed in touch with me instead of pretending I didn't exist when you were over in Milan with the French, *thennnn* you'd remember that I don't sling *dirt* or *gossip*. No shade." She looked over to the waitress coming our way and said to her, "Be a dear and get me another martini, please." She then returned her attention to me. "Next conversation. Please and thank you."

I stared at this bed bouncer like she was half-crazed.

The waitress quickly returned with her drink and Rich drained it in one gulp. Practically slamming her glass on the table, she spat, "Why are you recklessly eyeballing me? Do I need to snap for security?"

I cleared my throat, then took a deep breath and made an attempt to start again. "You know, Rich, we haven't seen each other in forever, and haven't spoken because *you*'ve been too busy to stay connected with *me*. And not once have you asked me how Milan was. Or welcomed me back."

She bucked her eyes. "*Whaat?* Clutching pearls! Is *that* why you invited me out for drinks, so this could be all about *you*? You selfish slore! Is that all you think about, yourself? Jeezus, London, nine-one-one, what's *your* emergency? Whatchu need, a hug? Besides, everyone knows London's her own greatest cheerleader. You don't need me screaming 'Give me an L! Give me an O!' What an epic fail! Humility is the new black, London. You better get into it."

I banged my glass down on the round table in front of me, then took another deep, slow breath. I was three seconds from tossing the rest of my drink into Rich's flawless face, then slamming my purse upside her dome.

She waved a finger at me, shaking her head. "Oh no, oh no, I don't do violence! I'm a damn lady, honey, and I suggest you get your manners together. Is that what they're doing over there in Peru?" She paused, as if she really expected me to answer that. "London, when I graciously accepted coming out with you I didn't expect you to get all ghetto and low budget. Banging glasses, who does that? It's not my fault that you have to wallow in self-pity, knowing you weren't missed. Do you know how many years I spent at Hollywood High without you? What, did you think I would die? Girl, bye." She gathered her purse, standing up. "I'm outta here. Thanks to you, my stress level is on ten and the only thing that will calm me at this moment is a pitcher of beer and some damn hot wings! Good day, ma'am! I'm trying to make moves and I *refuse* to be associated with rebels in heels."

I pulled in another deep breath, counting backwards in my head. *Ten, nine, eight, seven...* I was really, really, on the verge of slipping out of my heels and slamming Rich to the floor. But I was trying my best to hold on to my damn cool. "Rich, wait. You're right. That was so unladylike. Sit." She folded her arms, narrowing her eyes. "Please," I added, forcing another fake smile.

She dusted invisible dirt from the sides of her black pencil skirt, then flopped back down. "Oh, I'ma sit. But. Don't. Do. It. Again."

I bit into my bottom lip as I opened my purse and pulled out my compact and a tube of Lip Rewind. I tossed my hair, composing myself. "Rich, girl. I'm stressed." Well, that was true. "I've only been gone for two weeks and it feels like I've been gone for months." And that was true, too. "Someone sent via courier"—I pulled out the two photos I'd had folded in my bag—"these anonymous pictures of some nasty whore's fat ass while I was over in Europe. And I have no idea who the tramp is."

I attempted to show them to her. She frowned and shifted in her seat, ignoring my outstretched hand. I shrugged it off and quickly stuffed the flicks back into my bag.

"Hmph. Well, don't take it out on me. Stress kills. And being a freak does as well. So what is your obsession with walking around carrying naked booty pictures of another chick, anyway? Is that *no* homo or *all* homo?"

I frowned, trying to contain my annoyance. "It's *no* homo. And I am *not* obsessed. I was simply sharing with *you*, someone who is *supposed* to be my best friend."

"Yeah, *supposed* to be. That's what I've been telling myself. That's what I thought. Well, you know what? I'm tired of being the perfect best friend to everyone else. And I get nothing but backstabbers in return. All these tricks wanna do is turn on me. Talk to me crazy. Bang glasses down on tables before me like some backroom hoedown showdown! Which is exactly why my motto is *no new friends*."

I blinked, stunned. "Wow. Where's all of this coming from? Before I left we were besties, closer than ever. And now...seems like I've missed a lot since I've been gone." I pulled the cap off my lip gloss then twisted a few clicks until a dollop of pink liquid popped out of the tiny sponge applicator. "I see you and Spencer are back cheesing it up. How'd that happen?" I glided the applicator over my lips. "Last I checked she was your enemy."

Rich frowned. "Clutching pearls! Spencer was never *my* enemy. She's *yours*. Spencer and I have been down from day one." She paused. "And since when do you start questioning me, anyway? You're the one who chose to chase dreams over the Italian rainbow. Tryna be the black Kate Moss. No, no..." She twisted her lips, shaking her head and clearing her throat. "Wait. Wait. *Waiiit for it*...Let me get my Mr. Westwick voice together in the same way he had when he told me over tea in his office how he had to set you straight. Tryna be 'the Next Top Flop.' He dragged you for filth with that, honey. Dead to the bed!"

I rolled my eyes. *Screw Mister Westwick! And screw you!* I popped my lips together, tossing my lip gloss back into my purse. I was seething inside. How dare this cheap, sleazy, slut muffin try to do me! Still, I managed to keep a phony smile plastered on my face.

Rich snapped her fingers to get the waitress's attention and once the waitress turned around, Rich said, "Sweetie, I need another drink and this time can you bring me a pitcher of beer? These martinis aren't doing a thing for my stress. God, I need me a glass of corn liquor to the head."

"Coming right up." The waitress gave a tight smile.

"Oh, and bring me a small platter of hot wings. Extra sauce. I'm eating light tonight." Rich looked back at me. "Look, London. No shade. But don't come back here two weeks late and wrong, after you've been play-pretending to be some famous nobody, trying to interrogate me like I'm some low-down jewel thief. You *had* the number-one slot before you left. And now you've been dropped down to number three. If you keep it up you'll drop off the list."

I shot her an incredulous look. "Are you serious? Ohmy-

god! And how am *I* now number three? And let me guess,
Spencer's number two, huh?"

This flesh eater!

"Girl, bye. If that's what they're teaching you over in
the land of milk and honey and snow-covered hilltops,
then take the wheel and spin off a cliff because *you* are out
of control. Tryna do me. The fact Spencer's number *one* is
none of your business. All you need to know is, I'm keeping the number-two slot empty for someone who's worthy
of it. So count your blessings that you're still in the top
three... for now. And I recommend *you* not becoming my
next top enemy."

"Or *what*, Rich?" I rose up in my seat, placing a hand up
on my hip, ready to slap this trick into next week. "You've
been nothing but goddamn nasty to me since you got here
and I've put up with it. But now it's working my nerves.
Now, what is wrong with *you*? I've been nothing but loyal
to you. Obviously something *you* know nothing about."

She turned her lips up. "You know what, London? You
stay hatin'. Why would you care if I decide to be nice to a
trickazoid? Spencer's my homegirl. Always has been, always will be."

In spite of myself, I couldn't help but laugh at this silly
clown. "Mmph. Really? *Spencer's* your homegirl? Wow." I
shook my head. "You two chicks are real amusing. Mmph.
I guess she *would* be your homegirl; both of you are two
peas in the same damn *ho* pod. I read all about the two of
you trickin' it up. You hookers are full of stunts. But it's all
good. I just can't believe that you'd want to be friends
with someone who tried to break you and Knox up."

She rolled her eyes, flicking imaginary dirt from beneath
her fingernails, slowly shaking her head. "Uh-uh. Spencer

didn't do that. I know her. She's two thousand and one messy things, and yeah, she likes being the cleanup woman, neck bobbing someone else's man, but the one thing I *know* she *didn't* do is try to turn Knox against me. No. That was someone messy and desperate."

I shifted in my seat.

She glared at me. "You and Spencer are the *only* two who knew. So I'm going to ask *you*. Were *you* the one who told Knox I had an abortion?"

I gave her a stunned look; feigned hurt that she'd even accuse me of doing such an awful thing. Then told her emphatically, without blinking an eye, "No."

She stared at me long and hard. "Well, *someone* told him. And I *know* it wasn't Spencer. Knox wouldn't tell me who told him. But he did tell me I needed to watch the company I keep."

"Well, I was the one who told you Spencer couldn't be trusted. To watch her."

She grunted. "No"—she tilted her head—"who I *need* to be *watching* is the messenger. But I'ma let it go...*for now*."

I eyed the barmaid as she finally returned with a platter of hot wings glazed to perfection, a pitcher of beer, and one frosted mug. The waitress set the platter down in the center of the table, along with two plates and two forks and a stack of napkins. Then she filled Rich's mug to the rim with beer. The waitress turned to me and asked if I wanted another martini. I told her I'd have a pomegranate one this time, and a glass of sparkling water.

I shifted in my seat, feeling my stomach knot as Rich dug into her wings. My lashes fluttered several times before my lids finally popped open. She licked her lips, dipping a wing into blue cheese sauce and sliding the whole thing into her mouth. When she pulled back, the bone was clean.

I took my drink from the barmaid as she handed it to me and took two deep gulps. Rich looked up from her platter of wings, raising her brow. "What? I know you're *not* even thinking about sliding your fingertips over onto my platter for any of these. I only have ten wings. Everyone who really knows me knows I don't play with my money, my man, and my hot wings. So wipe the drool from your mouth because there's only enough for me. And I'm stressed too!"

I shook my head. "I'm not interested in any of your wings. So carry on and be gluttonous all you like."

"Glut *whaaat*? You wait one damn minute, London. Don't even get cute, which I know is already hard to do, and try to do me. You have a lot of nerve cursing me. Not once since we've been here have I said one nasty thing to you or about you."

I rolled my eyes dramatically at her delusions, crossing and uncrossing my legs. "Of course you haven't. Forgive me."

She blinked. "See. There you go. Do you even know how to spell forgiveness?"

"No, Rich, I don't," I said sarcastically. "Why don't you tell me how?"

"Ohmygod, London. Really? You're going to disrupt my snack time because you can't spell?" She snatched up a napkin, wiping her fingertips. "It's the number *four*, then G-I-V-E-N-E-S-S. Now I see why Spencer calls you Deebo. You're all feet and no brain."

I bit into my bottom lip. Eyed her as she lifted her mug, taking two large gulps. I glanced at my timepiece. It was now a quarter after five. I had to get out of here soon. So it had to be now or never. I needed to know about her and Justice.

I steadied my nerves, then pushed out, "Have you spoken to Justice?"

She frowned, making a ridiculously ugly face at me. "Justice? Who's that? I don't know a Justice." She wiped her mouth and pushed her empty platter to the side. Every wing, gone!

I raised a brow. "I don't know how you don't know who he is when you practically threw yourself at him in my suite, calling him your FBD, future baby daddy."

"*Whaaat?* Clutching pearls! You lying! Bish, please. I only have one future baby daddy. And his name is Knox. So, *no*, I don't know what or who you're talking about." She slid a manicured finger around the edges of the platter, swiping up remnants of sauce, then slid it into her mouth. She smacked her lips. "Oh, wait. You're talking about that sweet piece of chocolate, that stud daddy, who you acted all stank and overprotective over? The one you wanted to introduce me to?"

I cringed. "Yeah, him. Justice, who you practically seduced in front of me."

"Girl, bye. He's cute and all. But I'm not checking for him like that. That boy has issues. And I don't do issues. I thought you said you knew him."

I blinked. "I do know him. I know him very well. Why?"

She grunted. "And how *well* is that?" She waited for an answer. I didn't give her one. So she continued, "Well, *obviously* you don't know him well enough. Otherwise, you would have *known* he's real thirsty. No shade. Well, all shade. I think he has abandonment issues. Why would you try to hook me up with some crazy jerk like that? He doesn't even know how to play the sideline. He's too busy tryna be all front and center. I can't mess with him. He'll ruin my life. And disrupt my get-right with my man. And I can't have that."

"What? *Thirsty? Justice?* He's not even the type."

"Girl, bye. Like I said, obviously you don't know him as well as you think. That crazy mofo sweats me to no end. He stays in my neck trying to get all up in my goodness. I don't do that! I don't cheat on my man."

I felt the room spinning. "D-d-did you sleep with him?"

"Ohmygod, catch that tea! I just told you. I *don't.* Cheat. On my man. You're real messy, London. What, do you like him or something?" Rich eyed me suspiciously. "You're sitting here asking *me* some mess like that! Did I sleep with him? *Mmph.* Girl, bye. I'm a grown woman. Only some thirsty trick is gonna ask some mess like that. And you still haven't said if *you* like him or not. But don't bother. I already know the answer. I see it all in your eyes. It's all up in your face. Mmph. So that's why you were acting all possessive that day I met him up in your room and I gave him my number. You want him for yourself."

I blinked. I was fighting like hell to keep my emotions in check. "All I was going to tell you, *if* you did like him, which I hear you saying you *don't*, is to be careful. That's all. He's a user."

"*Scrrrreeeeech!* Stop the lies, London. I can't tell. You acting like your feelings are hurt. Maybe I should be asking if *you* slept with him."

"*What?*"

"Yeah, *Millie.* It's obvious you like him. And want him.

It's all in your voice. You're sitting up here interrogating me like I'm Olivia Pope. What, you riding him? Is that it?"

"No. I told you. He's a user."

She raised a brow. Tilted her head. *"Really?* Is he a user? Or is it that he doesn't want *you*? What, are you a reject? You didn't make the cut, is that it? Or am I standing in the way? Honey, relax. If you want that boy, you can have him. He can't do a thing for me. I gave him a lil taste of goodness, a lil slice of heaven on earth, and he couldn't even handle the heat. Four minutes and twenty-seven seconds into riding cowgirl, his toes curled and he was howling like a—"

"Did you use a condom?" I asked, cutting her off.

"Whaaat?" She slammed her mug down onto the table, drawing attention to us. "You are out of order! I already told you that boy was dead to the bed! A bore! You must really wanna bussa-bust with him too! Well, before you fulfill that fantasy, hon, I'm here to tell you, be prepared to count sheep!"

I felt myself shrinking in my seat. I was practically choking on my rage. And before I could block out the camera-ready gawkers and the flashing lights, I slung my drink in her face. And Rich leapt up from her chair, snatched the pitcher, slinging suds of beer into my face. Next thing I knew, Rich and I were swinging fists, yelling obscenities, and gripping hair. Tearing Club Tantrum up. And, although it wasn't an easy feat, I was doing my best to beat every moment she'd spent with Justice out of her.

20

Spencer

"**M**mph! My money down the shitter!" I heard Kitty snap as I made my way down and around the spiral staircase leading into the kitchen. I could hear papers rattling. As I got closer to the bottom landing, I could see Kitty at the table with newspapers and gossip rags spread out on the table and slung across the floor. And her face was tighter than a buffalo's booty cheek.

I silently rolled my eyes up in my head. Just by her huffing and snorting, sounding like some constipated baby panda, I knew Miss Fifty Shades of Crazy was going to try to serve me a bowl of her nuttiness.

"Good morning, snickerdoodle-doo. Who tinkled in your kopi luwak this morning?" I said, walking over toward the center aisle and plucking a strawberry from a fruit platter. I leaned over the enameled lava-stone countertop, dipping the strawberry into a bowl of plain yogurt and biting into it.

I moaned. "Mmmm. This is sooooo juicy." I swiped my

tongue over my glossed lips to catch the juices. I reached for another strawberry. Dipped, bit, and moaned again.

Kitty snorted, lifting her personalized KITTY LIVES mug and taking a sip of her beloved muddy-poop drink. Ugh! One of the world's most expensive coffee beans pooped out by the Indonesian civet—a furry-faced beast who eats the red coffee beans, then poops the inner part of the bean out, and natives go around digging through these animal's droppings for the beans, which sell for a whopping six hundred dollars a pound.

Kitty was a mess! Drinking animal poop! Ugh.

She glared at me over the rim of her mug.

I glared back at her, then rolled my eyes. Two could play the eyeball game.

She slammed her mug onto her saucer. Picking up a magazine, she said, "I could spit fire right now! Hollywood trash swept up in handcuffs!" She slung the tabloid at me. "I told you this would happen. Heather is wild and out of control. Not to be trusted. I told you she was still using. But *noooo*. You insisted she was clean and sober. You insisted she was ready for a big break. But you didn't listen..."

I frowned. "Mother, please. Not today, okay? Now who sneezed in your yogurt? I have no clue as to what in the world you're talking about. And I don't have time for your foolery." I reached for a crystal pitcher and poured myself a glass of pomegranate juice. "I need my strength and energy to fight through this rush-hour traffic in order to make it on time to the set for Heather's pilot taping."

Kitty slung another gossip rag at me. "Have you not heard a word I said? There is no set! There is no pilot! It's all gone to hell! Canceled. Luda Tutor, from what the tabloids are saying, is in the hospital with a broken face, severe rug burns, and a fractured rib."

"*Whaaat?*" I shrieked, covering my mouth with a hand. "Why in the sneezusjeezus would you have Luda Tutor laid up in a hospital bed? That makes no sense to me, Mother. That was"—I stamped my foot—"*not* written in the script. I'm so sick of you doing *what*ever in the hocus-pocus hell you want without consulting me. Heather was supposed to be dropped off in the guts of Brooklyn, forced to navigate her way through the gritty streets of the hood to find her way back home. Think *The Wizard of Oz* meets *The Neighbors*. You know, that TV show where the family is surrounded by aliens. What, do you want to call it *Luda Tutor Does Hospital Beds*? Some cheesy spin-off of *General Hospital?*"

She slung another magazine at me, almost hitting me in the face. "Oh, for the love of God, Spencer! Stop being a bimbo idiot! Must you take everything so literally? I swear the wet nurses I hired to breast-feed you must have been eating paint chips and drinking gasoline because you can be so brain-dead sometimes. Must I spell everything out for you? Do you need me to say it in sign language? I'm talking about *Heather*, for Christ's sake! Your precious junkie project! The *supposed to be* star of the now defunct Luda Tutor pilot! You know, the pilot that never got shot because of your ridiculous idea to rescue some pill-popping binger. *That* Heather is in the hospital!"

I gave her an incredulous look. "In the hospital for what?"

"For being a junkie mess! For being the daughter of a washed-up drunk! For being a confused, whorish mess! Take your pick, Spencer! The point is, you're too busy trying to be Captain Save A Junkie. And you had me use my resources to do it. Do you know what kind of strings I had to pull to make this happen? Do you? And I told you, if she screwed this up, it was going to cost *you*. It's your fault. Now what, Spencer?"

I blinked. *"Excuuuuuse* you? What are you blaming *me* for now, Mother?"

"I'm talking about this"—she snapped the newspaper open—" 'Teen star Heather Cummings gets molly-whopped with a two-piece and a foot stomp by her once famous but now forgotten Hollywood-starlet mother.' "

I blinked, walking over to scoop up one of the articles. I gasped. There was a photo of Heather's blood-streaked face splattered on the front of page three of the teen society section of *Teen Talk Trash*. The caption read: DRUGGIE VS. DRUNK!

I read on.

> Teen star Heather Cummings was beaten and dragged through a filthy room at a motel known for drug dealing and prostitution. A source close to the troubled teen star reported that she was ambushed by her mother—the once famed Hollywood actress, Camille Cummings—in a drunken tirade as she wielded a rusty knife in one hand and an empty bottle of Johnny Walker Black in the other, demanding money from the teen idol...

Ohmygod! This can't be happening!
Kitty read another news headline: " 'TEEN STAR HEATHER

CUMMINGS ROLLED OUT ON STRETCHER! STOMPED OUT IN DRUG MOTEL BY OUTRAGED MOTHER!'" She slung the magazine at me. "What a mudslide of a mess! My money wasted! My time wasted! You'll never take the helm of my empire at the rate you're going! You'd have my whole media dynasty down in the gutter with your pickle-brain ideas. That's it!" she snapped, banging a hand on the table. "This is part of your scheme to ruin me! To destroy my reputation! Why, you hateful little tart!"

I narrowed my hazel eyes. Strike me down and singe my panties, Kitty was effortlessly beautiful, but I wanted nothing more than to soak my fingernails in a bowl of Clorox and scrub out the whites of her eyeballs.

I stamped my heels into the floor, slinging the magazine back at her. "Shut your pie hole, you nanny!"

"I'm not your damn nanny!" she snapped back. "I'm your mother, who you continue to disrespect and try to sabotage!"

"You are a nanny! You ole hoof-heeled goat! If I wanted to sabotage you, dumbo, I'd simply dig up all the dirty pairs of boxers you have buried around your precious rose bushes outside! You floral floozy! Now don't make me put my fist in your..." I caught myself from getting violent. I sighed. "Mother, all I'm going to say is, you better shake it fast...*watch* yourself, before I show you what I'm working with! And I do...*mean*"—I dipped two fingers into the yogurt, then slung it at her—"show you."

A nice white glob splattered atop one of the magazines she had spread out across the table. I stuck my fingers in the yogurt and slung more at her.

"Spencer! That's it! You heathen! I'm shipping you off to the wilds of the jungles to be with your father, where you can swing from trees and eat with your feet! I'm sick of your—"

I jabbed a finger in the air at her. "Kitty, shut it. Up! I'm not going anywhere! Now go on out to the playground and find you some boy toy to ruin, because I. Am. *Not*. Hearing. You. It's too early in the morning for you to be attacking me! You're telling me all about Heather lying in some hospital bed and I don't know anything about any of this nonsense. Do I *look* like Nurse Jackie to you, huh, Mother? Jeezussneezus! I wasn't there changing her bandages. Now let me read in peace!"

I picked up another magazine, *GlamDivas*. There was a piece written by some heathen bunny about Heather and her mother, with a full-page photo of the two of them. Heather's face was bloody. Her hair was wild. Her lips were swollen. Then there was Camille's ugga-mugga face. Her pale skin was blotchy. Her eyes were wide, bloodshot, and crazed looking. Her lips were curled up into a snarl, showing her front teeth.

"MyReese'sPiecesNutterButterpiecrusts!"

Kitty grunted. "Don't act surprised, you little trollop! I told you she wasn't ready for another show! But *noooo*, you pressed me to no end. And look at the result. A pilot canceled! And you will transfer that three million dollars back into my account for being so ridiculous as to think that some misfit would have worked the program instead of letting the program—or should I say her counselor—work her."

I gasped. "Mother, how dare you! I told you about Heather's panties dropping down around her ankles for her counselor in confidence, you low-down snakeazoid! I told you to keep it on the hush-hush. And there you go yapping your gum line."

She gave me a blank stare. I got so sick and tired of her and everyone else giving me that same empty look as if they don't understand English.

Jeezus! My patience was really running on E with this woman. But one of us had to be the rational and sane one, so it might as well be me.

I took a deep breath. I had promised Daddy when I spoke to him two days ago—although after fifteen minutes into the conversation he kept getting distracted and started calling me some dang Cleola, whoever that ole country biscuit was. But, whatever! When Daddy finally got his mind together, I gave him my word that I was going to be loving and kind to this sea witch. And in turn, he was going to buy me my very own yacht.

Kitty huffed. "Don't you get pissy with me, Spencer. If you don't want me repeating anything you say, then perhaps—as hard as it may be for you—*you* should learn to keep your loose lips shut."

I blinked, deciding it best to block her out before I made it rain on her head. I glanced at another headline. LOOKS LIKE ANOTHER TKO FOR HOLLYWOOD ACTRESS CAMILLE CUMMINGS. Then started reading the article.

> Mayweather who?
>
> Camille Cummings is the new heavyweight champion in this bout between mother and daughter. The Academy Award–winning actress slugged her teen star daughter, Heather Cummings, over money and booze. Sources closest to the paparazzi-starved mother-daughter duo say the washed-up Hollywood starlet became enraged when Heather ar-

rived at their sleazy motel room, driving a '57 Chevy with her longtime pal Co-Co Ming— the androgynous son of five-star sushi king, Ying Ming—then flaunted her ten-thousand-dollar Brazilian butt lift in her mother's face as she packed her belongings. According to sources, the two exchanged heated words that led to the elder Cummings attacking her daughter, pounding and stomping her with her fists and feet. Sadly, while the younger Cummings screamed for her life, her rainbow buddy stood biting his painted fingernails before running out of the room yelling for help...

The multi-award-winning teen star, who is well known for her long-standing role as Wu-Wu Tanner on the now canceled but highly popular sitcom, *The Wu-Wu Tanner Show*, was slated to star in an upcoming pilot as Luda Tutor on Kitty-Kitty—the television network owned by media mogul Kitty Ellington...

My nose flared. *That two-faced hussy!* How dare she flounce her big ole bubblicious booty over to that dang egg noodle without making it her business to check in with me *first!* Co-Co Ming didn't give a damn about Heather the way I did. And this was the thanks I got! I should have been the first person she called and visited to gleefully show me my investment.

"I need to get to the bottom of this," I snapped.

Kitty pushed back from her seat, standing to her feet.

She snapped a hand up on her hip. "This is your mess! And you had better find a way to clean it up. That pale-faced, zebra junkie and her drunken mother are—"

I frowned. *"Didn't* I tell you to shake it fast and watch yourself, huh, Mother? Now I won't stand for your name-calling. Don't you dare call Heather a zebra. Zebras are too beautiful to be cheapened to the likes of some hyena who can't keep her snout out of the mud."

She shook her head, putting a hand up. "Enough! I don't want to hear another word out of your filthy mouth because, *obviously*, the only thing it's good for is blowing on some boy's trumpet. And I'm not talking about the ones in music class!"

Kitty prissed past me, slinging her hair and almost slapping me with the curled ends as she exited the kitchen in dramatic fashion; stage left, her heels angrily stabbing into the floor.

Ole spoiled pudding pop!

"Oh, so this little sea monkey wants to go hunt, huh?" I said to myself as I dug through my bag, yanking out my cell. "I'll show her! Trying to play me for some ole stale biscuit. I warned her!"

I waited for Heather's phone to ring. The line rang twice, then…*Oh nooooothebotholywax she didn't!* The crusty *beeeeyotch* sent me straight to voice mail. "Heather! This is Spencer! You have officially bent over and yanked your G-string off! You need to call me *ASAP*! Do you hear me? Do not have me slice into that new booty of yours, Heather! Because you *know* I will deflate your airbags! Now fiddle me a new roof if you want and I'll set it on fire up in here!"

21

Heather

Slowly, I eased the gleaming silver spoon from this morning's food tray and lifted it to my face. I could see my reflection clearly. My paper-bag-brown skin was blotched with purple bruises.

My nose: broken.

My scalp: stung.

My lips: due to burst into flames at any moment.

My stomach: sore.

My new Brazilian ached, but thank God my implants were still intact.

Camille tried to kill me.

Ruin me.

Destroy me.

Annihilate me.

And if it hadn't been for the nurses' station outside of my room, I would've sworn she had. But she hadn't.

I was in the hospital with some dumb blonde standing at the foot of my bed.

"Heather."

I lifted my eyes and peered at her. Her skin was the color of skim milk and the navy blue dress she wore made her look opalescent. Her dark, narrow eyes were draped with concern and I knew by the way she held her lips that whatever she had to say she'd practiced a million times before.

"I'm Mrs. Neilson," she continued. "From Child Protective Services." She attempted to hand me a business card. I let it dangle in the air. After seeing that I made no effort to reach for it, she tucked it into the side of the notebook she held. "I'm a social worker from the department of Child Protective Services."

My job is to keep you safe...

"My job is to keep you safe."

And I'm here to talk to you about what's been going on.

"And I'm here to talk to you about what's been going on."

My heart thundered. I knew the script. Knew each line word for word. And I knew how the story unfolded. Ugly. Harsh. I'd been forced into the role, lived it, once before. My breath quickened as fear crept in.

Relax.

I can't.

You're not five anymore.

I feel five.

But you're not!

Then why am I scared?

And why can I barely breathe?

Blondie took a step toward me and gently placed a hand over mine.

I froze.

The last time a social worker took my hand, I was five

and she was squeezing my wrist, dragging me into foster care. That was not about to happen. Not this time! I didn't give a damn what I had to do or say... I was *not* letting this translucent, ghostly child-snatcher drag me away from my life. From my newfound freedom. I'd slice her first before I'd let that happen again. I snatched my hand from beneath hers and her thin fingers slipped over the bed railing.

She glanced at me in shock and I could tell that she'd swallowed her first sentence. Instead of saying how she really felt, she proceeded with the rest of her practiced speech. "I'm not here to hurt you."

Oh, I know that. Because I would fly kick you in the chest first.

"I'm here to help you."

I don't need your help! I got this!

"You're only sixteen—"

Sixteen and a grown woman. And have been grown. For years.

"And you deserve to be safe—"

I don't want your safety. The last time they—Child Protective Services—called themselves keeping me *safe*, they'd placed me in a home with a foster mother who kept sneaking into my bedroom, slipping out of her nightgown and sliding into my twin bed, telling me it was okay for her to force my hands into unthinkable places, brainwashing me into believing that it was okay if I let a woman touch me, while whispering nasty promises to make me feel good.

No, bish! Eff you and your safety!

"Where is my mother?" I demanded, choking back tears. My lips felt like quivering five-pound weights.

Blondie's brow creased.

"Where is my mother?" I screamed.

"Calm down," she said in a soothing tone.

"Don't tell me what to do! Now where is my mother?"

"She's being detained for physically abusing you."

Under any other circumstances, imagining Camille in jail would've made me smile. Trust. I wanted nothing more than to lose her. To be done with her. Rid of her. But not like this. No. It had to be on my terms. My way.

Think... Think... Think...

I don't know what to say.

You better say something. And quick!

I hate Camille! She's the cause of all this mess!

Then leave her in jail and be carted off to some god-forsaken foster home—or worse, a group home. God knows what'll happen to you there!

Think... Think... Think...

"What?" I spat, feigning shock while shooting poisonous daggers at her. "Are you frickin' stupid, lady? *Abusing* me? My mother? Get out of my room with your lies! My mother never beat me! Ever!"

"When you were five she was a raging alcoholic..."

What did she say?

She continued, "And she beat you until the skin curled off of your back." She gave me an intense stare and I could tell that her comment was payback for me calling her stupid and crazy. "She was the reason we removed you from her care the first time. And she's the reason you'll..."

I tried to chew the left corner of my bottom lip but pain shot through my face. Instead, I closed my eyes and did all I could to erase the memory of Camille slashing me with a hairbrush across my tiny back, simply because I didn't want her to drink anymore and poured all of her scotch into the toilet.

But. That was the last time that happened.

I opened my eyes.

I've been fighting her back since then. And I would've gotten the better of her this last time had she not snuck me. And had Co-Co's Fruity Pebbles helped me fight Camille, instead of standing there acting like he'd just won third runner-up in *RuPaul's Drag Race*, I wouldn't be the one laid up in this hospital bed.

Technically, this was *his* fault.

He was the real reason why I was in here like this and why this blond bish stood over me like she was God. Like she was my savior. Trick, please! If I wasn't so sore and laid up in this hospital bed, I would find Co-Co, slap *shim* to the floor and drag Miss Thing around the room!

"First of all, Miss Know-It-All," I snapped defensively, "back up outta my face. Then go get your facts right. My mother isn't the reason I was taken from her; you people are. But it worked. My mother learned her lesson and she has never put her hands on me since then! End of discussion. She's a wonderful mother!"

She tilted her oversized head. Gave me one of those "yeah right, try again" looks. "Oh, really? Since when? Is that *before* or *after* her first drink? She *does* still drink, doesn't she? And not so long ago your mother was arrested!"

Oh, this ghost-face was way out of order. I balled my hands into tight fists. I was ready to take it to her forehead.

"I said she didn't touch me!"

"Well, someone did. And when the police and I arrived on the scene, you were passed out and the young girl who was there with you was screaming about how your mother beat you to death. She said your mother was always beating you."

"It wasn't a *she*. It was *he*. A *shim*!"

"Well, *he*, *she*, *shim*, also said that your mother spent all of your money and that the two of you were now homeless."

I can't believe Co-Co turned on me and snitched. Now he needed to get stitched! I took two deep breaths. "Co-Co's a liar," I calmly stated. "I fell into the wall. That's what happened to me. I wasn't beat by my mother."

She didn't respond. She stared at me long and hard. Blinked. Then waited for me to offer her more. I quickly dug into my virtual Wu-Wu bag and pulled out one of my scripts of lies.

On cue, tears sprang from my eyes. "I can't believe that drug-dealing fiend would spread those lies about me! I've been nothing but a friend to that boy! If anyone needs help from you, it's Mr. Confusion! I could have left him for dead when I found him passed out from a pill overdose. But I didn't. I stayed true to him. I was there for him when his own family wasn't. And this is how he repays me. By spreading malicious lies about my mother. His daddy kicked him out and he tried to kill himself! And you want to believe the word of some homeless high school dropout who ran off to live in K-town, where he sells drugs..."—I paused, shaking my head and dabbing my eyes with the back of my fingertips—"*and* sells his boy parts to the highest bidder."

She frowned. "I'm not here to discuss him or his plight. This is about *you*. The hospital is ready to discharge you, but you have no family members willing to take you in, or whom you can be released to. So until we can find a more suitable arrangement for you, I'm here to take you into custody."

"Over my dead body!" I cried out. "*Bish!* I told you my mother didn't touch me! We were attacked!"

"Oh, now you *both* were attacked, huh? A few minutes ago, you reported that you *fell* into the wall."

"I *was* thrown into a wall! Six masked men bum-rushed into my motel room and tried to rob us for what little we have. My mother and I fought them and—"

"You're both lucky to be alive," a voice said from the doorway. "Don't say another word, darling."

Pasty Face and I both turned to look. It was Kitty, Spencer's mother.

I hid my surprise. A painful smile slid across my swollen lips and a lone tear fell from my eyes. Real tears this time! The Devil was here to pull me from the fire! "Auntie!" I bawled. "Oh Aunt-Aunt-Auntie Kitty! They're trying to take me! Please don't let them take me!"

Kitty rushed over to me, placed her handbag beside my right thigh, and draped an arm over my shoulders. "Oh no no no, my darling." She pulled me into her embrace. "You hush. Auntie Kitty is here. And no one is taking you anywhere." She looked up at the social worker. "And who are you?"

"I'm Mrs. Neilson." She handed Kitty her card.

Kitty scanned the words on the card. "Oh, I won't be needing that, so you can tuck that back into your little billfold. Now how can I help you, Miss...?"

"Nielson," she repeated dryly. "I'm from Child Protective—"

"Oh, I know *where* you're from," Kitty stated, easing up

off the bed. "I want to know *what* are you doing here badgering my niece?"

"We were called in. There was a report of physical abuse by—"

"Aunt Kitty, I told her that my mother never touched me! But she won't believe me. Instead she believes Co-Co and the police."

"Co-Co?" Kitty said, surprised.

"Yes! And she said that she was taking me with her and I had to go to a group home." More tears, this time with snot and spittle for effect.

A cunning smile eased across Kitty's face. I didn't know what she would pull out of her bag of treachery, but I knew she would skin Pale Face alive.

"A group home?" She batted her lashes. "And what family did you call, may I ask? Because clearly no one even bothered calling me. Nor did anyone from your agency bother to speak to my sister..."

Blondie blinked. Even I had to blink at that one. If I weren't in a desperate state I would have burst out laughing at the thought of Camille and Kitty being sisters.

"Yes, dear," Kitty continued, eyeing Blondie, "you heard me right. My. Sister. My beautiful, white-chocolate, adopted half sister, whom you clearly forgot to pay a visit to before making your way here. And you, Mrs. Lawson—"

"It's *Neilson*," she corrected.

Kitty flicked her a dismissive wave. "Whatever it is. You are out of line coming up in here interrogating my niece. Do you have a court order?"

"Well, no. But—"

"No 'buts,' Miss Princeton," Kitty said, putting a hand up to stop her from speaking. "You come up in here, flaunting your authority but with no court order. And I *know* you have not contacted any of her other relatives in West Virginia."

That's because they don't want me. Some half-black, half-white mutt.

"Well, we, uh..."

"*Well* nothing, Mrs. Jamison. You've crossed the line. I will not hesitate to call John Carrington, the head of your agency and a dear, dear, darling friend of mine, and have not only your job but your social-work license as well. And by the time I'm done with you, Mrs. Jenkinson, you'll be sweeping floors! You'll be shoveling hay to horses on some animal farm." Kitty spun on her heel. "Now, let me show you to the door." She stopped and turned to face Blondie. "But of course you could always stay and test me. But I promise you, dear. You won't like the end result."

Pow! Now kick rocks, beyotch!

All the blood rushed from this trick's face and her skin went from skim milk to crimson.

"Choice is yours," I said, curling the corners of my swollen lips into a smile.

Kitty shot me a scathing look. I lowered my lashes sheepishly.

The bish swallowed and said, "It was very nice meeting you two. I think you better stay away from walls, young lady. You two take care."

Kitty smiled. "You as well, Mrs. Williamson."

My dimples sank into my cheeks as I turned to look at Kitty, who was closing the door behind the social worker.

"Thank you," I whispered, reaching for a few napkins and wiping my eyes then blowing my nose.

Kitty charged over to me and roughly snatched my aching

chin. I tried to move away but I couldn't. *"Thank you?"* she
sneered. "You shut your filthy pill-trap, you sniveling little
snot. You ungrateful little witch. You have lost your damn
mind going missing for three weeks! Drugging your
guardian! Attacking reporters! Tricking up money! And
then coming back here and talking all slick-tricky to
Camille when she confronts you. That little charade was
not about saving you, little girl. *That* was about looking
out for *my* money. *My* investments! And there are three
things—and you had better start taking notes—that I
don't take kindly to anyone screwing with: my ratings, my
money, and my boy toys. And not always in that order."

She glared at me through slits of fire. I knew one wrong
word, one wrong look, one rash move, and she'd finish
what Camille failed to do. Kill me.

"I had arranged for you to have your fast tail on the set
of Luda Tutor, a major production. And instead of you
being on your best behavior, staying clean and focused,
you take the first dollar you get and snort it as if you think
I don't know. Then you go to that rathole you and Camille
were staying in and you attack her!"

"I didn't attack her!"

"Oh yes, you did!"

"She dragged me around the room!"

"You deserved it! I've been too kind to you, Miss Missy.
And you have done *nothing* but act like a spoiled, entitled,
broke-down little Hollywood brat! I will *not* have it! Do
you know how much money I have lost behind you, huh?
Do you?"

"I can still be Luda Tutor," I reasoned, sniffling.

She scoffed. "Are you crazy? Silly girl. Disney doesn't
want to touch you. You're too much of a liability. Your face

is all over the gossip rags, the blogs, everywhere! Everywhere! And do you know what the headlines are saying? 'Heather Cummings, Child Star, Turns To Drugs Once More!' And the source closest to you says that this time you're snorting some new street drug called *murder*."

I felt a dropkick land in my chest. I'm going to kill Co-Co!

"No, you will not be Luda Tutor, Miss *Murder*! I've already given that part away to a clean and wholesome girl. No. *You*, little Miss Pill-Popping Junkie, will do reality TV."

"What? I'm not—"

"*Not* is *not* a part of your vocabulary when you're addressing me. So don't you ever tell me what you're *not* going to do. Whether you believe it or not, you sold your soul over to me. And my name is Kitty Ellington!"

She glared at me and pressed the tip of her sharp nail up to my eyelid.

Oh my God! Now I know where Spencer gets her craziness!

I was mortified.

"My name is *not* Camille. Or should I say Norma Marie. I'm *not* a junkie or a drunk. Therefore, you *will* do what I tell you. And the only words I expect to hear come out of your mouth when speaking to me are *please* and *thank you*. If *not*, I will pluck your eyeballs out. Have you reading braille, wondering what your cellmate looks like when I have you shipped back to the detention center. Cross me and see what happens next. I will have them put you away until you're twenty-one! And I, my darling, have the money, the power, the resources, *and* the connections to do it." She snapped her fingers. "Just like that."

I swallowed and my tears dripped over Kitty's finger.

She viciously flicked them back into my face. "Save the crocodile tears for the cameras," she jeered.

Maybe I should've gone with the social worker. Yes, that's exactly what I should've done. "Wh-wh-where's my mother?"

"In a two-day detox; apparently where you need to be."

"I'm not using drugs. I swear to you, Aunt Kitty."

"I'm not your damn aunt. And you can stop with the lies. You silly little girls are out of control. I don't know what's wrong with y'all, especially *you*, Heather. I had high hopes for you. Out of all of you, *you* are the one with the talent—*true* talent. But instead of using it, you choose to piss it away. Snort it away. Do everything but what you need to do—which is be the star you are destined to be and make this money.

"You are a beautiful girl! Beautiful! Mmph. But look at you. Laid up, all beat up, looking a hot crazy mess. What a waste. But since your mother is too busy drowning her demons in booze, I'm here to help you get your mind right, or help you find your way to the nearest gutter to crawl down in. The choice is yours. But know this: I will *not* tolerate you messing over my kindness. Now, you *will* be on reality TV. You will be paid one hundred thousand dollars per episode. And you *will be* happy about it." She eased her fingernail back, flung my chin out of her hand and paced.

Reality TV? Was she crazy? She had to be! I wasn't desperate.

"Camille will never agree to that!" I blurted out, feeling the walls around me starting to close in.

"She already has." Kitty stopped in her tracks and faced me. "In fact, who do you think called me from jail? Therefore, you *will* be grateful to me. And you will *not* spit on my money." Hand on hip, she stalked back over to me, narrowing her gaze. Her catlike eyes spooked me. For the first time, I felt a chill being alone in the same room with her; something I'd never felt before. "Cross me, disrespect me, and you *will* suffer the consequences. You will feel my wrath."

I swallowed, hard. Blinked back the tears that weighed heavy on my lids.

"You want to be ratchet?" she continued, glaring at me. "You want to be ghetto trash? Then be just that. But know this: You and all of your ratchetness is going to air on television. And *you* are going to make *both* of us money being the little ooga-booga cockroach you seem so comfortable being. But if you cost me one red cent, I am going to *shut* your life down. You'll *never* step foot on another set again. I promise you. Screw up and the next time anyone hears the name Heather Cummings, or sees your pretty little face on a flat-screen, it'll be you eating out of a garbage bin, or somewhere with a needle dangling from your arm. Is that the life you want?"

I swiped tears from my aching face. My tongue felt heavy. My jaws felt stuck together. I had no words for what this cruel witch of a woman was saying to me.

Before I could flinch or get a word out, she had my chin in her clutches again. "Answer. Me!"

"N-n-no," I stammered.

"I thought not." She let go of my face. "Now get out of this bed and get dressed. The driver is downstairs to take you home. You know. The one Co-Co said you rented in 90210."

22

London

"Wow, you look…amazing." Daddy beamed proudly as he flipped through the pictures from my Pink Heat photo shoot. "My little girl is really growing up." He looked up and smiled at me. "I'm so proud of you, London."

Not for long you won't be. Not after you learn about the brawl Rich and I had at Club Tantrum.

Daddy and I were sitting at a table having dinner at one of my favorite Japanese restaurants in West Hollywood, Nobu—just him and me. And as bad as I wanted to enjoy our father-daughter time together, as bad as I wanted to delight in my sumptuous meal without the prying eyes of my mother staring down my mouth and counting my calories, I was struggling to keep it together.

I was on the edge of a cliff, dangling on a thin thread of sanity. And, at any moment, my fingers would slip open and the shell of my body would fall into a dark pit.

That was all that was left of me. My body.

My heart was already snatched. Gone.

And now my mind was slowly going.

I felt it. Slipping in and out, seesawing back and forth between past and present. Snapshots of my entire sixteen years of life fast-forwarded and rewound and played over and over in my head.

I was fighting to hold on. Fighting to keep my emotions in check. Fighting to keep this fake smile I was wearing like a plaster cast mounted on my face. But it was beginning to crack.

My life was in shambles.

Rich and I still weren't talking. Our fistfight at Club Tantrum happened several days ago and I still wore the bruises from our brawl. I had pretended to be ill so that my dinner date with Daddy could be postponed long enough for them to fade. I wanted another round with her. I was still pissed at how she'd treated me. Nasty. Talking sideways to me, and being condescending. Her bitchy meter had been cranked all the way up from the moment she sat down, and I had no clue as to why. I still didn't.

And now I didn't give a damn. We'd fought before. And we'd had our share of arguments. But we'd always made up right after we finished tearing each other up. Either right afterward, or no more than a few hours, or a day later. But we never, ever, went this long without making up. No. This fight was different. It came from a very different place. Anger. It was a rage that bordered on hate. We punched and kicked and slapped and cursed each other like enemies, like two chicks who had something to prove. We tried to beat each other to the death. And neither of us wanted to go down.

I'd fought her over Justice.

Not because she'd said she *wanted* him. No, *he* wanted

her. But she'd slept with him. My man. Then disrespected him to my face. So what if she didn't know he was mine? She *knew* he mattered to me. And even though I'd asked her if she'd slept with him, she didn't have to be so crass about it. It'd already killed me sitting there, knowing in the back of my mind that it would eventually happen— them, her and Justice, sexing. But to hear it, that she'd screwed him, sliced right through me. I didn't want to share him. Not like that. Not without me having some control over it.

But I had none.

In the blink of an eye, everything had blown up in my face. And without even knowing it, that bitch, Rich Montgomery, was the one who'd pulled the trigger.

But it was all a moot point now. My friendship with her was over.

Dead.

I hated her. And, obviously, she hated me...for whatever reason.

Then there was...*Justice*. I still hadn't seen him since I'd been back. Still hadn't talked to him since he'd sent that text message and broken up with me. I still couldn't believe he'd dumped me. Couldn't believe that he refused to talk to me. Refused me the opportunity to understand what I'd done for him to push me away, to shut me out like that. He denied me the chance to, at the very least, explain myself—well, given how emotionally needy I was, *beg* him to take me back.

But it didn't look like that would happen. Not now. Maybe not ever. Not after the way he'd treated me this time. Now I sat here feeling like a jilted ex-girlfriend on the verge of a nervous breakdown. And the pounding in my head told me what the aching pain in my heart didn't want to know, didn't want to accept. That Justice had meant what he'd said. I mean, texted. He was done.

It was over.

And the fact that he'd deleted and blocked me from his Facebook page, and blocked my number from calling him—something he'd never done before—it was crystal clear. The message was piercing.

He wanted nothing else to do with me.

After I'd given him every part of my mind, my body, my heart, my love, my life; after I'd lied and schemed and defied my parents and was willing to risk losing everything to be with him, he turned his back on me.

And, as if that wasn't already enough salt rubbed into my wounds, Anderson told me he wanted me. That he wanted to love me. But he wasn't going to share me; he wanted all of me, including my heart. Not pieces of it. All of it. But I didn't have it to give. I tried to tell him that there was nothing else left of me. That Justice had taken everything that I'd freely given, and what he'd given back, what he'd tossed back at me once he was finished using me up, was destroyed. Damaged. Pieces. Shards of broken spirit, slivers of a shattered heart, shavings of broken promises, that's all that was left of me. But Anderson wouldn't hear it. And when I couldn't make a choice—him or Justice—he kissed me one last time. He walked out on me in Milan, leaving me standing in the middle of my suite with my robe around my feet, naked and rejected, with burning tears in my eyes.

Now I had nothing. No one.

The only thing left for me to do was to wait for him to tell my parents that it was over between us, that he'd dumped me because he didn't love me, then lower my head down into the guillotine and wait for the blade to come down.

On cue, Daddy's voice floated into my consciousness. "Your mother tells me the ad for the perfume...uh, Pink Heat, right...?"

I nodded absentmindedly. I wondered if he even noticed that I'd disappeared from the table; that I'd mentally checked out of the room.

"Right, right. She tells me it's on a rush schedule and is going to start appearing in magazines in the next few weeks. Are you excited?"

I blinked. I no longer had to wonder. Either he was clueless, like everyone else, or I hid it well. Yeah, maybe that was it. I was good at pretending. Good at hiding. Good at keeping secrets.

I shrugged. "I guess so."

God, I just want it all to end. Be over. Finished. I'm so tired of hurting. So tired of having my heart crushed. So tired of feeling empty and alone. I'm so tired of all this pretending...

"Your mother is excited. I haven't seen her this happy..." His voice drifted off as if he'd gotten lost in his own head for a moment. He ran a hand over his handsome face. "Wow. It's been that long." He let out a chuckle that sounded more pained than not. "Once this ad starts appearing in magazines and on billboards, my little girl is going to be a star. Are you ready for all the attention? Should I get your autograph now or later?" he said jokingly.

I didn't laugh. But I forced another smile. I wanted desperately to share in his enthusiasm. I wanted to be happy and excited with him, but I couldn't. I had nothing to be enthused about or to be excited over. I was the joke. The dancing court jester on a string. And everyone was laughing at me.

London the dancing fool.

"God, you look so much like your mother when she was your age, modeling. I really hadn't noticed just how much until now."

I cringed. Hearing *that*—that I looked like my mother— was the last thing I needed or wanted to be reminded of. I still wasn't speaking to her, unless I had to, for slapping me. But I'd already decided, agreed to, committed to, resigned myself to, being *her* property without any more fighting. I was tired. I was returning to Milan with her next week, in time for my fittings and rehearsals for the upcoming fashion show, and I would work the runway as she'd demanded. I'd give her and the fashion world something they'd never forget. She wanted me under the bright lights and in front of the flashing bulbs, so I'd give her exactly what she wanted.

Still, I was pissed at her. And I blamed *her* for taking me away from Justice. Again. Even if she didn't know I was with him, this time. She still snatched my happiness away from me. She dragged me overseas to chase some damn dream that wasn't even my own. Had to disrupt my whole world. Destroy my life. Kill my love.

She gave Justice the time and space to stop loving me, to stop wanting me. And it was all her fault. Or maybe it wasn't. Maybe it was Rich's, or some other ho's doing. Maybe it was mine, for not doing enough. I don't know.

All I know is, had I still been here, had my mother not forced me to go, I would have had a fighting chance to keep him. Maybe. But I wasn't here. And now...

I blinked. Blinked again. Suddenly aware that Daddy's gaze was locked on me, I averted my eyes. I couldn't bring myself to look at him. I stared at my half-eaten shrimp and picked-over salad, glanced around the restaurant, fidgeted in my seat. Did everything but look into his face. The tears were coming. I could feel them welling up from somewhere deep down in me. My chest was tightening.

I had to get out of here. I needed an escape.

The molded smile I kept mortared on my face was cracking. I could hear the plaster fracturing. The mold was splitting open. At any second, the mask would fall off. And Daddy would see me. My lies. My loneliness. My hurt. My dejection.

He'd see my ugly scars. My insecurities. My fear. My secrets.

I felt light-headed. I was starting to feel disoriented.

Daddy's brows furrowed. He searched my face. "Sweetheart, is everything all right? You look like you're on the verge of..."

I quickly swiped a hand across my eyes. Lied. Told him I had something in my eye. Then, unconcerned with making a graceful exit, abruptly excused myself, practically sprinting in my six-inch heels toward the bathroom before all of my emotions came pouring out. And the minute I locked myself in the stall and slid down to the floor, everything inside of me erupted. The storm had come. A monsoon of tears flooded my eyes. I was drowning in it. And I had no one to pull me free.

I cried.

And cried.

And cried.

I didn't know how long I'd been in the stall, on the floor with my knees bent up to my chest, sobbing, when Daddy's voice startled me on the other side of the door. He was in the women's bathroom. Tapping on the door. His voice filled with concern. Trying to get to me.

"London? Come on out and tell me what is going on, sweetheart. What happened? Why are you crying? Are you hurt? Is this about you and Anderson breaking up? You didn't have to keep that from me, sweetheart. Breakups happen. It wasn't your fault."

God, he already knows! Anderson couldn't even wait!
I sobbed harder.

"I just got off the phone with him. I know it's..."

"I don't care about that, Daddy! It was my fault! All of it!"

"What, sweetheart? What was your fault? The breakup? No, it wasn't. Anderson told me—"

"I don't care about what *he* told you!"

"Then what is it, sweetheart?" he asked, sounding exasperated. I could tell by the tone of his voice that standing on the other side of the door listening to my tears and not being able to do anything was more painful than seeing me... like this. A broken mess! Distraught. Snotty nose. Swollen eyes.

"London, please, sweetheart. Talk to me. Is it about your modeling? I know it's a lot of pressure on you, but isn't this what you wanted?"

I wailed louder. "I don't care about that!"

"Then what is it? I can't help you if you won't let me. Talk to me, *please*."

"All I want is to be wanted and to feel loved! I don't want to keep hurting! I don't want to keep having my heart broken!"

"London, sweetheart, you are loved. Your mother and I love you very much. What is this about, huh, sweetheart?" The door shook. "C'mon, London, open the door. I don't want to see you like this, please."

More tears splashed out of my eyes, stinging and staining my cheeks. I coughed and cried out in agony. "Then why does Mother want to drag me to a plastic surgeon to have a bunch of surgeries to get rid of my breasts and butt? Why is she always ridiculing me? Why, Daddy, why? Nothing I do is ever good enough for her! Never! If she loves me, why is she *always* trying to change me? Huh?"

"Say *what*? Your mother did..." Silence. Even he was at a loss for words.

I croaked out a groan and wept louder.

"Your mother couldn't have been serious about that, sweetheart. You're perfect the way you are. There has to be some misunderstanding."

"There is no misunderstanding! I'm FAT! And UGLY! And WORTHLESS!"

"London, you *are* beautiful, sweetheart."

"NO, I'M NOT! I'm an AMAZON FREAK! A BIG FOOT! Everybody hates me!"

"No, you're not. Who told you that?"

"Juuuuuustice!" I growled out his name between heavy sobs. I hadn't meant for it to happen. But it had. And Daddy had heard it, too.

"Justice?" he repeated.

I couldn't hold the rest of this pain in any longer. It was eating away at my insides. Burning me like acid. Justice had hurt me deeply, this time worse than ever. His name was hot fire in the back of my throat, blazing around in my head. "Yes! Justice! Justice! Justice!" His name shot out of my mouth over and over, hot and angry and filled with hurt and sadness and defeat and lots of spittle and snot. "JUSTICE!!!! *He* is the reason Anderson broke up with me! I hurt him, Daddy! And now he hates me! My own mother hates me! Justice hates me! I hate me! And n-n-now *youuu hate meeeee*!"

"No, I don't, sweetheart. Please." He sounded frantic. "Please, London. Stop crying. And come out. I could never hate you. I love you."

"Yes, you do. I know you do! I just want to close my eyes and never wake up. I want everything to be over."

I was sinking in anguish. Being swept under by emptiness. I couldn't move. I felt paralyzed. My arms, my legs, everything felt heavy.

"London, please. You've got to come out of there." He violently shook the door. I could hear the alarm in his voice. I'd never heard him like this. Frightened. Scared for me. Nervous. Maybe I was imagining it. Maybe I wasn't. Maybe I needed it to be real.

But it was. Real. The minute the door swung open and my father scooped me up into his arms and carried me out—not caring who was looking or how many cameras were flashing, while I screamed and sobbed and held on to him for dear life—the minute I looked into his face and saw his own tears brimming in his eyes, I knew. It was real.

And he knew.
I was at the end.
He was losing me to it.
The raging war inside of me.
I'd given up.
I'd dropped my white flag...and surrendered.

23

Rich

Dear Diary,
Jazmine Sullivan's "Lions, Tigers, & Bears" is my theme song at the moment. I'm listening to it now and I've had it on repeat all week. And every time I hear it, I get lost in it and a million ~~wanted~~ unwanted thoughts of Justice bombard my mind and demand all of my attention.

I've tried everything.

Apologizing...

Texting him.

Calling him. Over, and over, and over again. All from different numbers and each time he blocks me.

Replacing the windshield that I kissed with a brick.

Replacing the entire car with a brand-new 2015 black Maserati with a red bow on top.

He sent the car back. Bow still intact.

I've done it all.

And still…nothing…but dead silence.

This is killing me.

And seeing Knox and being with Knox is no longer soothing me and distracting me long enough to keep my thoughts at bay.

And yes, I love Knox…

But Justice…

Maybe everybody is right.

~~Maybe I need to be single.~~

~~Maybe I should…~~

I refuse to be single. Seriously, why would I choose to be without a boo? I know chicks who would slice their wrist to have a dude, but everybody thinks I should just choose to be alone? And then what?

Just because I have a man and a few side jawns does not make me a ho. And I'm tired of being called one. I like sex, yes. I like boys, yes. But am I easy? No. I'm not in a relationship with every dude I run up with. How desperate is that? Seriously, I'm not one of these needy chicks who's emotionally open and on the prowl to be every boy's wife. I know the difference between those you're supposed to bed and the one you're supposed to wed. Why do you think I hold on to Knox so tight?

That's my husband.

I'm his wife.

Period.

It's just that at the moment, I'm sixteen and choosing to live my life.

What's wrong with that?

And my mother—this stupid broad, around here

committed to a man who's cheating on her every
chance he gets—of course she doesn't understand.
Like really, that ain't fly. That is so, so whack.
Everybody knows my father keeps a stable full of
hoes and that his office is his stroll. And instead of
my mother attending to her man, she's posted up all
in my grill and all in my business, telling me what I
better do. Kick rocks and drop! When you get a handle on your man then you can step to me. Until
then, have several seats... waaaaay in the back!

I got this.

Besides, ever since Spencer and I went on that
faux run—when we thought she killed Justice—and I
returned home two days later, Shakeesha's been acting funny. I sit down for breakfast and she gets up.
Leaving me, my daddy, and the chef looking stupid.
The other day my daddy—this hoodbugger—said to
me, "Seems you really messed up this time."

I was a cross between pissed and shocked. First
off, I didn't like him coming at me all sideways. And
why do I always have to be the one to do something?
Shakeesha turns it up too. Trust. And second, my
daddy never, ever starts a conversation with me. The
most he says to me, if he's not spazzing because of
some unwanted press, is "How much is it, daddy's
girl? You can have the world."

That's it. Nothing more. Nothing less.

Our relationship is based on staying away from
negative press and finances. Period.

Anyway, he went on to tell me how he admired me
and that I reminded him of himself at my age.

I almost hit the floor with that. Dead to the bed! I couldn't believe he'd actually noticed me long enough to compare me to him. And just as I'd thought I was about to have the best conversation with him, his phone rang, and a woman's voice echoed "Hey, baby," and in two seconds flat he was up from the table and out the door.

Meanwhile, in the spa room his wife is clueless...

But whatever...that's not my problem...

Missing Justice is my issue...

I want so bad to call him.

I'm not about to sweat him.

And to think that the last time we were together it was the perfect date...

He'd called me...randomly...and said, "Why don't you come and chill with me?"

"Chill with you?" I know he could hear me grinning through the phone.

"Yeah." I heard his smile. "Chill with me. I was thinking 'bout you and I wanted to take you out for a minute. Meet me at my spot and I'ma take us for a ride."

I did.

And we ended up at Twin City Roller Rink in East Oakland. Of all places. And he knew I didn't do the hood, but he promised me a good time—media- and drama-free. "Yeah, but will I need security?" I'd asked him.

He laughed...and oh, what a sexy laugh! "Love..."— I loved it when he called me that—"the most you'll get in the hood are some giggles and waves from a few little girls. Other than that, nobody will be on it like that. I promise. Now, if this was Hollywood or L.A., then you'd need to be afraid."

I believed him.

And just like he promised, I got no more than a few giggles and waves...and truthfully, I'd never felt so free. There were no paparazzi hanging in trees. Nobody pointing, whispering, and giggling about me. I was with my baby, and while we danced and skated—well, I danced and he watched me—I teased him with the roller-skating version of the wobble. Then I topped that with the running man.

I skated over to him. "You didn't know that I could bust it like this, did you?"

He placed his hands on my waist. "I never doubted your skills, love."

"So why do you keep looking at me with a side grin?"

" 'Cause I'm loving this. I'm loving being with you like this. You're not all amped up. You're just chill."

"That's 'cause I'm here with you." I slid my arms around his neck. And we slow danced while skating.

"You think we could be like this forever?" he asked.

"Yes, baby."

"Then I'ma need you to leave your man..."

Whomp...whomp...whomp, straight crickets after that. And no, I didn't answer him then. And yes, I answered him later that night—when he was sleeping and I eased out of his apartment—leaving a Yeah Boo letter behind.

Leaving Knox was not and would never be up for discussion.

Then why isn't it enough...?

Knox used to be fun...but what we used to laugh at he no longer finds funny.

Now he gets pissed when I'm on the blogs or in the gossip rags.

There was a time when I could tell him anything... everything...and now...I don't know what to tell him.

He's always complaining.

He's always telling me how to act and what to do.

I got a nagging mother for that. I get enough from her!

And dear God, his routine! Strangle me now! Shower by 6 a.m. Gym by 7 a.m. Class by 8 a.m. Return to the dorm by 3 p.m. Chill with Midnight from 3 to 5 p.m. Eat dinner by 6 p.m. Do homework by 8. Chill with his frat brothers by 9. Call me by 10. Tell me he misses me. Loves me. Then sweats me about where I've been, who I've been with, and why I haven't called him, blah...blah...blah...End nag session with me by 12. Talks sweet and tells me he loves me again by 12:15, and by 1 a.m. he's in the bed asleep.

This is Knox. All day. Every day.

Yawn...stretch...yawn!

Nothing new. Nothing different.

Just stale.

And to think, if I wanted some excitement out of him I'd have to tell him my period is late.

He'd be sure to lose his mind then.

But I'm not in the mood to watch him squirm.

So I'ma just leave it alone.

I love Knox…but I just want the old Knox back. The one I could call and tell anything to. The one who used to drive by here and invite me outside and we'd chill, laugh, and just have fun. That one. I want him back now. Pronto. Because if not, then I may have to…

I'm not leaving him.

But what if he's never enough…?

Am I the only one who thinks it's an impossible task…?

I dropped my blue Tiffany pen and watched it roll over the page to the edge of the bed as I lay back, arms stretched above my head, and prayed that the urge to track down Justice went away.

It's Thursday. He plays the Kit-Kat Lounge and if I leave now…

No.

Eff that.

I'm not sweatin' him.

I'll get through this.

The blaring of my ringing cell phone interrupted my thoughts.

Ten p.m.

Knox.

As usual.

I rolled my eyes up in my head. "Hey, poo!" I answered my phone and added the extra amp for good measure.

"Wassup? I missed you today."

"Awwwl, poo. I missed you too. I was just thinking about you. Watching the phone and waiting for it to ring." I twisted my lips.

"Why didn't you call me earlier?"

"I don't know, baby. I was so wrapped up in this home-work and everything. You know Logan stays sweatin' me."

"I know."

"Were you thinking about me today?" I asked him, rolling my eyes in my head again. *Of course I was thinking about you. I think about you all the time.*

"Of course I was thinking about you. I think about you all the time. You know what else I was thinking?"

"What?"

"Why don't you come down here and chill with me tonight?"

I paused. "Tonight? On a Thursday? You usually want me to come on Fridays."

"What? I can't switch up?" He laughed.

You never have before. "Okay, baby." I smiled. A gen-uine smile. "I like the thought of you switching it up."

"Besides, tomorrow I won't be here."

And where is he going? "Where are you going?"

"Vegas."

I don't believe this. "Vegas? And you didn't ask me to go?"

"Jealous?"

"Never."

"So are you coming down here to see me?"

Hell, yes. "I'm coming now." *And not so much because I want to see you, but I need to clear my head.*

I grabbed my keys off of the nightstand and stepped into my pair of broken-glass-encrusted Marc Jacobs sneak-ers. Instead of pulling my hair back into a ponytail, I let it flow over my shoulders. I grabbed my Louis Vuitton hand-bag and couldn't beat it out the door fast enough.

One good thing about my mother acting funny, she wasn't sniffing around my door hounding me and I didn't have to wait all night for the right time to sneak out.

I tossed my purse on the passenger seat of my car, placed Knox's call on speaker, and took off for the highway.

"Rich, are you in the car already?" Knox chuckled.

"Yes, I am." I laughed. "You know I love being with you. And I'm sorry that the last time I was there I had to leave before you got back from class. But you know Spencer, the drama queen, she just had to get sick. Probably from all that drinking she does."

"Spencer?" he said, shocked.

"Umm, yes. Spencer. Don't let that innocent face fool you. That's my girl, but she will drink a grown man under the table! That chick will knock off pitcher after pitcher of nothing but beer."

He laughed. "Speaking of beer. Wassup with you and London? I see the blogs have nicknamed the two of you 'The Beer Brawlers.' What happened?"

Dear God. I rolled my eyes quickly to the car's ceiling and then looked back to the highway. "I don't want to talk about that."

"You and these blogs."

Here we go.

He continued. "I'm just saying. You need to stop showing up on them every week."

Whatever. "I know."

"I'm serious, Rich. It's too much..."

For the next forty-five minutes I tuned him out and instead of continuing south toward San Diego, I took the exit for Manhattan Beach.

"Ohmygod!" I interrupted Knox's lecture.

"Look, I know you don't want to hear me telling you this over and over again—"

"That's not it," I said, aggravated. "It's a fifty-car pileup out here!"

"What?" he said in a panic. "Fifty cars?"

"At least!" I said, pulling into Justice's apartment complex. "And the police are making everybody get off the highway. Telling us to turn around! I'll never get there, poo." I parked in the back of the parking lot, diagonally across from Justice's assigned spot, so that when he pulled in—at whatever time tonight—I'd be able to spot him.

"I was looking forward to seeing you, too," Knox said, clearly disappointed.

"I could always join you in Vegas," I said, turning the engine off.

He laughed. "Vegas is for the bruhs, baby."

"I understand."

"I'll stay on the phone and we can talk until you get back home."

And stay past your one o'clock bedtime? No, thank you, sir. Go to bed, on time, like you always do. "Don't worry, baby. Plus my battery is dying and I forgot my charger."

"Call me when you get in then."

"I will."

"I love you, Rich."

"I love you more."

I turned off my phone, nixed the inkling of guilt that tried to convict me, and waited.

PUT YOUR DIAMONDS UP

Ni-Ni Simone
Amir Abrams

ABOUT THIS GUIDE

The following questions are intended to
enhance your group's reading of
PUT YOUR DIAMONDS UP.

Discussion Questions

1. What did you think of the way London's mother pressured her to be perfect? Do you know anyone whose mother treats them like this?

2. What did you think of the way London feels about herself? Do you know someone who has low self-esteem, or who doesn't like who they are?

3. Heather has had a serious battle with drug use since the beginning of the series. Do you believe she can ever be completely drug free? Do you think drug addicts can ever truly change their lives around? Why?

4. What did you think of Heather's relationship with her mother? How was it different from all the other girls' relationships with theirs?

5. Rich can't seem to keep her love life straight. Why do you believe she continues to make bad choices? Do you think she'll ever be with one boy? Do you think Rich knows what true love is? Why?

6. Why do you think Spencer continues to save Heather time and time again? Do you think it's because she's a true friend? Or because she's lacking something in her own life?

The Pampered Princesses are at it again in the
4th installment of the Hollywood High series

1

Rich

2 a.m.

I will not be played.
Or ignored.
And especially by some broke side-jawn.
Never!
I don't care if he is six feet and hey-hey-hollah-back-lil-daddy fine.
Or how much I scribble, doodle, and marry my first name to his last name.
He will never be allowed to come at me crazy.
Not Rich Gabrielle Montgomery.
Not this blue-blooded, caramel—thick in the hips, small in the waist, and fly in the face—bust 'em down princess.
Psst.
Puhlease.
Swerve!

And yeah, once upon a time everything was Care Bear sweet: rainbows, unicorns, and fairy tales. He was feeling me and I was kind enough to let him think we'd be happily ever after.

But. Suddenly.

He turned on me.

Real sucker move.

And so what if I keyed up his car.

Tossed a brick through his windshield.

Kicked a dent in his driver's side door.

Made a scene at his apartment building and his nosy neighbor called the police on me.

Still...

Who did he think he was? Did he forget he was some gutter-rat East Coast transplant?

He better stay in his freakin' lane.

I've been good to him!

I replaced the windshield and had all the brick particles swept from the parking lot.

The next day, I topped myself and replaced the entire car with a brand-new black Maserati with a red bow on top.

The ungrateful slore sent the car back. Bow still intact.

I've done it all.

And how does he repay me?

With dead silence.

I don't think so.

I'm not some ratchet ho.

I don't have to take that!

And if I have to sit here in my gleaming silver Spider, in this dusty Manhattan Beach apartment complex, and wait another three hours for Justice to get home, I will.

4 a.m.

> *I should leave.*
> *Go home.*
> *Call my boyfriend, Knox.*
> *And forget Justice.*
> *If he can't appreciate a mature, sixteen-year-old woman like me, then screw him.*
> *No. I can't leave.*
> *I have to make this right.*
> *No I don't.*
> *Yes. I do.*

5 a.m.

> *Where is he?*

6 a.m.

> *There he is.*
> *But where is he coming from?*
> Was he with some chick?

My eyes followed a black Honda Accord with a dimpled driver's door as it pulled into the half-empty parking lot and parked in the spot marked 203.

The red sun eased its way into the sky as I took three deep breaths, doing all I could to stop the butterflies from racing through my stomach.

> *I should go home. Right now.*
> *After all, he is not my man.*
> *My man is at his college dorm, thinking about me.*

I chewed on the corner of my bottom lip. Swallowed. My

eyes moved from the brick, two-story, U-shaped, garden-style complex Justice lived in to the small beach across the street where an overdressed homeless woman leaned over the wooden barrier and stared at the surfers riding the rough waves.

"What the hell? Are you stalking me?"

I sucked in a breath and held it.

Justice.

I oozed air out the side of my mouth and turned to look out my window. There he was: ice-grilling me. Top lip curled up, brown gaze narrowed and burning through me.

Say something! Do something!

"Can I, umm...talk to you?" I opened my door and stepped out. "For a minute? Please." I pulled in the left corner of my bottom lip and bit into it.

"Nah. You can't say ish to me, son. What you can do, though, is stop stalkin' me 'n' go get you some help. Thirsty. Loony bird. If I didn't call you, it was for a reason. Deal wit' it. Now get back in ya whip 'n' peel off."

Oh. No. He. Didn't! This scrub is outta control!

"For real? Slow down, low-down. When did you become the president? You don't dismiss me. This is a public lot. I ain't leavin'. And you will listen to me. Now, I have *not* been waiting here for seven hours for you to come out the side of your neck and call me a freakin' stalker. You don't get to disrespect me. And loony bird? Really? Seems you've taken your vocabulary to new heights; now maybe we can work on your losin' career. And yeah, maybe I've been waiting here all night. But the last thing I am is some *loony* bird."

Justice arched a brow.

"Or thirsty."

"Whatever." He tossed two fingers in the air, turned his back to me, and walked away.

Unwanted tears beat against the backs of my eyes. But I refused to cry. "Know what, I'm not about to sweat you!" I shouted, my trembling voice echoing through the early morning breeze. "I'm out here trying to talk to you. Trying to apologize to you. Trying to tell you that I miss you! That all I do is think about you! But instead of you being understanding, you're tryna do me!"

Justice continued walking. Just as he reached the stairs, I ran behind him. Grabbed his hand. "Why are you doing this?"

He snatched his hand away, spun around, and mushed me in the center of my forehead. "I'm sick of your ish, ma. Word is bond. You don't come runnin' up on me." He took three steps closer to me. And we stood chest to chest, my lips to the base of his neck.

"Justice—!"

"Shut up!" His eyes dropped eight inches.

I need to go. I took a step back and turned to walk away. He reached for my hand and quickly turned me back toward him. Pulled me into his chest.

The scent of his Obsession cologne made love to my nose and I wanted to melt beneath his large hands, which rested on my hips.

He tsked. "Yo, you selfish, you know that, right?" He lifted my chin, taking a soft bite out of it. "Word is bond. What's really good witchu?" He tilted his head and gazed at me. "Just when I start to treat you like no one else matters, you turn around 'n' play me. Leavin' me Yeah Boo letters 'n' money on the nightstand, like I'm some clown mofo. I don't have time for that. And then you get mad 'n' eff up my ride, like that ish is cute. You lucky I ain't knock-in' you out for that, for-real-for-real. Yo, you a real savage for that."

I sucked my teeth, feeling the light ocean breeze kiss my face. "I was pissed off!"

He released his hold on my hips. "Oh word? So every time you get pissed you gon' jump off the cliff? Is that it? Yo, you crazy if you think I'ma put up wit' that." He paused and shook his head in disbelief. "Yo, I gotta go. I'm outta here." He took a step to the side.

"Wait, don't go!" I stepped into his path. "Justice, please!"

He flicked his right hand, as if he were flinging water from his fingertips. "Leave."

I ran back into his path, practically tripping over my feet. "Would you listen to me?" Tears poured down my cheeks. "Dang, I'm sorry! What else do you want me to do?"

"Nothing."

I threw my hands up in defeat. "I keep calling you and calling you! And calling you!"

"And stalkin' me. Playin' ya'self. Comin' over here bang-in' on my door like you crazy, then keyin' up my whip. What kinda ish you on, yo?"

I felt like somebody had taken a blade to my throat.

Play myself?

Never.

He had me confused. "I don't deserve—"

"You deserve exactly what ya greasy hand called for. You really tried to play me, yo. You got the game jacked, yo. I ain't no soft dude, real talk. I will take it to ya face." He paused and looked me over. "*Then* you had ya dude roll up on me and sneak me? Word? Are you serious? That ish got me real hot, yo." He paused again. "I shoulda burned a bullet in his chest for that punk move." His dark eyes narrowed. "You lucky I ain't knock ya teeth out."

Was I having an out-of-body experience? No boy had ever spoken to me like this. Ever. I was stunned. Shocked. Confused. Desperate. Scared . . .

I didn't know if I was quiet because I couldn't think of anything to say or because I felt a tinge of fear that told me I needed to shut up. The bottom of my stomach felt like it had fallen to my feet. I watched him take three steps toward me and I wondered if this was the end.

He yanked my right arm. "Let me tell you somethin'. I don't know what you standin' there thinkin' 'bout or what's 'bout to come outta ya mouth, but it better not be nothin' slick." He paused and I swallowed. "Otherwise, you gon' be pickin' ya'self up from this concrete. Or better yet, the evenin' news will be 'bout you floatin' facedown in the ocean."

"I-I-I-I," I stuttered, doing all I could to collect my thoughts. "If you would just listen to me! I didn't have anybody sneak you. I didn't do that!"

His eyes peered into mine. "Well, somebody hit me from behind. Now who was it? *Who?*"

Without a second thought. Without concern. Without regard or a moment of hesitation, I answered, "London!"

That's right. London.

That crazy ho.

My ex-bestie.

Another one who turned on me. Tried to take hate to new heights by inviting me out to Club Tantrum and attacking me. For no rhyme or reason.

"London?" Justice repeated in disbelief. I could tell by

the look he gave me that he was taken aback. He frowned. "Are you serious? London?"

"Yes, London! She's the real thirsty loony bird. Real crazy! She even jumped me the other night! I know you had to see the blogs."

"What the . . ." He quickly caught himself. "Do I *look* like the type of dude checkin' blogs?" He pushed his index finger into my right temple, forcing my neck to the left. "Now say somethin' else, stupid."

My kneecaps knocked, my heart pounded, and my throat tightened.

I should leave. This was a bad idea. Apparently, he can't appreciate me standing here, trying to woman up and handle our situation.

"Do you hear me talkin' to you, yo?" he screamed in my face. "I *said*, what you mean, it was London?"

I hesitated. "She just came from nowhere. You and I were standing there talking and the next thing I knew you hit the ground and there was London hovering over you with nunchucks in her hand!"

I searched his eyes to see if he believed me. The truth was it wasn't London. It was Spencer, my real, loyal, ride-or-die bestie. She'd snuck him. Hit him in the back of his head. And when he didn't move, Spencer and I got scared, took off, and left him for dead.

But none of that was the point. London deserved to wear this one. Especially since I was done with her. "I'm telling you it was London! She came from nowhere. You hit the ground and she was there with a bat in her hand!"

"London?" he repeated, shaking his head. "I thought she was over in Italy somewhere."

"Lies! She was never in Milan. That lunatic was home all

along, curled up in the bed! And I just knew she killed you! I just knew it!" Timely tears poured down my cheeks. "I'm sorry that I left you. I am. I was *sooooo* scared. You should've seen the look in London's eyes. That girl's crazy! I didn't know what to do. I called the hospitals! I called the morgues. I was even willing to pay for your funeral. I'm just so sorry. And when you were on that ground, motionless, I tried to shake you and you wouldn't move. London took off! I heard sirens. I got scared and I just ran!"

I boldly took a step toward him and pressed my wet cheeks into his chest. "You gotta believe me, Justice. I just knew you were dead. I really did and I didn't know what to do. I thought the police were coming. And I didn't want them to think it was me who killed you so I ran too! It was stupid." I stammered, "I-I-I left my car. Everything." I wept into his chest and he wrapped his arms around me and squeezed.

I batted my wet lashes. "Baby, did you do something to that girl?" I asked.

"Oh, so now I'm ya baby?" he asked in disbelief.

"Yes, Justice. Yes. Of course you're my baby."

"Really?"

"Yes. But why does London hate you so much? Did the two of you used to be a couple or something? I thought you were only friends."

"Yeah, we used to be friends. All that's dead now." He wiped my wet cheeks with his thumbs. "Now, back to you." He lifted my chin and placed a finger against my lips. "The next time you come outta pocket, tryna slick-talk me, I'ma slap ya mouth up." He tapped my lips lightly and I kissed his fingers. He snatched his finger away. "Nah, I don't think so. You still in the doghouse wit' me. Now what you gonna do to get outta it?"

"What do you want me to do?" I whined. "I'll do whatever."

"What you *think* I want you to do?"

I slid my arms around his thick neck and whispered against his chin, "I can show you better than I can tell you. Can I come inside?"

"Yeah." He ran his hands over the outline of my body. "Right after you call ya man." He pulled his cell phone out of his back pocket. "And dead it."

My heart dropped. "*Whaaaaaat?* Clutching pearls!" My eyes popped open and I felt my breath being snatched.

"Ya heard me. Call that punk now." He pushed the phone toward me.

I took a step back and he took a step forward.

"You said you'll do anything, right? So do it. You said I'm ya baby. Then prove it. 'Cause, real ish, yo...I'm second to none."

"You being second to none and me breaking up with Knox, my soul mate, my future husband and future baby daddy, are two different things. He has nothing to do with this."

"Oh word?"

"Word. No. He. Does. Not." I shook my head and placed a hand up on my hip. "You need to learn to play your role as a side piece, 'cause you are all out of control. Appreciate the time I'm spending with you instead of standing here and thinking about my man. Like really? Who does that?"

Justice popped me on the mouth, just enough for it to sting but not enough for it to hurt. "Let me be real clear wit' you: You ain't gettin' upstairs. We ain't kickin' it. I ain't effen witchu till you dead it wit' dude. Got it? Now poof. Outta here." He forcefully turned me around, practically yanked me back to my car, snatched open the door, and pushed me inside.